HORTON'S TEST

HORTON'S TEST

by

David Petri

'A highly inventive tale which cricket addicts will find hard to resist'

CHRISTOPHER MARTIN-JENKINS

Other books by David Petri:

CURTAIN OF NIGHT	Dell Pub. Inc., New York U.S.A.	
	Rotabook Pub. U.K.	Oct 1982
	1st reprint	Nov 1982
FORTUNE OF THE CREEDS	Rotabook Pub. U.K.	1983
TENDER SKY	Rotabook Pub. U.K.	1983
CATS IS DOGS	Rotabook Pub. U.K.	1983

HORTON'S TEST
Cover design Barbara Walton
Photograph Roger Pennington
Printed by Richard Clay PLC (The Chaucer Press), Bungay, Suffolk, England.

Enquiries to ROTABOOK Publishing
Heathfield, Sussex TN21 8NL, England.

British Library Cataloguing in Publication Data

Petri, David
Horton's Test
1 Title
I.S.B.N. 0 946 382 018 (Paperback)
0 946 382 034 (Hardback)

Published by
ROTABOOK Publishing

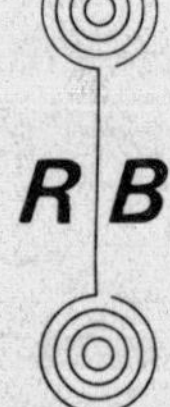

HORTON'S TEST

THE
AUTHOR

Born in 1924, David Petri was raised in the environment of the Regular British Army and was educated at Downside. After visiting Hong Kong in 1939 he travelled back in the very first convoy of the war to complete his education and then volunteered for the Royal Artillery. Commissioned, he served in India, Burma and the Far East, in a Self Propelled Field Regiment and flew Austers in Air O.P.

He played cricket for the British Army in India in 1944 and 1945 – mainly in inter-state and university matches. His most noteable achievement was for the Viceroy XI versus Lindsay Hassett's Australian XI at Poona in 1945 where he not only made a 'pair' – but put no fewer than 5 catches on the ground. This stimulated Abdul Hafeez to comment, 'if only the Umpire would send him off!'

Petri's entrepreneurial activities cover sporting goods, publishing, printing, invention, design and, of course, writing.

Since the first words of HORTON'S TEST were put on paper I had no doubts whatsoever that the book must be dedicated to my father

Lieut. Colonel A. V. 'Peter' Petri

who was alone responsible for instilling in me my love of cricket.

This love took in not only watching the game and, of course, playing it, but also what I call the 'imagination' of cricket.

At a very young age I would lie in bed at night half asleep and being bowled to by Fleetwood-Smith pitching on the leg stump and going away to off and I would mentally lean back in the bed and cut viciously, fine of point, so that the ball tore past the bedside table, by my desk, past the wardrobe and thudded into the wainscot of the wall. Petri D. moves up to 87 and England are 156 for 4.

In advanced middle age I don't count sheep but instead face Thompson as he thunders in from my dressing room. It is a vicious bouncer and I duck instinctively on the pillow as the imaginary ball flashes past and thuds into Marsh's hands behind the headboard. The next one is another bouncer. I go, literally, up on my toes and hook ferociously high in the air and the ball flashes past the telephone by my bed, high over the green carpet, by the window, over the chest of drawers and smacks into the wall that represents the Mound Stand at Lords. I sleep the sleep of a man on 52 not out.

About 55 years ago, my father wrote what was, I believe one of the finest short cricket stories I have read. He was a soldier stationed at Colchester and living in rooms. As a serving officer, he was forbidden to write under his own name, so adopted the pen-name Norman Hillbrook. He sent the story to the magazine of his choice and sat back waiting many weeks to hear of its destiny.

At last, near desperation, he asked his landlady if there had been any letter for Norman Hillbrook.

'Why, yus,' she replied at once, 'a letter came for Mr. 'illbrook but as he don't live 'ere I 'ad it sent back.'

Preferring to live in the world of imagination, my father left things as they were, so if any publisher has a credit to Norman Hillbrook's account I would be interested to hear.

Sadly, my father died 17 years before HORTON'S TEST was written, for I believe he would have enjoyed the tense and cliff-hanging incidents. It is strange that a game which can, at times, be boring to many people, will, under given circumstances, raise itself up to be so thrilling that those who know nothing of its finer points can be on the edge of their seats with excitement. Perhaps this is one of the attractions of the game.

My father, no mean exponent himself, was a coach par excellence. His 'hold your catches and you'll win your matches' introduced me to a lifetime of every ball – while it was still in the air – being a potential wicket which one chased till one sweated blood.

Life would have been a sadder place without my cricket and I therefore dedicate HORTON'S TEST to the person who led and guided me to it –

My father.

PLAY!

They'd crossed by Hovercraft from Dover.

They didn't like it. Not a bit.

True the speed was good – the timing better than the boat. It got them to their old hotel in Amiens two hours earlier than usual. But the noise, the bustle and the movement of the craft were unpleasant. You missed the casualness of the boat. The slow approach to France. The growing excitement of a holiday begun. It was like an instant wine compared to a Chateau Yquem.

They took the Autoroute for much the same reason as they'd taken the Hovercraft. For speed.

They wanted to get South. Among the sun.

The first three hundred miles were but a drudge. A penalty to pay before the bliss of getting right away.

They didn't waste their time on Amiens.

Michael drove. Fast but with care. The needle around ninety. Easy for the Rover 3500. He preferred to drive his own car. He always did. He'd drive throughout the holiday. That was accepted.

They stopped for lunch by courtesy of M. Jacques Borel. Michael ate too much. A pizza and an enormous chocolate thing. He wondered if Meg would complain. Pointing out his slightly sagging middle. His somewhat rounding shoulders. His tendency to weight. She didn't.

He drove on round Paris easily and onto Autoroute A6 for Baune.

The day was overclouded. Cool. Ideal for killing off three hundred miles of boredom.

Michael settled down. He eased his seat back. Drove with his arms near full stretch. Relaxed. If he had a migraine then he had a migraine. That's all there was to it. He'd suddenly lose sight upon one side. It would give him time to slow down and drive gently to the hard shoulder. There, for half an hour he'd suffer zigzags with his sight. Then that would go. That's all the eyesight problem he would have. The headache? Yes, that would follow. Perhaps for twenty hours. That, with a beaten feeling as if one had been coshed. It was, on and off, part of his life. He now accepted it. It was a bore. Nothing more.

They stopped twice again on the A6 before turning off the automatic road at Macon for the Swiss border and Geneva.

Meg had slept most of the way from Paris. She was tall and very slim. When at last she got out of the car she'd look as neat and immaculate as when she got in. She'd flip her head and her fair hair would fall into place. It was one of the features of which Michael was most proud. Another was that she looked nearly ten years younger than her forty-five. He was still in love with her after twenty years which continually surprised him.

She woke up on the side roads where one saw the country and the little towns. Where it was not just mile after mile of the same view flashing past.

They stopped for a café cognac at Poncin in the foothills before climbing up to descend onto the lake and the city of Geneva. The Café was small with only three tables on the roadway. The sun was fighting to get through thick cloud. It was cool – but it was only early March.

They sat and smoked and watched the daily life going on around them. It was early for the tourists. The GB on the car still drew attention.

The café was good. The cognac poor. Not just rough. They wouldn't have minded that. That was part of the fun. Rough, cheap cognac. This was bad.

They flashed down the winding hills, past the idle Customs Posts and into Switzerland.

The sun had won. It beat the clouds. It flickered on the lake, the snow covered mountains around. The town was clean. A glistening in the air.

They turned left at the Pont de Mont Blanc, waiting for a stream of bicycles and mopeds roaring across their front.

They stopped outside the Hotel Angleterre. A porter came. Meg, looking marvellous, walked through the automatic doors. Michael, tired, a little flustered, organised the luggage. The porter took the car. It disappeared.

The factory could go to hell.

He'd not told them where he was.

They'd get by somehow. They couldn't go far wrong.

God knows it was small enough. Any fool could run it.

Piss to them.

He'd four days freedom in Geneva. And then the South of France.

He followed Meg into the luxury.

Geneva did them proud.

By day they drove up to St. Cerque and into France, Megéve.

The skiing was still good.

Meg, young and athletic still, skied by herself. No flashing expertise. Just elegant and competent enjoyment. She'd take the ski-lift to the top and spend the middle of the day coming down in stages. Stopping to drink in the loveliness of it all.

Michael, in the town, would wander round. He ate too well. He drank a little. He claimed he wasn't fit enough to ski. At 53 he wasn't. Just after the war, thirty years ago, he'd have done the Grand Pis twice in the day at Megéve. A keen athlete – tennis, cricket, golf – he'd lost all that. It faded from his scope. 'Overweight and underkeen' he excused himself.

They ate expensively and well. They ate cheaply and well. Another thing he liked about Meg. She was quite unpretentious.

They left Geneva satisfied.

Another glorious spring day.

They drove through Annecy to Aix Les Bains. The blossoms out. The greeness of the land. They stopped for lunch and had it on a pavement overlooking yet another lake.

The streams they passed were rushing, full. The melting of the upper snows.

Grenoble tedious with traffic and up onto the ancient road, the Route Napoléon. The road that winds and weaves its way south over the Alpes Maritimes. The road you can't relax on. Every curve to the right countered, instantly, by yet a greater to the left. Then back again. Climbing, climbing into the blue sky itself.

Michael Horton kept a steady speed. The car was big enough and had the power to beat this road. The thing demanded was constant attention. Michael gave it all he had. He sacrificed the pleas of Meg to look at that and see down there. He sold himself to driving.

Only when they stopped at what must surely be the top and drunk their coffee from a flask was Horton able to view the true magnificence around him.

They started down. Michael found it more tiring than the climb. He didn't want to wear the brakes. He drove upon the engine, changing gear repeatedly.

'Mielle – Honey. Do let's stop,' said Meg.

They did.

She bought a kilo pack and ate it by the spoonful taken from the picnic basket.

'How about me?' asked Horton.

She fed him one, then two.

'By God, that's good,' he said. 'I could live on that.'

'I wish you would.'

'Oh Meg, love, give it a break. On holiday.'

'I wish I could.' She loved the slim man, twenty years ago.

'Well try.'

It was dark as they drove along the coast to Sainte Maxime.

The hotel was there. Exactly as each remembered it.

Five years ago? – no six.

La Hostellerie des Bon Amis.

It was perched right on the sea. In the moon they saw the private beach running down to the blackness that was the Mediterranean.

They had a room at beach level with wooden doors where a window might have been. A patio outside was six inches off the sand.

The restaurant where they dined, after a bath, was nearly empty. So early in the season. It too overlooked the sea. The moon shining from above St. Tropez made its usual pathway on the water.

They both loved France. This was excitement for Meg. Relaxation for Michael. They both knew they'd blend in their holiday.

The kids would be all right. Mary, sixteen, staying with the Honniman's and going daily. Stephen, still at Downford, in his last term. So tall and slim – like Michael used to be. Eighteen now.

They went to bed. Ten days of peace before them.

The holiday went to pattern. The weather was glorious.

They'd breakfast on the patio, late. Sit stripped in the sun all morning – even taking a plunge in the still cold Mediterranean – and have drinks on the beach. Meg went a beautiful golden tan with the aid of Ambre Solaire. Michael tended to a dark skin anyway but his shoulders and thighs got red and angry. They'd read and write and busily do nothing. Michael fought to keep his work outside his brain.

They'd lunch at the hotel and walk to St. Maxime. They window shopped. They bought as well. They had their tea at one of many cafes on the harbour-side. Meg, with her thé citron and Michael, beer and luscious sticky cakes, with the Financial Times.

They postcarded their friends, the children, relatives.

The evening was bathing, dressing slowly off a brandy and out to dinner in the car, mostly on Michelin's advice – but sometimes at their own.

So ran a week.

Then Madamoiselle Du Cos stopped Michael in the bar.

'Are you going to the Fête at St. Plaque, Monsieur?'

'No idea. Where's that?' he asked.

'For three whole days, it starts tomorrow. It's only fourteen kilometers on the Le Luc road from here. It's very happy.'

'We might look in. I'll ask my wife.'

Meg was not enthralled.

'Some ghastly village do. What can she mean "it's very happy"?'

'I've no idea. Let's see what the weather's like. If it's fine, I vote stay here.'

'Me too.'

The day was overcast and cool.

The beach was out of the question.

St. Plaque it was.

They drove up in the car at mid morning. The road grew crowded as they neared the village. Cars – mostly Renault, two chevaux – carts, people on bicycles, on foot, prams. They crawled at walking pace to reach the village square. That was packed. They parked in a field beyond the village and walked back.

The square was the Fête centre. With hurdy gurdies playing for merry-go-rounds. Stalls for shooting, next to market stalls. A ring for dancing to an accordion band next to a ring for boxing bouts. A fair and a market rolled into one. Flowers, vegetables, wine, clothes. Card sharpers and, no doubt, pickpockets. St. Plaque en fête.

Meg and Michael walked around.

They spent a franc here – a franc there, amused by the crowds and their obvious enjoyment.

They sat for a moment outside the Café Des Alpes on a corner of the square. They had a beer. Suddenly Michael stood. He looked across the crowds.

'Hang on a minute, Meg. I'll be back.'

He smiled at her and moved off through the mass.

She lost him in a second.

At the corner of the Rue St. Jules, Vittorio ran his ball game for the children.

He had a roped off section, ten meters deep. He stood at the back with a net full of balls. Tennis balls, soft rubber balls, hard rubber balls – a mixture. He'd take a ball and flick it from his hand. It flew towards the children gathered at the unroped end of his square. The ball would bounce and, spinning madly, twist away from the grabbing hands. The children laughed and if, as happened once in twenty times, a youngster caught a ball, a sous would flick from Vittorio's hand to land and cause a scrum.

Then on with the ball game once again.

Michael stood and watched. Not the children, but Vittorio and the balls.

The place they bounced was flat – not pavé. The spin came from Vittorio's extraordinary wrist. Michael gazed as each ball flew. He watched it bounce and flick away. The softer balls went egg-shaped with the spin.

Michael joined the children. He stood towering above the group. A ball would come, he'd move towards it and it shot away from his outstretched hand.

He watched the wrist with fascination. He tried to read the spin. He couldn't. There was no logic in the moving wrist and fingers.

He stood back again and let the children have their play. Vittorio saw him watching and put on a special exhibition of spin control. Vittorio sensed a drink.

'Ces tous,' he dropped his hands and gathered up the balls.

The children faded in the crowd.

Vittorio filled his net with the balls. He wrung his fingers to ease the strain. He looked the tall Englishman in the eye. He smiled. A little man but a big smile.

Michael Horton walked across.

'Bonjour,' he said, hesitatingly. His French was poor.

'Goods day to you, Zair,' said Vittorio, showing off his English and his knowledge of the international world.

'Ah, good. You speak English.'

'Much Inglis, yis.'

'Would you like to join me for a drink?' asked Michael.

'I am much pleasure, zair. Sank you.'

They walked across the square. Six foot one of bulky Englishman and five foot one of Vittorio, slim and lithe.

Meg had disappeared. Their drinks, his gloves and cigarettes were on the table. Michael pulled up another chair.

'Sit down. Your name's Vittorio?'

'Yis.'

'What will you drink?'

'A glaz of vine. Rod pliz.'

Michael called a waiter. Ordered wine and beer and turned to his guest.

'Are you Spanish, Vittorio?'

'Italiano, zair. And you are Inglis, yis?'

'Yes. My name is Michael. My wife is just called Meg.'

'Mig. Zat is nice.'

The drinks arrived.

'Santé.'

'Santé.'

They sat in silence.

Michael spoke.

'I'm very interested in the way you throw the balls.'

'Pliz?'

Horton repeated his remark.

'Oh, yis. It is amusement. No?'

'How did you learn? Your wrist,' he touched the Italian, 'is quite remarkable. It is what we call double jointed.'

'I am zi Great Vittorio. Wiz my bruzzers I was once the idol of zi circus rings. Zi Music Halls, you say. Of all Europe zi greatest jugglers are zi sri Grazzini Bruzzers. In Ingland no. But zi rest of Europe. Si. We go to zi United States. Zere I learn zi Englis well.'

He paused and sipped his wine. He looked sad. As if about to cry.

'And then?'

'And zen. My two bruzzers zey are kilt. A car smash. Only Vittorio is left.' This time the tears came and he threw the rough wine down his throat.

'Another one, Vittotio?'

'Sank you. Yis,' he mopped his eyes.

He must be my age thought Michael looking at the creases in the little man's face. The hair was pure black but dyed.

'How old are you, Vittorio?'

'Am serty-seven, zair.'

'The truth.'

'Am serty-seven, zair. Zat is se trus.'

Michael looked at him.

'Were you born with that jointed wrist?'

'Wis zis. No, no. I have uncle. Vera clever man. A dottori. He make for me. He is genius, no?'

'You mean an operation?'

'Si. Very simple. One week. Two maybe. Vera clever. I have, how you say, the bone removed. Two, three special bone. Now he twist. Like zis, see?' and Vittorio made his wrist spin in the most incredible fashion. Both ways.

Horton was staggered. So damned easy.

He saw Meg coming through the crowd carrying, of all things, a fire back.

'I'll come and see you tomorrow, Vittorio. You'll be here?'

'Yis. All day, zair. I see you,' he swilled his wine and rushed off in the maze of people.

Meg arrived.

'Who was that?'

'Just one of the entertainers. I bought him a drink.'

'Why?'

'He amused me. That's all. What have you bought?'

'A fire back. It's lovely. For your study.'

They drove back slowly to the hotel. Meg was rather glad to get away from the noisy Fête. She had a headache.

Michael was pleased to get away too.

He wanted to think.

The next day was glorious. Real beach weather. They were bathing by ten thirty.

At eleven Michael announced he was getting dressed and going for a drive.

'Where?' asked Meg.

'Oh, around. Not sure. Inland a bit.'

'Want me to come?'

'No, you stay here. Soak up the sun. I'll be back in time for lunch.'

He took the Rover and drove up to St. Plaque. It was as crowded as the day before but a procession of the Virgin Mary was taking place and the fairground noises rested.

Michael found Vittorio sitting outside the Café Des Alpes. He looked pleased to see the Englishman.

They talked of this and that. Of where Vittorio had done his act. Of Europe and her problems. Of the Lira and the Pound. Then Michael aimed the conversation.

'Your Uncle – who operated on your hand – he's still around?'

'Oh, yis. He has a fine clinic in the hills behind Geneva. He iz a great man the dottori.'

'Does he do many operations like your wrist?'

'Oh, no,' Vittorio laughed. 'That iz sumsink special he do for me. He take away zi pains in bones. Zat is fat zi dottori do.'

'Could he make for me a wrist like yours?' Michael Horton leant over and tapped Vittorio's right hand.

'You are making zi jokes, zair,' Vittorio looked worried.

'No I'm not. I've decided. I would like to have a wrist like yours. Would your Uncle do it for me?'

'Santa Maria. He means it.' Vittorio talked to the air. 'I sink I haf anozer vine pliz.'

'I do mean it.' Michael ordered the wine and a beer.

'Why, zair?'

'I have a special private reason. I do not want to copy you. I will not spoil your acts. It's a reason quite apart from what you do.'

'Zat I do not mind. I am a'finished now. Wizout my bruzzers I am nossing. I live wis zi Circus. I am 'appy. But to ask my uncle – so – it iz not so cheap you know. He charge a'plenty for zi operation.'

'How much?'

'I do not know. Two hundred thousand lira perhaps. And zen zi stay in zi Clinic. I sink half a million lira. Less if you pay in dollars.'

Michael worked it out. Three hundred pounds. Plus the air fare and recuperation. Say six hundred pounds. It was worth double to him.

'If you can fix this for me Vittorio there is two hundred pounds in it for you. Quite apart from what I pay your uncle.'

'You are crazy, zair. Why are you paying me?'

'Because I want it all kept very secret. I want no one to know about this. Not in England or Europe. It is to be between you and me and your uncle. You understand?'

'No, zair. I do not. But I agree. What's it matter if I do not haf zi understandings. When you want to have zis operation?'

'In ten day's time. No later. Can you arrange that?'

'I see. You lend me fifty francs – an advance, zair – I telephone my uncle tonight. He sink me crazy but he sink you crazy too. You haf zi half million lira?'

'Yes, yes. Of course. I'll pay in dollars or in pounds or lira. I don't mind which. I just want a wrist the same as yours within three weeks.'

'You come tomorrow here. Zi same time. I talk wiz my uncle. If he agree, O-kay. We got ourselves a deal.'

They had another beer and wine to seal the contract.

Michael drove back down to St. Maxime.

Vittorio wandered over to his net of balls.

The next day. The last of their holiday, Michael again drove up to St. Plaque. Meg could not understand this absorption but it didn't bother her unduly. Whatever was involved she didn't think it was a girl.

Michael saw Vittorio. All was agreed. His uncle, who spoke the most fluent English, 'just lika me' said Vittorio, was waiting for a call from Horton. Any time in the next week. He could take him into the clinic when it suited and the whole operation would cost five hundred thousand lira paid in advance.

'What happens if it doesn't work for some reason?' asked Michael.

'That's a'too bad,' said Vittorio, 'but it will my friend. It iz zo zimple. Nossing can go wrong. Ze dottori iz a fine man. Vera clever.'

Michael drove back to the Bon Amis with Doctor Grazzini's number in his diary. He'd ring immediately he got back to the office. Another fortnight off would be a bore but it couldn't be helped. He'd got to go through with this thing.

They left the Hostellerie Des Bon Amis in the morning and drove to Aix for lunch. They went on up the A6 with Michael driving fast and Meg asleep. They spent the night at Baune.

Keeping to the Autoroute they rounded Paris to the east and cut off for Rouen. They made Dieppe at eight and spent the night and caught the early ferry. By four o'clock they were at home at Deighton near to Horsham.

With the children away, the house was quiet. To save Meg cooking they went out to the Three Horses for dinner. They got home early. Tired but happy. A good break. They'd both had fun. They still got on so well together.

Today was Sunday. Tomorrow Monday – and the office.

Michael Horton was back in harness.

Firstly, he had his Accountant in. They spent the morning going through the books and finance details. All seemed well.

He lunched with Jeff, his General Manager. Not more problems than had been expected had arisen. Jeff had handled things well. A good man. Reliable.

The first thing after lunch he went into the Stringing Shop. He talked with the girls. Joking. He checked the output charts. Gave congratulations where it was called for and went on to the racket finish plant. The staff were glad to see him back. He gave a sense of security. There was a problem with a transfer that cracked. He made a suggestion. 'Of course, why had they not thought of that.'

He moved on to the plastic pressing shop. Here the Shinguards in all colours of the rainbow poured out. He stopped and talked and checked the work. He wandered round to show he had returned.

At half past three he had George Maxwell, the Sales Manager, in. They spent an hour with George reporting. Running through the forward orders. Checking gut that had caused complaint. Talking policy and plans.

By four thirty he was free.

He rang the Grazzini Clinic at Alba on his private line.

A girl with an America-Italian voice answered.

'Doctor Grazzini please. I'm calling from England.'

'One moment, please.'

It was too.

A deep voice came on the line.

'Grazzini.'

'Doctor. My name is Michael Horton.'

'Oh yes. Vittorio's English friend. How do you do?'

Thank God he really does speak fluently, thought Michael.

'Your nephew has explained I think.'

'Yes, that is so. The young rogue has told me what you want. I won't ask why. I can do it if you are serious.'

'I am. Very,' said Horton. 'When can you take me in?'

'Next Sunday if you can be here by then. I'll want you for ten days.'

'That's fine by me. Where do I come?'

'I'll send you details if you let me have your address. You come to Turin. I'll have you met. It is all very easy. Did Vittorio tell you the price?'

'Half a million lira.'

'That's right. What are you paying Vittorio? Knowing him it won't be nothing.'

'He seemed reluctant to take anything. I'm paying two hundred pounds.'

'Clever fellow. He's getting sixty out of me.'

They laughed together. Michael's spirits soared. This man sounded genuine.

'Everything must be kept secret please,' said Michael.

'I do agree. I'll only do it on that one condition. You sign a paper to say you will not reveal who or where you had the operation done. This is a trick I do on you and my work is serious, not a game of tricks.'

'Agreed,' said Horton and gave the office address. 'Please mark your letter "Private and Confidential".'

'I will do that Mr. Horton. See you on Sunday.'

'Thank you and good-bye.'

Michael felt relieved. He had done the plunge. Now he'd got a week to plan things in.

He called in Mrs. Ware, his secretary, and started on his routine work.

On Tuesday morning, when he'd been round the factory and offices, he got his day to day work behind him as fast as possible. He then rang Henry Sanger, the Managing Director of Chiddock Nets Limited. He'd known Sanger for years, generally meeting him at English and overseas trade fairs. Michael liked Sanger. He was a go-getter.

'How are you, Henry?'

'Well, Michael. What can I do for you?'

'I need some of that netting junk you make.'

'You mean the best nets in the world?'

'If you go on price, I presume they must be,' joked Horton. He went on to describe roughly what he wanted and the fact that he needed it fast.

'Young Hertford's in Sussex now,' said Sanger. 'Would you like me to get him to call in on you tomorrow? You can show him exactly what you need and he'll fix all the details with you on the spot.'

'First rate. Yes, that would suit me marvellously. Can your chaps do the fitting for me. Both the nets and the matting?'

'Certainly. At a price.'

'Oh come off it, Henry. I'm going to buy a load of stuff from you – you can bloody well rig it for me.'

'Do it at cost. How's that?'

'No wonder you make such ruddy big profits.'

'All right. I'll give you an extra ten percent off across the board. That's my last offer.'

'O-kay. I accept. Have Hertford here by nine thirty will you? I've got a busy day.'

'Shall do.'

'Thanks, Henry. Bye.'

Michael was satisfied so far. Now to get Jeff in.

'Look here,' he said, as the General Manager entered his office. 'What's happening in the old gut drying room now?'

'Nothing, Michael. You remember we closed it down in October and it's virtually empty. We've got some sacks in there. Not much more. We thought of leasing it out for storage but there's no decent entrance and it's such a rotten shape.'

'What size is it?'

'Ninety-six feet by fifteen. It's nearly thirty feet high.'

Thirty-two yards by five thought Michael. Perfect. And the height too. Exactly what he needed.

'How's the floor?' he asked.

'Damned good,' said Jeff, 're-concreted last spring. Done by Williams. Really good job. The lighting's pretty good too. All artificial but plenty of long tubes. It's a good shop but unsuitable to us except for storage and we've plenty of that.'

'Well I want all entrances padlocked up except the one from outside. I want a Chubb lock fixed on that by tomorrow evening and I want all the keys. Got it?'

'Yes. Doing something secret in there?'

'Yes. I am.'

'May I know what?'

'Not yet Jeff. Be a good chap and don't ask me. I'll tell you as soon as I can. You know that.'

'Of course. I'll get the sacks removed and have it swept and hoovered. Check the lights too. They're about twenty-five feet off the ground. Is that too high?'

'No. Perfect. If there's anything else I need I'll let you know. I'll be tied up in the morning from nine thirty onward. Is that O-kay?'

'Sure. I'll see you're not disturbed.'

After Jeff had gone his immediate, and for the time being, plans were simple. He sent for Mrs. Ware.

'Mary, would you get onto Mr. Magson and ask him to let me have four dozen Slazenger tennis balls some time tomorrow. Usual terms. Give him my compliments. And would you keep them for me until I ask.

'Then contact Baldwins and say I want an open Air Ticket to Turin for Sunday next. Don't care who I fly with. Return. About two weeks. I'll confirm the time I want when you get the schedules. May have to go to Milan. I don't know. You'll gather I'm off again. Sorry about this but you all seem to do pretty well without me. Call a meeting of Jeff, Collins, Accounts and yourself for tomorrow, two thirty. I think that's all.'

Now all he'd got to do was to handle Meg. She'd want to know what he was up to and he didn't want to say yet. He wasn't ready. He'd think up something and put it to her this evening.

After dinner he broached the subject.

'I'm thinking of going over to Italy for a few days.'

'Where abouts?' asked Meg, surprised.

'Oh Milan, Turin, Genoa – that sort of area.'

'But we only just got back from near there. Why on earth didn't you go when we were in France?'

'The idea didn't crop up until yesterday. I've been thinking about it. There's a firm out there with a new gut polishing machine. A centreless grinder would cost about forty thousand pounds now. This gadget can be put together for less than five thousand pounds. It seems a good idea.' Michael took refuge in the fact that he was not lying. There was indeed this new gut polishing machine and it would save thirty-five thousand pounds if he wanted it. But he didn't. Their own grinder was still satisfactory.

'Also,' he went on, again truthfully, 'we're having some trouble with Pastacci. He's meant to be our Sole Agent and he's been acting for a couple of other sports goods companies. I don't like it and I think I better deal with him. He's only in Como. All same area.' Michael, again, didn't feel guilty. They had got this

Pastacci problem but he felt that a good stiff letter would probably sort it out.

'How long are you going for?'

'Leave on Sunday. About fourteen days.'

'Couldn't someone else go? You must be needed here after our time away.'

'Not really,' said Michael, answering both points. 'There's no one else available and they seem to be getting on quite well without me.'

'So I must do the same,' said Meg.

'I'm sorry, darling. It wont be long really. You know I wouldn't go if it wasn't damned important to me.'

'Where will you stay? With Pastacci?'

'No. Not under the circumstances. Oh just around. Depends where I am.'

'Well keep in touch love, won't you? I like to know you're all right.'

'Of course I will. Don't I always?'

The problem was virtually overcome. Michael hadn't had to lie really at all. Just bend the truth. He hated to do even that to Meg but he'd make up for it later on.

The next morning the private letter came from Doctor Grazzini. It gave him every detail of how he would get to the clinic in the hills above Alba some forty miles south of Turin. He was to fly to Milan – Flight number and time given – and then be collected by car. A long drive on the Autostrada but the quickest way.

Michael Horton sent a cable agreeing and prepared himself for getting away.

Young Hertford of the netting company came sharp at nine thirty. Michael and he spent three hours in the old gut drying room. They planned the nets Horton needed and how to hang them. They decided on tarred twine as opposed to synthetic. Indoors it would be quite good enough. Some parts had to be double thickness, Michael insisted. Hertford agreed. He made detailed drawings and notes. He was a precise young man.

The matting was easier to decide on, even though Michael needed it so wide.

By twelve thirty they'd done their job. The work would be completed well before Michael got back from Italy. He arranged for Hertford to have the new Chubb key to the outer door.

At two thirty, when the meeting with Jeff, Collins, Accounts and Mary Wane took place, Horton felt that things were falling into place.

The Italian visit was easier, more pleasant and enjoyable than Michael Horton had thought possible.

He arrived at the clinic in the late afternoon. Whatever he had expected in the way of some village building he was wrong. The clinic was a long low white hospital with a verandah the whole length of the south side. It had a green tiled roof. Very modern and very attractive.

As he mounted the steps following the driver carrying his bag, a woman approached. A strong Boston accent asked 'Are you going to be the next cure?'

'I hope so,' said Michael.

'You will be. For eleven years I had trouble walking with my knee. Five weeks under Il Dottori and I'm doing six kilometers a day. He'll cure you. What's the trouble?'

'Oh, er, a wrist. I've tried everything.'

'Il Dottori will fix. He's pure genius.'

So it proved to be.

He had a small white room with every luxury he could want. The service and the nursing were excellent.

The Dottori turned out to be, not a tall distinguished man as Michael had visualized him, but a gnome like little fellow with really beautiful hands. They both signed the document denying the operation from being passed on to any third party and on the third day the job was done.

When Michael came round in his room, his right arm was strapped to a board and his hand was held in a plastic device with his fingers spread out.

He stayed like that for four days. Doing everything with his left hand. The Dottori visited him twice a day. He was delighted with the operation.

'It is going to be most successful. I feel it. Even the cut is down the line of a crease on your hand. It is indeed a beautiful piece of work. I am pleased.'

On the fifth day the hand came out of the splint but Michael had to wait two more before Il Dottori would allow him to move it. When he did he was disappointed. It didn't hurt but it was stiff. Awkward and uncontrollable. Grazzini told him it was perfectly normal and that now he would begin exercises. The first exercise Michael did was to write on plain paper to Meg. He'd already sent one letter before the operation, which the staff posted in Milan. This letter would go from Turin. He succeeded in saying nothing very much in two pages.

By the twelfth day, even Michael knew it was a howling success. His wrist was virtually treble joined. The muscles were toughening up again and he could twist his wrist into astounding shapes with the greatest ease.

Il Dottori, as Michael now called him, produced an old squash ball for Horton to exercise his right hand.

'I do not know what this ball is for,' Grazzini explained, 'but a patient from Monte Carlo sent it to me. It is a wonderful piece of exercise equipment. I wish I could get more.'

Michael explained exactly what it was and promised to send Il Dottori a dozen Zodiac Long Life Squash balls – the best the company produced.

On the fourteenth morning, Horton stood with Grazzini on the verandah steps waiting for the car to go to Milan Airport.

'You may never hear from me again. If I succeed, however, I may send you a press cutting. No letter of course. We have never met, have we? But you might like to hear of your work if it is successful.'

'If it depends on your wrist, I will hear from you I am sure. You have a wrist better than Vittorio's.'

*

Michael had to concentrate on keeping his right wrist in a natural position. It now only had a small length of tape on the cut but he found it enough to remind him not to twist the hand in public – and specially not in front of Meg and the staff. Not yet. In a week or two perhaps. But not yet.

He arrived home in great form. Meg put it down to a successful business trip. The staff at the factory didn't know why. No real business seemed to have been done. They soon forgot about it.

Michael parcelled up twelve Yellow Spot Zodiac Squash balls and posted them to Il Dottori himself. He put nothing in the box but the balls.

Each evening when the office closed, he'd spend half an hour in his netted and matted sanctum. He began very slowly by spinning the tennis balls in the air 'til his wrist gained strength. After about a week he could throw a ball fifty feet and spin it in the most incredible way. The balls would go quite egg-shaped in the air and cut away viciously on landing. He could turn them from the left or right. He could make them rip forward with top spin so that they hardly bounced at all or he could loop one up high and have it bounce back towards him even from twenty yards away. He was greater than the Great Vittorio.

It was incredible.

By the twenty-eighth of April, three weeks later, he was ready for Ben Hendricks.

Michael had known Ben on and off for years. Ever since he had played such wonderful cricket for Essex and England. Ben the batsman who was always there when a debacle occurred. Ben, who in the years after the second world war, was a household name. He was now a stockbroker in London.

To keep his interest in the sport he really loved, Ben Hendricks was cricket adviser to Michael's company. They used to meet every few months deciding on the policy of selling the cricket gear and also designing new and modern equipment from the vast range of lightweight materials now available. Ben was ready to rush to Horsham to see Michael at the shortest warning.

Michael rang Ben.

'Look here old chap,' he said. 'Could you get down on Sunday for a few hours. It's rather important.'

'Something new?' asked Ben.

'Yes. Well something quite different to our usual line of talks.'

'I think so. Yes. Are you going to give me lunch?'

'If you like. We could meet at the pub about one and come on here afterwards. And Ben. There's one thing I'm going to ask of you. I want you to sign a short document swearing not to divulge what I show you.'

'I thought we had a gentleman's agreement on all that.'

'We do. But this is different. We've got to keep it under wraps.'

'Right. I agree. See you Sunday at the pub.'

That evening Michael extended his half hour to two hours. At weekends he'd spend most of both days in his sanctum.

He'd mastered soft and hard baseball balls and could make them do almost anything. Cricket balls had been a problem. He was now using both wrist and fingers to spin the balls and when he first bought twenty-four cricket balls he found the shine on the new balls defeated him. After several day's frustration he let himself into the buffing shop and sanded off the shine 'til they looked as though about a hundred runs had come off them. It made all the difference. He could grip the balls well and apply maximum spin. It was all going exactly as he'd hoped.

Ben came down by car. They met at the Three Horses. Michael ate very little and drank tomato juice. Ben was surprised. Michael liked his pub lunches.

'What have you got new, Mike?'

'Just wait and see.'

They drove separately to the factory. To Ben's surprise they didn't go to the offices. Michael led the way to the back of the factory and a door into a long, high, narrow building.

Ben was astounded. The whole room was one large cricket indoor school. The matting wicket was double the normal width with the nets surrounding it. That was the most noticeable thing. The incredible width of the wicket.

By now Michael had a full twenty-two yard wicket laid out. Creases were painted at each end. Weighted stumps with spring returns were in place. The netting surrounded the area and the roof of the structure.

'Are you opening a school?' asked Ben.

'No. Now sign this. Be a good chap.'

Ben read the document and signed.

Michael had spent hours working out his run up.

He had to keep it to the minimum to prevent fatigue. Equally, he needed enough impetus to get some speed on the ball. Too slow would be no good at all. He'd settled on an easy five step run. Three long strides and two short paces at the moment of delivery. One-two-three – four five. He could already keep that up for eight overs of six balls before his efficiency went off badly.

He went and changed into a pair of studless boots. Ben was examining a table with a deep ledge holding the twenty-four cricket balls. It saved Michael bending down to collect a ball each time he bowled. He stood Ben three paces behind the bowler's stumps, roughly where the umpire might be.

'Now watch this, Ben.'

Michael went to his painted mark.

He came up in his shirt sleeves. One-two-three – four five and bowled.

The ball flew high to the left and hit the netting halfway down the wicket. It fell dead.

'Most impressive,' said Ben. 'Now what.'

Michael said nothing. He was cursing himself. He selected another cricket ball. Regained his mark. He came in again. One-two-three – four five. The ball hummed as it went through the air. It landed on a good length about three feet outside the off stump. It kicked like mad to the right. Really sharply. And clipped the leg stump.

Ben was silent for a moment. Then he moved forward.

'You've got a hell of a lump in the matting there, haven't you?'

He felt about with his foot. It was all as smooth as any wicket could be.

'Or have you re-invented the Googly Ball?' he said picking up the ball from the mat. He examined it closely, weighing it in his hand.

'It's M.C.C. approved if you want to know,' said Michael. 'And there are no lumps or bumps in the wicket.'

'You mean you can do that again?'

'Yes. About ten times out of twelve.'

'Let's see it again.'

Michael overpitched the ball slightly about two feet clear of the leg stump. The ball bit in and turned sharply across the face of the stumps just missing the off peg. A phenomenal break by any normal standards.

'Mike. That's the most astounding thing I've ever seen. I wasn't watching your hand so I can't say whether I would have read the type of spin or not. But even allowing for that to turn a ball that amount on a matting wicket is quite fantastic.'

'It is really. Isn't it?' Michael said. 'But I'm doing it.'

'Would you bowl a couple of overs and I'll watch from behind the net at the back of the stumps. I'd like to study this.'

Horton bowled the twelve balls. Three were pretty bad and wild. The other nine were superb. He bowled leg and off breaks of enormous bend. He did a couple of top spinners which shot through an inch off the ground and one gigantic back spinner that sat up like a dog begging from just over a good length. It fell dead as a stone.

'By God Mike, if I hadn't seen it I wouldn't believe it. It can't be done. But you're doing it. I'm lost for words.'

'Could you read my hand as I bowled? I mean did you know whether an off or leg break was coming?'

'That's almost the best part. I hadn't a clue.'

'That's what I've been concentrating on. Hiding the give away of the hand.'

'How did you learn to do this – and how the Devil do you do it?'

'Oh no. That's my secret. You just happen to be the first person to see it. You're not in on the act. That's my province.'

'Could you teach someone?' asked Ben. 'One of our young spin bowlers I mean.'

'No. Couldn't teach anyone. There's more to it than meets the eye.'

'I can see that. Your wrist looks damned odd as you bowl.'

'I'm bowling properly. Not throwing, I mean.'

'Hell no. You're not throwing. Elbows perfect. It looks all wrist and finger spin.'

'That's right. It is.'

'Mike. What are you going to do with this. It's got potential. No doubt about it.'

'I'd like to get Peter Ames behind the stumps and see if he can 'keep' to it. It might be more than he can deal with even as Kent and England's wicket keeper.'

'Well let's try. I agree,' Ben said. 'He's available now and I think we should go one further. I'd like to see Ivor Hughes of Glamorgan batting against you. He's probably the best player of slow spin we've got and he should play against the Australians this year. Would you like me to set it up? They'd have to sign secrecy of course, as I did, but I think it would be fascinating. I don't see how the Devil they'll deal with it.'

'O-kay. Let's try it that way. I'm available any time so you fix Ames and Hughes and just give me a day's warning. I'd like to get on with this.'

Ben drove back to London bubbling. He'd never seen anything so fantastic in his whole cricket career. This middle-aged, rather fat, business man tossing up spinners that he reckoned were virtually unplayable by normal methods. God, life was exciting. Good old Mike.

Meg would have said that Michael had not changed much over the years except for his growing so much stouter and of course ageing. In other ways he was the same man. Generally kind and considerate but very taken up with his work. The success or failure of it over the years would be reflected in his general attitudes but this was so normal for all entrepreneurs – which, of course, Michael was.

Now Meg was worried.

She'd begun to be when he kept going off to that place St. Plaque during their holiday. She felt sure then that there was no question of another woman. She was really pretty certain about it. Now she wasn't so sure at all.

The extraordinary trip to Italy when even the staff at the office weren't sure what he was up to. She'd had two fairly normal letters from him but the vagueness of it all was suspicious. After all he was at an age when –? Now this so called staying on at the office after hours. True it was sometimes only for forty minutes or so but lately it had become one or two hours.

She hated snooping but she'd rung the works when it was closed but Michael was supposed to be there. She'd done it several times. She got no reply from him. Just the Message Recorder assuring her of its attention. She'd rung off.

Once. Very concerned. She'd driven down to the office to find it all locked up and no sign of Michael nor anyone else. But his car was there.

She began imagining the set up. This other girl would pick him up leaving his car in the park. Then she'd drop him back to drive home. They'd had their fortnight in Italy and were now satisfied with odd moments grasped. That meant she must live round Horsham. Perhaps he'd known her for years. Perhaps Meg knew her herself.

Then Michael's eating habits suddenly changed. Meg got it first from Derek the barman at the Three Horses. She went in for some cigarettes one day and stayed to have a sherry.

'Mr. Horton gone off his usual fodder,' said Derek.

'How do you mean?'

'Well you know he's had our steak and kidney pudding for lunch for years. Now he has an egg salad and a tomato juice. Wondered if you were trying to slim him off a bit.'

'No, I'm not.'

'Well perhaps it's his own idea. He is carrying a bit isn't he? Due respects.'

Now she noticed it at home. She'd make a rhubarb crumble and he would normally have two healthy helpings loaded with sugar and cream. She'd made one last week and he had one small portion with very little sugar and no cream at all. For some years she'd been pleading with him to cut down on the heavy goods and try and get his youthful figure, that she so admired, back, and now he seemed to be doing it she was worried to death. It wasn't, of course, for her he was doing it. It was for someone else.

Then, horror of horrors, he started doing a few exercises in the morning. Nothing very obvious but things like deep breathing. She was certain he was trimming himself up and it wasn't for her. Who was it for then? God, she was worried.

She didn't dare mention anything to Michael. In a way she didn't want to know. In a way she did.

She noticed small things. He didn't cut down on his smoking but he took fewer puffs and stubbed the cigarette out hardly touched. He still had a whisky in the evening, maybe two, but much weaker than he used to. He even walked to the office occasionally. An unheard of thing. He asked for green vegetables that he'd hardly touched before. He gave up eating slab chocolate which he loved.

Meg decided there was definitely someone else even though he was normally kind and considerate with her. Perhaps more so – and that was a bad sign.

She made up her mind she had got to find out.

Peter Ames, wicket keeper for Kent and England, slipped on his inner gloves. He put on his vivid blue gauntlets and pushed down on his box. He did several knees bends behind the wicket in Horton's sanctum.

'What are we to expect?' he said. 'Nothing too dangerous with the Season starting next week, I hope.'

'Don't think you need worry,' Michael replied. 'The pace won't really trouble you. I'll just bowl a dozen or so to you then we'll have Ivor in and see what happens.'

'What's the mystery?' said Ivor Hughes, very tall and powerfully built, 'no one's told me a damned thing. Just had to sign a bloody document. That's all, man.'

'Be patient and watch Peter at work,' Ben Hendricks said. 'You've got the advantage of summing up the bowler before you bat. Peter's the guinea pig.'

'O-kay,' said Michael, 'we're off.'

He came in from his mark. One-two-three – four five and bowled a straight slow medium ball just outside the off stump. It did nothing. Just went right through and Ames, standing up, took it and flicked at the baleless spring stumps.

No one spoke.

Michael came in again.

The ball was almost identical but just outside the leg stump. It did nothing at all. It didn't swing and it didn't break. Ames flipped it back to Horton.

'Very impressive, I must say,' said Ivor Hughes. 'I've come a long way to see this.'

Ben said nothing.

Ames smiled.

Michael came in. One-two-three – four five. It was a slower ball and pitched well outside the off stump. Two feet or more. Ames moved across behind the ball to take it. It spun madly to the leg side and shot past Ames who was left standing without even putting a hand out. He looked stupid.

'There's a bump in this wicket,' said Peter, walking forward in front of the stumps and pressing the matting with his studless boot.

'Where was it? Somewhere here.'

'The wicket's o-kay,' said Ben. 'Get back behind the stumps.'

Ames did.

The next ball pitched just outside the leg stump and to Peter Ames' horror, shot through about two inches off the ground and eighteen inches below his waiting hands. This was embarrassing.

'Look here,' he said. 'Have these balls got something wrong with them – or what?'

'It's "or what" Peter,' said Ben. 'The balls are quite standard M.C.C. approved. The wicket's like a billiard table. It's your keeping that's ruddy lousy. Didn't you know that?'

'Shut up joking. Let's try a few more,' said Ames. He crouched down beside the wicket using all his concentration.

Michael bowled. He bowled eight balls which did everything bar hit the wicket and Ames completely missed seven of them. He missed them by a mile and got more and more frustrated.

'Even with good slips that's twenty-four byes so far,' said Ben. 'Now what do you think?'

For a moment Ames said nothing. He looked hard at Michael. Then at the wicket. Lastly he took off his outer gloves and felt the balls.

'Do you know,' he said, 'I wouldn't have believed it if it hadn't happened to me. I mean if someone told me this, I'd just say "balls" and ignore it. The really extraordinary thing is I tried to read his hand and I couldn't. You'd never be able to keep wicket to this without a code between the bowler and the keeper. You'd never manage. Well, I'm buggered.'

Ivor Hughes was silent. He stood behind Michael and slowly tapped his bat against his pads. He, too, had watched Horton's hand and he couldn't tell what was coming either. What on earth would it be like to bat against? How would you deal with it? There must be some way. He was longing to get to the crease.

'What are you actually doing?' Ames asked Michael.

'Mostly wrist spin with some finger.'

'Yes, but I mean it's unplayable.'

'I'm not sure of that,' Michael said. 'I know it's almost hopeless to keep wicket to, but a batsman who uses his feet might overcome it. That's why Ivor's here. He's terrific on slow spin. Let's see what he can do.'

Hughes walked slowly to the far wicket. Peter Ames left the net and stood behind with Ben Hendricks.

'It's bloody marvellous,' he whispered to Ben.

‘We’ll see now just how good it really is,’ Hendricks replied.

Michael gave Hughes a leg stump guard. He marked it with a piece of chalk. Michael walked back to his mark. He came in steadily.

The ball was going to pitch two feet outside the off stump but Hughes took two lightning steps forward and cracked it full toss into the netting between where cover and extra cover would have been.

‘I’ll take four runs for that.’

Michael came in again.

To beat Hughes leaping out to take the ball full toss he pitched it two feet shorter. Ivor stood his ground. The ball kicked high to the leg giving the batsman time to watch the ball closely and crack it hard, fine of square leg.

‘And four makes eight,’ said Hughes.

Michael had known that with a batsman of top calibre facing him he’d have a real challenge. Right. He’d got to use his head as well as his wrist and overcome this problem.

He ran up. One-two-three – four five.

A faster ball. Dead straight on the centre stump, just a shade short of a length. Michael followed up running fast towards Hughes. The batsman lunged right forward to kill any spin on the ball. Only he didn’t. It was a vicious back spinner and lifted off the angled bat. Even so it was never more than six inches off the ground as it came back down the wicket. Michael was there. His right hand scooped the ball up to catch Ivor Hughes.

‘That makes it eight for one wicket, I think,’ said Horton.

‘Sod it,’ said Hughes.

Ben Hendricks smiled and relaxed slightly.

Peter Ames was fascinated.

The battle went on.

By using his feet and all his guile Ivor Hughes succeeded in killing or even scoring off four balls in six. Of the other two he was completely lost and was bowled by one, hook line and sinker, behind his legs.

This just didn’t happen to England’s top player of spin bowling. No one knew it better than Hughes himself.

As they went into the second and third overs, things got worse for Hughes – not better. One ball, three feet clear of the off stump he left alone and it kicked in and flicked the top of the off stump. Bowled without even playing a stroke! And he couldn't blasted well read Horton's hand. That was the worst of it.

The four of them sat in a quiet corner in the Three Horses an hour later. Peter Ames was very quiet. Ivor Hughes full of questions.

'Could you teach someone to do it? Young Overton for instance or Baggley of Leicestershire for example. They've got lots of cricket to come. It'd be a sensation.'

'He can't teach a soul,' said Ben. 'He can just do it. That's all.'

'But if one of the England team could only just do half of what Mr. Horton's doing, we'd be in a terrific position. The Australians wouldn't know what hit them.'

'Overton and Baggley and all the others will be good spin bowlers but they'll never do what Michael's doing. Don't you understand?'

'Well, it's a great pity Mr. Horton isn't twenty years younger – if you'll forgive me, Sir. Why weren't you doing this then?'

'It never occurred to me,' said Michael, 'and I didn't get the chance.'

'If there was only some way of teaching the others,' persisted Hughes. 'Couldn't you even put them on the right lines?'

'Not a hope,' said Horton. 'You can wipe the idea out.'

Ames came to. He sat up and leaned forward.

'How many overs can you keep this up for, Sir?'

Michael smiled.

'About six at the moment. I begin to go off pretty soon after that.'

'You say "at the moment". Are you improving?'

'Yes. Slowly. It takes quite a bit out of one.'

'I'm sure it does,' said young Ames, 'but have you thought of playing again? I mean it's obvious you used to be fairly good, isn't it?'

'I never played really good cricket. Certainly not County stuff. School. University. Yes. But just playing again would be rather a waste of this spinning wrist. Just village cricket or whatever.'

'May I ask how old you are, Sir?'

'I'm fifty-three, Peter. Thirty years your senior, I think.'

'Um,' said Ames. 'Are you a batsman?'

'I was. Never bowled much – 'til now. I haven't played at all for eighteen years. It's a long time. I was a fairly useful slip fielder. Adored fielding. Could certainly only field in the slips now. I'd never be able to run for a ball without a load of training.'

'Could you train?'

'Not too much, Peter. Fifty three's a bad age for sudden exercise. I'm doing a bit.'

'Well, I think it's damned interesting,' said Ames. 'I'm very grateful to you and Ben for bringing me in on it at this stage. I don't think it's the end of the affair at all.'

'Neither do I,' Hughes added. 'Something ought to be done about it. But I haven't a clue what. That's up to you.'

As the young cricketers left together by car for London, Ben turned to Michael.

'Great success, Mike. Take my hat off to you. What next?'

'What next indeed,' Michael replied.

Dr. Martin Gillespie finished his surgery at seven thirty.

He telephoned Michael Horton.

'Mike. I'm free now. Do you want to come down and have a drink over it?'

'I'll be along in about ten minutes.'

Horton had known Gillespie for a decade. He was a young doctor who'd done very well in the district and had helped Michael a great deal with the stresses and strains of the business. In spite of a difference of fifteen years in their ages, they were close friends and if the Horton's or the Gillespie's had a party the others were likely to be there.

Michael didn't take the car down to Gillespie's. It was only a quarter of a mile. He walked. Jog trotting for some of the way. He was a bit blown when he got there.

'Come on in, Mike. Forgive the shambles. Kids. What'll you have?'

'Bitter lemon, thanks.'

'Good God. Are you trying to impress me?'

'No. Myself.'

'Seriously?'

'Yes. Bitter Lemon. With ice if you want to lace it.'

'Very impressive. What is all this? I mean getting me to check you over. Cutting down on drink. There's not much need for it. It doesn't disagree with the pills you're on.'

'I know. Well. What's the verdict?'

'You are eager beaver, aren't you? I thought this was a social call.'

'Business and pleasure. Let's have the business first.'

'Oh, very well,' said Gillespie. 'You know we didn't do a really comprehensive run of tests on you but I did give you a pretty good running over.' He took a sip of his drink. 'Very roughly, you've got the body of a man in his middle fifties who could have treated his body more wisely. You're a bit overweight. Funnily enough not very much. About a stone.'

'Christ,' said Michael.

'It doesn't matter yet but you should get it off in a year or two. Doesn't help the ticker you know.'

'How is the ticker as you call it?'

'Pretty fair. Can't truly tell with the tests done. I'd say quite good for your purposes.'

'And what are my purposes?'

'Well you know. Not over straining it. Nine holes of golf instead of eighteen. Walking down here – not running.'

'How did you know I ran?'

'Guessed it. What are you up to?'

'Never mind that yet, Martin. What about the smoking. Cancer – all that.'

'No patches yet but you do smoke too much. About four hundred percent too much. No. You seem fairly clear. Blood's o-kay. Urine and sugar balance well. Your lung power's a bit weak but I wouldn't expect anything else.

'As I say, you're about average – possibly a bit above average, physically, – for your type of life style. I wouldn't recommend changing it though.'

'Why not?'

'Well I don't think it's too good a plan to start mad activity at your age. It's the tricky period you know.'

'If I lost some weight quickly?'

'You'd do yourself little or no good. Lose it slowly. That's another matter. I'd agree with that.'

'Not good enough.'

'Now look here, Mike. Why not come clean with me. It's all off the record. I'd like to help. What is it that's bugging you?'

'You'd never believe me or else you'd certify me.'

'Let's try it and see.'

Michael sat swinging his ice round the tumbler of Bitter Lemon. He drank some. Looked up at Gillespie.

'I want to play cricket.'

'You what!'

'I want to play cricket. Pretty serious cricket. Not regularly. Just occasionally. This summer. Maybe . . .' he hesitated, '. . . well let's say three day matches. Or two on the trot.'

'Are you serious?'

'Oh bloody hell, Martin. I've just told you.'

'You couldn't begin to. You blew yourself just running down here.'

'I only ran a bit of the way.'

'Exactly. And your pulse was going like hell when you arrived.'

'You never took it.'

'I could see it. In your neck.'

'Well you asked me what I wanted. That's it. Now what do I have to do?'

'I should try an undertaker. Not me.'

'Look, Martin. I can plan this out. Firstly, I don't have to bat. At least I walk to the wicket and back again. Out for a duck. Both innings. Any idiot could manage that. Agreed?'

'That you could do. Yes. I now think you're mentally deranged. I really do, Mike.'

'You deal with the medical side. I'll handle the planning side. I don't have to make a run. O-kay?'

'Bloody useful to the team, poor sods. But yes. That is within your physical capability. I should walk out and back slowly though. Don't want to rupture yourself.'

'Thanks. Now, fielding. I make a deal that I field in the slips the whole time and never run for the ball. Got it. Is that all right?'

'All day on your feet. Pretty good change for you. You spend all day on your arse. I'd have reservations about that but, to be serious, I think you could manage after some training. I don't like it. You'd be stiff as all hell by day two. I suppose you could do it though. This team seems pretty tolerant.'

'Yes. Now bowling.'

'Oh my God. No.'

'Yes. And this I can do. I've been at it for a few weeks at my indoor net. I can do six overs at the moment with breathers in between. I need to do twelve. Then, say, an hour off. I only run three or four paces and bowl slow tweeks. What do you think?'

'I think my drink must be too strong. Look Mike, you're talking a lot of balls – and that's no pun. Who's going to agree to such a set up – and even if some idiots do, I still think it's beyond you. Hell man you're fifty-three.'

'And how old was W.G. when he played?'

'But he played regularly and he was tough. You're just a modern office orientated business man.'

'I want to try it.'

'You better come clean and tell me the whole thing. You've got it on my Hippocratic oath not to divulge it.'

'You'll still sign this form to say you agree not to disclose what I tell you. Otherwise it's off.'

'Oh, you silly basket, Mike. All right. Give it here. If you weren't a friend of mine I'd kick you out with a flea in your ear. You're a maniac. Dangerous, I shouldn't wonder.' He signed the form. 'Now tell me. This should be really good.'

*

They were going to bed.

Meg was sitting at a kidney-shaped dressing table. She'd done her face and was examining it critically in the three-way mirror.

Michael was in his dressing room two steps up and beside the bathroom.

'Where did you go this evening?' asked Meg disinterestedly.

'Martin.'

'Professionally?'

'No. Had a drink.'

'You must have gone for some reason.'

'Why?'

'Because I wasn't asked.'

'Men's fun.'

'I'm sorry. I don't believe you.'

Michael came to the door.

'You what?'

'I don't believe you.'

'Ask Martin then.'

'I might.'

'Look Meg, you're being rather silly.'

'Am I! I don't think I am.'

Michael came down into the bedroom.

'All right. I asked him about my weight. Does that satisfy you?'

'Why the sudden interest in your figure?'

'Well, I like that from you. You've been at me for four years to trim down. Now I do something about it and you don't like it. That's really prime – that is.'

'If you wouldn't do it for me, who are you doing it for?'

'What's that got to do with it?'

'A hell of a lot, I should say,' she snapped at him.

He walked across the bedroom. Stood behind Meg and looked down at her in the centre mirror.

'Oh, come off it, love. What are we arguing about? It's absurd.'

'It's not absurd and you know damned well what it is.'

'I'm blasted busy down at the office. I have got some new

things on. I did go to Martin for a sort of weight check up. Does that satisfy you?'

'No it does not. There's more behind it than that and both you and I know it. You wouldn't do anything about your figure for me but you'll do it for someone else. I'd like to know who.'

'You must be joking. You think there's someone else – some other girl? Oh no, Meg,' he began to laugh.

'Don't bloody well laugh at me. You've been behaving most strangely for a month. Ever since our holiday. If you want to know, it all points to someone else. It certainly isn't me.'

'There's no one else – and you know it.'

'Would you tell me if there was?'

Michael thought for a moment.

'No. Probably not.'

'That's honest anyway.'

He was near to telling her the whole story. He wished he could come clean about the wrist and the bowling and his plans. He'd sworn to himself not to – yet. The time wasn't right to bring Meg in. He knew he couldn't trust her not to talk. It wasn't her fault. It was the way she was made. No amount of promises from her would guarantee her not letting the beans out of the bag. He very nearly weakened but just managed not to.

'All I can say,' he spoke slowly, 'is that I have got something new on but it's certainly not a girl.'

'That's your story.'

'Yes, it is. And I'm sticking to it. Just have a little faith in me.'

'I just don't believe you. If it's something else you'd say.'

'I will. When I can. Now let's go to bed.'

'I don't trust you, Michael Horton. You may as well know.'

'Oh sod it, then don't. You're being stupid.'

They slept badly and angrily beside each other.

The work went on at the office and factory. April was one of their busiest times. Horton didn't shirk his work. He was thoroughly involved as always and it was only at weekends and in the evenings – for two hours or more – that he devoted to his sanctum and training.

Early in May Ben Hendricks came down for a routine policy meeting. It lasted all day and it was only after a drink in Michael's office that they got around to Horton's spinners and what could be done with them.

'You know, Ben – and I do – that I can take wickets with this technique of mine. I don't mean local cricket stuff, I mean top class batsmen. We proved it with Ivor Hughes. Now the season's starting and I've got to get a policy going.'

'How are you physically, Mike?'

'Had a check over. Not bad. About average for my age. I'm carrying a bit too much weight but I don't think I'll fall down dead.'

'I'm thinking of batting and fielding. I know the bowling would get you into any team in the world but what about the rest? Test Matches are five days pretty solid going – even if you're fit.'

'Well they'll have to make up their minds whether they can carry me as a batsman and keep me in the field where I don't have to run. It'll be a bargain affair.'

'You really want to try for the Test team?'

'That's been my object all along. Couldn't care less about county cricket or anything else. I've set myself up to be able to take half a dozen wickets in any Test innings and I think I'm ready to do it.'

'God knows how we get you in. We can't have a trial or anything, or the cat gets out of the bag. Somehow we've got to impress the selectors. Ruddy hard.'

'We impressed Ames and Hughes all right. Why not Maurice Kerr and the crew? I've got to show them. That's all.'

'You make it sound so simple. Toss up a few balls and play me for England thank you.'

'That's your job, Ben. You know them all intimately. Can you get Kerr and Bebington and Tom Lipton – it he's going to Captain England – down and let's show them.'

'They'll think I'm mad.'

'What's it matter? You get them down and leave the convincing to me. Ivor Hughes would come again. He'd impress them.'

'I doubt if Ivor wants the selectors to see him being got out half a dozen times in as many overs. – No. We'd have to let them choose their own batsman to face you. Could be done I suppose.' Ben sounded reluctant.

'Do you want to opt out?' Michael said.

'No, no. Certainly not. I think what you're doing is fantastic. It's how to put it into practice that creates a bit of a problem.'

'Well, I can't do it,' said Horton. 'It must be up to you.'

'Suppose I ask for a meeting and put a hypothetical case – and see how that goes down.'

'I don't care how you fix it, but I would like the M.C.C. chaps down to see a Demonstration. I think they'd go for it.'

'I'll see what I can do, Mike. Give me a week at least. They're pretty busy now and even though I stand in well with them they don't exactly hop to my tune. I'll have a go though. I don't mind your batting letting you down but the fielding's a big thing. They need more than just ten men in the field.'

'I'm not bad in the slips.'

'You've got to be better than "not bad". You've got to be fucking good.'

'Not if I take six wickets cheaply.'

'No. Agreed. But if you drop three catches that makes a pretty poor exchange. Specially if you make a pair of ducks. No, Mike. It's not plain sailing at all. They're going to take a hell of a lot of convincing. But I'll do my best. I must push off now. Don't see me out. I'll be in touch as soon as I can.'

Michael sat at his desk depressed. It was true what Ben had said. Even taking wickets was only part of the job. He could balls up his whole advantage by poor fielding alone. He used to be good close to the wicket. But not Test stuff. Not even county. Because of his running he couldn't even be lost at Third man or somewhere. Bloody hell, he'd got to make the team. Somehow.

He went home in low spirits.

*

'And how was she?' asked Meg.

'Who?' Michael answered unthinking.

'Your girlfriend.'

'Oh fine. On great form.'

'So you admit it?'

'Yes. She had on a very smart trouser suit, had a small moustache and looked exactly like Ben Hendricks.'

'I suppose you think that's funny?'

'Come off it, Meg. I've had a tough day. The only woman I've seen is Mary Ware and she's not my type.'

'I've had a mind to walk out on you.'

'Well, be an angel and close the door. I'm perished.'

'Oh, damn you, Michael Horton!'

Sir Maurice Kerr, President of the Marylebone Cricket Club and the Secretary, Bob Bebington, sat on one side of the long board-room table. On the other were Ben Hendricks and the tall, six foot three, dark haired, Captain elect of the England Test team, Tom Lipton.

'Are you telling us, Ben,' said Kerr, 'that there is a chap who can virtually get Ivor Hughes out when he chooses?'

'Pretty well, Sir Maurice. You'd have to see it for yourselves. I can't really do it justice. But this chap not only applies greater spin then I've ever seen before, but does it so you can't read his hand. Young Peter Ames couldn't keep wicket to him at all. His good balls are all but unplayable. I wouldn't waste your time if it wasn't really phenomenal.'

'What do you say, Bob?' Kerr looked at Bebington.

'Sounds nonsense to me. I think we've got our plate full enough without chasing after some unconfirmed miracle.'

'Tom?'

Lipton looked up.

'I don't agree with Bob. If Mr. Hendricks thinks this chap is worth looking at in spite of all the obvious disadvantages then I respect his verdict. Gosh he's been in the game for long enough – and at the very top – we ought to pay attention to such a talent scout.'

'Well, my time's valuable, as you know,' said Kerr, 'but if you two can spare an afternoon I think we ought to look at this man.'

'Waste of time,' Bebington said. 'I'm busy too. If he's so keen, let him come up to the nets and show us what he can do. Why should we go to him?'

'Mr. Hendrick's already explained that,' said Tom Lipton. 'We're going round in circles. I can get away tomorrow afternoon. Our match will be over by then, worst luck, and I still think it's our duty to go. Hell, this chap may be as good as he's reputed to be. In that case I want him.'

'All right Bebington?'

'If you insist, Sir. Yes. But I don't approve.'

'I'll bring my kit down,' said Tom Lipton, 'and he can bowl at me. I'm not as good at slow spins as Ivor but it'll give me a chance to test him out.'

'Shall I talk to Hughes and Ames by telephone this evening?' asked Sir Maurice. 'Their views may help.'

'They're sworn to secrecy,' Ben told him. 'But I'll get the ban lifted for you. May I call you about six?'

'Yes, do that and fix a time for Horsham tomorrow. Around three if possible. That suit everyone?'

'I still think we're wasting our time,' Bebington persisted. 'So don't say I didn't warn you.'

'I won't,' said Lipton.

'Neither will I,' said Ben.

At the time the M.C.C. Selection Committee was meeting, Michael Horton had a migraine. It was quite a standard one for him. First of all he found he could see nothing low down to his right. There was just a blank every time he tried to look there. He stopped working on the Sales Figures and put them aside. He rang Mary Ware and just said,

'Migraine.'

'See you tomorrow,' she replied sympathetically.

Michael closed his office and went down to the car. By now he had a jazzy light flickering on his right-hand side. It would last for half an hour, he knew. Meanwhile it was safe to drive slowly and super carefully. He was angry with himself – the worst possible treatment, he was well aware.

The three quarters of a mile to Keystones took an unusual five minutes and as he parked the car in the double garage, the headache began. It was rather as if someone had chopped him sharply on the back of the skull with a jagged axe. The ache wasn't quite straight. It jazzed a little, like his sight.

As he went in the door, his daughter, Mary, came down the stairs.

'Are you alright, Daddy?'

'Why darling?'

'You're home so early and you look awful.'

'Migraine.'

'Oh no, I'm sorry. I was going to be horrid to you but I won't.'

'What have I done?' Michael asked.

'You forgot to take me to Haywards Heath this morning.'

'Oh my God. How thoughtless of me. It went right out of my mind.' He was always forgetting to do things for the children and for Meg. He'd got too bloody much on his mind to be a good father or even husband. He needed a Personal Assistant he decided. Someone young and active. To take the strain. If only Stephen wasn't going up to Cambridge but into the firm. That would be ideal. Still he'd be more use later on, with a degree. Meanwhile, this cricket activity was loading the dice a bit but that he was determined to go on with. He'd promised himself that.

Mary looked very young and pretty on the stairs. Her fair hair a bit like Megs was, loose and long. She was dressed for tennis. Good looking girl thought Michael.

'Is tomorrow any good for Haywards Heath?' he asked.

'Yes. The afternoon if you can do it?'

'About three. From the office?'

'Yes. Thank you, Daddy. That's sweet of you. Now go and lie down.'

'I'm going. Sorry about today, Love.' He dumped his briefcase and climbed the stairs.

'Sod this head,' he said aloud.

Stephen came out of his room.

'What's up Dad?'

'Migraine.'

'Oh damn. What bad luck. Had many lately?'

'No. Not for a month or so.'

'Any reason?'

'God knows. I don't think so. If He does know He's not telling me. Where are you off to?'

'The nets. We're practising.'

'What do you do when it's wet?'

'Hang around and talk. It's a ruddy bore.'

'I may have an answer to that problem of yours fairly soon – in the Summer anyway,' said Michael.

'Sounds interesting. Building a sports centre?'

'Not quite. But I might have a net for you.'

'Marvellous. Can I tell the others?'

'Not yet. It's just an idea. You'll be o-kay today anyway. Enjoy yourself. I'm going to lie down.'

The telephone rang.

Stephen answered it.

'It's for you, Dad. Mary Ware.'

'Oh hell.' He took the telephone beside his bed.

'Yes, Mary.'

'Sorry to worry you with a migraine. You know I wouldn't if it wasn't very urgent.'

'I know. Go on.'

'Mr Hendricks' been through. He says Sir Maurice wants to talk to Ivor and Peter this evening. Have they your permission to discuss the project? I don't know what about but Mr Hendricks was most insistent that I contact you.'

'Yes. Quite right of you, Mary. I'll ring Ben Hendricks myself. Have you got his number by you? I'm not seeing so well.'

Mary Ware read out the code and number for Hendricks.

'Can I do anything else to help?'

'No thanks, Mary. I'll handle this.' He rang off.

'Stephen,' Michael shouted. 'Have you gone?' The shouting hurt his head.

'No. Still here, Dad,' came a voice from downstairs.

'Be a good chap and come and dial a number for me. Can't see properly.'

Stephen arrived at the double.

'What's the number?'

Michael told him.

Stephen dialled and passed the purring telephone to his father.

'O-kay now?' he asked.

'Thanks. Yes.'

Hendricks answered the telephone.

'Ben, It's Michael Horton. What's up?'

'Hear you're not well.'

'From whom?'

'Your secretary. Mary whatsit.'

'Interfering ... I'm alright. Slight migraine. That's all.'

'Well I'm sorry to trouble you but things are moving. I've seen Maurice Kerr, Bebington and Tom Lipton. Saw them this afternoon. The play is quite clear. Tom Lipton is very keen. Sir Maurice, well interested and Bebington very anti for no good reason. Typical Bebington though. Tom chewed him up pretty effectively.

'They want to see you do your act tomorrow at your place at three. Tom will bat and I have no doubt Bebington will bitch. Kerr is hoping it's as good as I said. That's the strength of it.'

'That's not bad, Ben. You've done bloody well.'

'I hope so. Well Sir Maurice wants to talk with Ivor Hughes and Peter Ames to get their reactions. Can I give them the go ahead to talk to Kerr? It won't go any further.'

'No. Certainly not. They both signed agreements and only a document under my signature releases them. What's the point of a signed agreement if we then undo it verbally? You can give Sir Maurice my compliments and explain the situation. He can talk to the boys after seeing me tomorrow.'

'You're being a bit niggly, Mike. We're only trying to do the best thing.'

'Well, the best thing is for the selection committee to make up its own mind on what it sees and then keep the whole thing under covers. My value is surprise. If I'm going to play it must be completely out of the blue. I'm certain Kerr would agree about that. Christ, I've been to enough trouble over secrecy. Don't let's spoil it now.'

'I rather agree. I'll speak with Kerr and explain. We'll be with you about three tomorrow. Where do we meet?'

'Not at the offices. Could you bring them straight round to my sanctum? Park out in the road. We don't want people recognising them. Specially Tom Lipton.'

'I'll put a blanket over his head,' laughed Ben.

'That's not a bad idea. Now I'm going to bed. See you all tomorrow and I only hope my head is better.'

They rang off.

Michael took four Codex and slept.

He woke at nine thirty p.m.

Meg was back from helping her sister move to a new house at Godalming. She was tired and dirty and had a bath.

The children had both eaten at eight and gone out again to some friends. Their holidays were full of do and go and Michael and Meg largely let them lead their own lives. It was hopeless trying to keep them on too tight a rein. Even Mary, at sixteen, was virtually grown up and resented any efforts at control.

Michael wasn't worried about Stephen. He seemed to have his head screwed on. Mary was more vulnerable and was going through a phase of fighting with Meg on any point at all where difference of opinion could be established. Meg didn't help herself. She fought back 'til she lowered herself to Mary's level, resulting in shouting matches about even the most insignificant things.

Michael opted out of the arena. He had his own relationship with Mary which he tried to keep on an adult level. Sometimes it worked. Often it didn't. But he preferred it to the screaming matches between Meg and Mary which he was quite unable to control.

He was glad the children were out this evening. There'd be no rows at least. He rated peace at home fairly high. He needed it badly after the battles of the business but he seldom got it nowadays. He supposed it must be his fault in some way but he couldn't find the answer. His only solution was a negative one of shutting himself in the study and doing his own thing.

He supposed he ought to tell Meg about this cricket business but it was pointless doing so and still trying to keep it under covers. Love Meg though he did, he still knew her weaknesses and however hard she'd try to keep the secret it would slip out. He must keep remembering that.

It was better that she thought there was someone else in the picture for a couple of months than to spoil the whole thing. He'd make it up to her later.

Michael had spent much of the past twenty years trying to make it up to Meg.

Things were all right now. The business was on its feet and fairly sound. They had the material things they needed and Keystones was a lovely house even though it was only pseudo Georgian.

Michael sat nursing his migraine after a late, cold dinner. He sat in the centre of a knowle sofa looking across the white carpet in front of the Adam fireplace at Meg working earnestly at a tapestry. She was a damned good looking woman. Tall, long legged. Beautiful ungreyed fair natural hair. Not pretty. Wrong word that for Meg. Good looking. Yes, certainly. And attractive.

They hadn't always had it so good.

Meg's people, the Whighams, were diamond brokers. Had been for three generations. Extremely well off. At first Michael had been rather frightened at their financial power and affluence. His own background was perfectly good but there was no money in it. He'd stayed on in the army after the war and done seven years before retiring, frustrated, as a Major. He'd started his own business with a gratuity and a thousand pounds put up by a friend. He made spectacle cases. It was then that he'd met Meg.

They'd both been at the Bingleys for a weekend up at Hornsley House one July. It was really tennis that brought them together.

Michael was good. Very good, and used to play the second level circuits like Surbiton, Cranleigh, Frinton, Winchester and Budleigh Salterton. The rest of the houseparty who played were rabbits but Meg Whigham was outstanding. Michael persuaded her to play in the mixed doubles at Surbiton and that's how the whole thing began. Michael was thirty-two. Meg, twenty-four.

Surprisingly, the Whighams accepted him as a suitable son-in-law. He couldn't really think why. He certainly had no money. Perhaps they were prepared to back the young couple. Anyway it was all arranged with a slap bang wedding in Wilton Place in London, with all the world and his wife there. They were launched.

A year later they had Stephen and the business went broke. Both events happened within three months.

Michael hadn't a penny behind him. They gave up the small house they rented at Byfleet and Meg went back to the Whigham's estate near Effingham, taking Stephen with her.

Michael searched for a job.

People weren't really interested in a thirty-three-year-old ex-soldier who had failed in business.

For two months he walked London living in a bed-sitter at the World's End. He knew then it was hopeless. He'd got to lower his sights.

He went to the Whigham's at weekends to see Meg and his son but no mention was ever made of helping out financially – not that Michael really wanted it, but he'd have welcomed the gesture.

In the end he landed a job at Wolverhampton as an export clerk in a bicycle factory, R.S.A. His pay was four hundred and fifty pounds a year. Less than nine pounds a week.

Inside a month he had found digs in Bilston where he could have Meg and Steven. It was a rather dirty hash house run by an ex-actress. She gave them a large cold double room, breakfast and 'tea' at six thirty p.m. For this she charged eight pounds a week.

Meg had guts. She came up and joined Michael. She brought her allowance of a hundred pounds that her father gave her, a full trousseau and Stephen. That was all.

Somehow they existed – and almost enjoyed life.

They managed to run up four week's credit at the lodgings which gave them a few pounds in hand.

Michael would walk as much of the way from Bilston to R.S.A. at Wolverhampton as he could to save on tram fares. He could only do it if it wasn't raining. If it was, the holes in his shoes let in too much wet and he caught colds. He built up the shoes with old cigarette packets soaked in a glue material he invented.

Meg could have a 'dinner' at the lodgings for four and sixpence and Michael had a sandwich for lunch at a pub.

They went nowhere. They did nothing. Even walks were out as they wore down Michael's only shoes.

For two years they lived like this with Michael Horton swearing that he'd make it up to Meg one day.

Michael's parents tried to help but a retired junior civil servant isn't so well off himself. The Whigham's did nothing but send expensive and useless birthday and Christmas presents. Meg was ashamed, but much too proud to ask.

In the two years Michael progressed. He ceased being a clerk and became area controller of the Middle East Market. His pay went up but the rent went up with it. The struggle continued and Stephen grew and needed clothes. Meg was a brick. She put up with the ghastliness of it all and supported Michael in his black fits of depression. She must have had faith but she was in love with him too.

Eventually he was promoted to Overseas Representative and a salary of eleven hundred pounds a year. They were able to move to better rooms. Michael bought a few new clothes. Meg's trousseau was still holding out. Life became passable and they'd go to a cinema or even the theatre in Birmingham. They felt almost well off.

After his final training, Michael was sent off abroad for a six month trip, all expenses paid. A chance to save money.

Meg had started having Mary.

It wasn't part of the plan.

She went to a school friend of hers in Northern Ireland for the six months Michael was away and more money was saved like that. Meg would not go home to the Whigham's.

Michael got back for Christmas. They spent it with his parents at Croydon. They'd saved nearly four hundred pounds and Michael's salary with R.S.A. went up to thirteen hundred pounds.

They returned to Wolverhampton full of hope.

The Company were good to Michael. They put down a deposit on a house in Dudley and fixed the mortgage for him. As far as R.S.A. was concerned he had arrived.

Meg had Mary in February. They moved into the new house in April when all spring was about. All the presents from their grand wedding came out of store and four blissful years followed.

Michael had made it up to Meg.

He did two or three long trips abroad before getting promotion to Comptroller Africa and Europe. His trips were then shorter and First Class. They had a very sweet Swiss au pair and Meg went on several overseas tours of up to a month with Michael.

Then Max came into their lives.

Max sold everything including kitchen sinks to the American Forces in Europe. It was big business and Michael had helped Max land a big contract for R.S.A. bicycles through Nuremburg. It was more than big – it was huge.

Michael didn't exactly like Max but he admired him. They seemed to get on together. Meg hated him.

For a year all on the Max front was good and they did several other R.S.A. projects together. Max was expanding. He was opening an office in Bond Street to sell American Automobile parts to British car manufacturers. He was really started. He needed Michael. To get him he offered five thousand pounds a year plus commission. A Directorship in the new Company and an Austin Winchester car and liberal expenses.

Michael was earning sixteen hundred pounds – with no side kicks.

It meant they could live in London.

It meant ease and luxury for Meg.

It meant good schools for the children.

It meant opportunity for Michael.

It was too good to miss – Michael decided.

He took it.

Once he'd got the job and was so obviously enthralled by it, Meg was delighted too.

They bought a house in Walton Street in Chelsea. They lived a quiet but unworried life. Meg had her friends round her again. Michael had time and money for sport – which he loved. They still had their Swiss au pair who had become a governess friend of the family. They even saw the Whigham's on level terms.

They lived up to their income but there was plenty more to come.

They were a successful family. They were happy. Stephen went to prep school and loved it. Mary was becoming a little girl. Meg was happy and that gave Michael happiness too.

What happened wasn't sudden.

It crept in like a dark cloud but somehow Michael didn't see it coming.

Max had bought an Import Export Company. It was nothing to do with Michael's side of the business. In fact Michael knew nothing of it until the new Company was in trouble. Max had invested to the hilt in Hong Kong. He'd bought plastic factories out there. He owned cotton mills and God knows what else – and they were all the wrong ones. He'd gone in blind and lost the lot.

Michael still didn't think he personally was in any danger. He kept on doing his job well and drawing his salary. Then one month no cheque came. He rang Max to find out why. He wasn't in the office yet. By lunch time everyone knew why. He'd shot himself in his flat the night before.

The Company couldn't stand. The whole group had gone and Michael's job with it. The car was collected and the office taken over. The house had fallen like a pack of cards.

The Horton's had nothing behind them but some small debts and a huge mortgage.

In ten days the house was on the market. A dull market with little likelihood of a quick sale.

This time the Whigham's made a small effort to help. They'd have Meg and Mary and the Swiss girl to stay and pay Stephen's school fees.

Michael was on his own.

At forty-three he had very little to offer in an effort to earn five or six thousand a year. He knew in a week of job hunting that he was back in the fifteen hundred pound a year class as a Sales Representative. Sales Directors of fallen companies were not popular.

He decided that his only real chance of building a secure and reasonable future was to go it alone. If any mistakes were to be made then he'd make them. If success was to be achieved, then he'd achieve it.

He rented a small dirty condemned factory in Battersea. He bought on hire purchase a new designed American racket stringing machine and he learned the hard way how to use it. He slept on a bunk in the minute office of the building and cooked on an open electric heater.

Somehow he lived.

He'd used all the miserable capital left to him in setting up this stringing business. It had just got to work.

At first he managed to get restrings and repairs from some of the local shops. They paid on his delivering the finished rackets back and he could buy food and pay his rent.

He worked long, long hours doing first class work and his name and his customers spread. He could now eat and pay the factory rent and send a few quid to Meg at Effingham. He saw her and Mary about once a month and Stephen if he was on holiday.

His hands, working on the machine and strings, became the hands of a labourer. He only bothered to shave when he was going to see customers. It was a slow, tough, heart-breaking start. But it was a start.

At her home, Meg had to put up with the criticism and even ridicule of her husband. What a useless waster he was. How much better she was rid of him.

She fought off all these attacks from her weak position and wrote almost daily to Michael trying to encourage him. To give him hope in himself and in her.

The moment arrived when Michael could no longer cope with

the flow of work. He had to have help. He took on a local woman to put the strings in the racket frames so that he could keep the machine working longer on the actual tightening. It worked. His output went up. But not enough. Somehow he got another machine on hire purchase. He taught the woman, Molly Welsh, to string herself. She'd work nine hours a day and Michael fourteen – but they still could not cope with the flow. He knew he was on a good thing. Perhaps even a winner.

More putters-in were taken on. Extra machines were bought with bank money and the small dirty factory thrived.

At the end of eighteen months he had seven machines and twelve workers. All his time was spent outside collecting and delivering rackets. He put his prices up. The work still flowed in. It came from outside London now. By post from Hull and Huddersfield and Hassocks. They had gone national.

Finally, one of the most famous names in sports equipment contacted Michael. Could he do a thousand tennis frames a week on a long contract basis? They could not cope themselves. It was the breakthrough. Solidity. Security. The seal of success.

He could do it. But not from Battersea. There wasn't the room. He still accepted the contract. By hook or by crook he would do it.

Just in time he found Horsham. The building was old but big. It was ideal. It was cheap. Seven of his workers came with him and he trained another twelve. They worked time and overtime.

He rented a small cottage out at Brankscombe and Meg came home to him. Their furniture came out of store again. They had to live carefully but they had a life together.

Now Michael owned the whole area that had held the large dirty factory. That had been knocked down six years ago and the new plant and warehouses had gradually gone up followed by the office block.

He was the Sole Distributor of a whole range of imported sports equipments and they manufactured more and more of their top quality goods.

Michael Horton Limited was a very strong company with some eighty employees and twelve salesmen on the road. Michael and Meg owned the whole concern.

Two years ago they'd bought Keystones after having watched it enviously for five years. It was a lovely comfortable house. A happy house. A real home to all four of them.

As Michael sat nursing his migraine he felt that again he had made it up to Meg – materially, at least – for they were comfortable and happy.

Now he only had to keep this cricket thing from her for a short while. Perhaps only a month or so, and then he'd make that up to her and settle down to be the middle-aged man he was becoming.

'Feeling?' Meg asked him.

'Better now, thanks. It's not a bad one.'

'I'm glad.'

He was glad she was glad. It somehow made her closer.

Sir Maurice and Bebington sat with Ben Hendricks on hard wooden chairs outside the netting behind the batting wicket, roughly where three slips would have been.

Tom Lipton was geared up and admiring the wide practice indoor net. He had been charming to Michael as had Sir Maurice. Only Bebington was cool and rather abrupt.

Ben was worried about Horton. He looked drawn and far from well. He certainly looked no athlete today. His forehead was badly creased and his eyes looked tired. His shoulders slumped.

He walked slowly over to where the balls were resting on their ledged table. Selected one at random.

'Can you give me leg stump?' asked Lipton.

Michael moved to the bowler's wicket. He indicated to England's Captain.

'That's it. One leg.' He walked back to his marker. Seemed to take a grip on himself. Squared his shoulders and moved in to bowl. One-two-three – four five. The ball hummed through the air.

Afterwards, Michael was to think that that ball should have been the one to settle the issue.

It pitched two foot six outside the off stump.

Lipton raised his bat and kept it held over his right shoulder. He stuck out his left knee to protect his wicket from nothing. As far as he was concerned it would go through wide to the off and was dangerously far from the crease to play at – for the first ball at least. He certainly saw no danger.

The ball cut in sharply to the right only about a foot off the ground. It hissed past Lipton's knee and rattled firmly against the middle and off stumps.

Of all the hundreds and hundreds of balls that Michael had bowled, it was probably the best.

Lipton bowled Horton 0. First ball.

Ben relaxed slightly.

Sir Maurice leaned forward.

Even Bebington looked surprised.

Lipton was rigid.

There was a moment of complete silence.

'That's it,' said Lipton. 'I'm out,' and he walked down to meet Michael. He stopped opposite him.

'Could you bowl that same ball again? Exactly. Before you treat me to your other tricks. I'd like to try and play it knowing what was coming. I want to see if it can be dealt with.'

'I'm prepared to try,' said Michael. 'I can't just serve up what's ordered any more than another bowler. I might get somewhere near the same.'

Lipton went back to his crease.

Michael came in.

The ball looked pretty like the first one.

It pitched just over two feet from the off stump. Lipton hardly lifted his bat at all. He shuffled quickly across towards the ball. It bounced. Michael had given it slightly more back spin. It rose quite sharply as it cut in towards the stumps. Lipton knew he was too close to the ball. He tried to withdraw his bat slightly. The ball flipped the edge of the blade and flew through the air towards Sir Maurice. If it hadn't been for the netting in the way, it would have gone clean down his throat.

Again Lipton would have been out. Caught third slip. Bowled Horton.

'That wasn't the same ball,' Tom complained.

'They never are,' said Michael.

For half an hour Michael kept up his one-two-three – four five. A few balls were very loose and wild. More than usual perhaps. But enough were astoundingly effective. He had Lipton 'caught' four times and clean bowled him twice more. For good measure he bowled a dead straight vicious top spin creeper which flashed through under the bat and rapped Lipton's left toe right in front of the stumps. It was Tom, himself, who said,

'All right. L.B.W. No need to ask.'

Lipton had not been as hard to bowl to as Ivor Hughes. He didn't use his feet so much and Michael knew that few runs had been scored off him. The migraine headache hadn't helped, but he'd put up a pretty remarkable show. He was well aware of that.

Lipton came out of the net. He walked up to Michael and clapped him gently on the shoulder. He said nothing. Just patted the shoulder and shook his head from side to side in wonderment.

They joined the others.

Michael sat down on a spare wooden chair. Lipton stood leaning on his bat.

Sir Maurice spoke to Tom Lipton.

'Do you want to discuss things now? Or do you need time to think about it?'

'Up to you. It's been a complete revelation to me. I can't read the chap's wrist at all. It's just guesswork and that's damned dangerous. The rest you saw for yourselves. He spins the ball a mile and seems to have pretty good control of it. It was better than I'd thought it was going to be – more incredible.'

'Bebington?' asked Sir Maurice.

'I think we should think about it. After all we've only seen

Mr. Horton working here on his own wicket with his own selected balls. I think it wants more thought.'

'Have you anything to add, Ben?' Kerr turned politely to Hendricks.

'It's up to you, Sir. You've seen Mike at work. Not at his best I might say . . .'

'Christ,' interrupted Lipton.

'. . . you must decide what to do from here on.'

Sir Maurice Kerr was a man of decisions.

'I'd like to see a full trial on grass. We could borrow a ground – perhaps Guildford – and put up canvas screens round the wicket. We must certainly keep this whole thing very, very confidential. I don't want a word of it to leak out. We'd lose the whole advantage of surprise if we did.

'Personally, Mr. Horton, I am most impressed but there are a whole lot of reasons for not introducing you into Test Cricket out of the blue. At the same time it would be absurd to put you "on the market" in County Cricket and expose the surprise element of your ability.

'Let's do a field trial with just us five and Peter Ames and Ivor Hughes. If that's a success we'll think again.

'What about one morning next week? Say Tuesday. Bebington can fix the details – can't you?'

'Yes, if it's worth it.'

'Of course it is,' said Lipton.

'I mean that Mr. Horton's age and fitness are against him,' said Bebington. 'I don't think we should be carried away.'

Sir Maurice Kerr poured oil.

'A trial isn't being carried away, I don't think. Just common sense. In the meantime the Selection Committee can consider the rather exceptional circumstances and see what we come up with. There's never been a case like this before – but by God it's exciting, isn't it?'

On that note they left.

Tom Lipton was full of thanks to Michael for the most fascinating and degrading afternoon. England's Captain was clearly impressed.

Bebington murmured his good-bye. For some reason he was anti-Horton.

Kerr was clearly impressed – with reservations.

They drove off from the rear of the factory as it started raining.

Ben and Michael walked round to the office.

Mrs. Ware had a message for Horton.

'Mary rang four times to ask if you were going to take her into Haywards Heath. Seems you'd promised to go at three o'clock. Did you forget?'

'Oh, my Christ,' said Michael. 'That's the second day I've forgotten her. Poor kid. Oh, I am a sod. Why am I so thoughtless?'

'It's all right,' said his secretary. 'I explained you were tied up and got Mannering to run her over in the van. They got away soon after three-thirty. She seemed satisfied.'

'That's not the point,' Michael complained. 'I said I'd do it and I forgot. I never even asked you to remind me. Oh hell. Sorry Ben,' he went on, 'come on in.'

They sat in Michael's comfortable office. He was tired. Nearly exhausted. Partly physical, partly nerves.

'What do you think, Ben?'

'Highly successful as an exercise. Whether it gets you into a Test team is another matter. The Selection Committee is really Kerr, Bebington and Tom Lipton, so we had the right people there. Unfortunately they work on the principle of hundred percent agreement in choosing the team and Bebington is not convinced. He's got a lot of power. Almost a veto. Sir Maurice wouldn't go dead against Bebington. That worries me. He's a bugger when it comes to stubbornness. Never did like him.'

'Oh well, let's leave it 'til Tuesday. I feel all in. Come on home and have a drink.'

'No thanks. You're too tired. Anyway I must get back to London. Don't lose heart. It went bloody well. You'll have more people on your side on Tuesday. I'll let you know the time and the place. You get some rest. Well done, Mike. I think it's still a starter.'

*

'Mary,' Michael called out as he entered the house.

'I'm here. In the study, Daddy.'

Michael walked slowly through into his favourite room.

'I'm so sorry about this afternoon, darling. I got tied up.'

'It's all right. I get used to it. I went with Mannering.'

'Did you get what you wanted?'

'No. They'd run out. We were too late.'

'I'm sorry love. We should have gone yesterday.'

'Yes. We were meant to.'

'What did you want?'

'A Denim suit. They're by Masons. Awfully nice.'

'How about London? Could we try there? Tomorrow, perhaps.' He looked at his daughter sitting on the floor.

'I am going to try London tomorrow. Mannering said he'd take me with your permission.'

'I'll do it. We could leave early and have lunch up there.'

'I'd sooner trust Mannering if you don't mind, Daddy. You see I really do want this suit and you might not be free – or something.'

Michael was silent.

He knew she was right.

Anyway he'd got a Staff Meeting in the morning.

'I'd like to buy it for you Mary.' Michael started taking out his wallet. The girl shook her fair head.

'It's all right. I've been saving up for it. I've got the money. It's just that I thought we were going together. That's all.'

'I'm sorry.'

He turned and left the study.

Meg was in the hall.

'You forgot Mary,' she said.

'I know. Something cropped up.'

'Of course. A message would have been kind.'

'Oh, cut it out, Meg. I know I've ballsed it up. No need to rub it in.'

'Isn't there?' she asked.

*

Michael tried on his cricket gear on Saturday morning when Meg and the children were doing the weekend shopping. He was pretty horrified.

Everything was very tatty. All right for his indoors net but hardly suitable for playing before England's Selection Committee – even behind canvas screens.

The trousers were far too tight and uncomfortable round his over-ample middle. They'd be hell to spend all day in. Everything seemed to centre round his stomach. Even the shirts, which were in quite passable condition, gripped his middle.

He was thoroughly despondent with his shape.

In the afternoon he ran down to Sloanes in East Grinstead where he wasn't known. He bought two pairs of comfortable and rather baggy whites and four shirts. Six pairs of good socks and a new jockstrap. He added a sleeveless sweater and a voluminous top sweater for good measure.

He drove back feeling better and left his purchases in his office.

That would make Tuesday easier and more pleasant.

Meg and Mary were having a slanging match when he got home. Something about Mary not helping with the housework.

He crept quietly into the study.

Tuesday dawned overcast.

The whole of the middle square at the Guildford County Ground was surrounded with green canvas seven feet high.

Even the groundsman didn't know the reason.

Tom Lipton, Peter Ames and Ivor Hughes had all managed to get to the trial. They met half an hour early and changed in the downstairs Visitor's Room.

They joked about this and that.

'Tell me, Tom,' said Ames. 'Do you think they're serious about this chap Horton? I mean that they might play him in a Test.'

'Hell of a thing to decide to do,' Lipton replied. 'Frankly I've never played against bowling like it. I can't read what the chap's doing at all. But what's his physical state? He's well over fifty. Carrying a load of weight. What do you do with him in the field? Can he bat? We want to know a bloody sight more. Could he last five days and come up bowling the same quality stuff? It's a hell of a gamble.'

Ivor Hughes intervened.

'I don't agree. It doesn't matter a sod if he can bat or not. God knows English numbers nine, ten and eleven never can. Then if he's nursed carefully in the field the stress can be taken off him. He's obviously got a damned good ball sense and he may be quite competent in the gully or lost out at mid on. We'd have to aim at fielding ten and a half men. I think his bowling would be worth the risk.'

'You tell Bebington.'

'Oh that miserable basket,' said Hughes. 'I might have guessed he'd be against Horton. No imagination.'

'You've got too much, Ivor. That's your trouble.'

'You need imagination in our position. We haven't beaten the Australians in five series. We've got as weak a team as we've had for four seasons. They're at their absolute peak and if we don't do something imaginative, the series will be over in three matches. I'm serious.'

'I agree,' said Peter Ames. 'Ivor's right. At worst we've got to win one and draw the other of the first two Tests. If they get on top we've had it. I think it calls for something outstanding like Mike Horton. I'd carry him. Cyril Washbrook played at over forty and was a tremendous success.'

'Cyril was fit and in regular play,' said Lipton. 'Quite another matter to a fifty-three-year-old executive. Don't think I'm not keen on Horton. I am. Bloody keen. But there's going to be plenty of opposition. Better drop it now. There's someone coming.'

They sat lacing their boots.

Michael walked in.

'Morning.'

The three players greeted him.

'Can I change here?'

'Of course. Shove up Ivor and make room for Mike.'

They were going to treat him as their own age.

Sir Maurice Kerr appeared at the door.

'Morning all. We'll start in about fifteen minutes. It's a bit damp on the wicket but that will make the trial more worthwhile. How are you Horton?'

'Fine. In top form. Looking forward to working on a grass wicket.'

'Good. Ivor will you pad up first and Peter will keep wicket, of course. Tom you can bowl a couple of overs to warm things up. Keep them outside the off stump and we'll put Horton at cover to loosen him up a bit. All right?'

He disappeared.

'Don't you run too hard, Mike,' said Ivor. 'Keep yourself for your bowling. They're crafty, these buggers.'

The cricketers walked out of the pavilion together. They entered the canvas surround through a flap.

Kerr, Bebington and Ben Hendricks were standing inside. The wickets were up. A dozen balls, some still in their wrappings, were on the grass.

Everyone seemed very serious.

Michael felt slightly sick.

Meg entered the sordid small office in the back streets of Horsham just as Michael was feeling sick.

There was just the one room with a single window looking onto the road. The glass was filthy, both inside and out and the hanging electric bulb in the ceiling always seemed to have to be on.

There was an old rolltop desk too full of papers to close down. Mr. Gingham sat at this in a wooden swivel chair. There was one other seat with a broken rush bottom and a table littered with junk including a kettle and equipment to make tea. A half bottle of Gordon's lay in the nearly full wastepaper basket with the split side.

'Come in, Mrs. Horton,' said Gingham, half rising in his chair. He was about as sordid looking as his office. A generally greasy-looking suit hung on his sparse frame. His face was hawk-like and his head bald, shiny and slightly dirty. He had a black wart above his left ear that he picked at.

Meg loathed him. She had for some weeks.

'What news, Mr. Gingham?' She didn't sit down.

'I fear we are wasting your money and my time, my dear lady.' He spoke with an appropriately greasy voice through his nose.

'How do you mean?' asked Meg.

'Well as far as I can tell, Mr. Horton does stay at his office when he says he does. At least he stays in the factory buildings though he may not be near a telephone.

'At first I thought perhaps the lady you had in mind worked in the office and stayed behind but I have checked the staff and that is not the case.

'My second idea was that the er, personage, came from outside and joined your husband there. This has also been a blank.

'Are you quite sure you are right in this matter?'

Meg ignored the question.

'What about when he goes out?'

'Nothing. That is, nothing we could call strange. He went to East Grinstead on Saturday, to a sports shop called Sloanes. He was there forty minutes and came out with some packages. He took these to his office.

'My man has followed him today. I don't think we will be lucky.'

Mr. Gingham coughed delicately and shifted some papers.

'Sometimes, Madam, ladies get mistaken about matters such as this. A little falling off in interest, shall we say, by the loved one and they think there must be another, um, lady in the picture. Do you think perhaps . . . ?'

'No I don't. He's being most peculiar. Secretive. I've never known him like this. It's not imagination.'

'Very well. We'll keep on trying. If you could give some guide perhaps. That might lead us.'

'I've told you, I can't. That's your job isn't it? You told me you could ferret out anything.'

'Just so, dear lady. Just so. Leave it with me. I'll ring you if anything comes up.'

Meg left the filthy office with the nauseating Mr. Gingham and breathed the fresh air of the street.

Michael took a full breath of the clean air of Guildford County Cricket Ground. It settled the queasy feeling he had.

Peter Ames walked down to the stumps at the North End and adjusted the bails. He did several knees bend and slapped the knuckles of his right glove into his left palm. He swung his arms, navvy fashion. It was cool.

Lipton selected a ball. Flung it at Ames who took it just above the stumps and tossed it to Michael. He wasn't ready – but he caught it. Flicked it sideways to Lipton who was pacing out his run.

No one talked.

Even Sir Maurice, Bebington and Ben Hendricks stood silently by the canvas surround.

Hughes came through the flap, padded up. Michael was pleased to see the Glamorgan player was wearing a pair of his firm's batting gloves.

Hughes took guard.

Ames crouched down.

Michael was at square cover. He moved in towards the batsman as Lipton came in to bowl.

The ball was on the off stump, overpitched, doing nothing.

Hughes played it simply back to the bowler.

For the first five balls nothing much happened. One went through fast to Ames off the rather damp wicket. Another was well short and Ivor cracked it hard round to square leg to rap against the canvas.

The sixth ball was a half volley outside the off stump and Hughes played hard down on it with perfect timing. It flew to Michael's left curving with the spin off the bat. He went down fast on one knee covering as wide an area as possible. His hands fumbled the ball but his right thigh stopped it.

'Good enough,' said Ivor.

Michael was shaking.

Lipton bowled another six balls but only one came near Horton. It was going like bullet past his right-hand side and he was far too slow to get at it. A top player would have got there but he hadn't a hope.

'Let's see Mr. Horton bowl,' called out Kerr.

This was it.

This really was the trial.

Tom Lipton flipped the ball to Michael. It was nearly new with a lot of shine on it. It was also slightly damp and hard to hold.

He dropped the ball by the small pile and picked up a worn looking cherry.

'What's wrong with the ball?' called out Bebington.

'Too new,' said Michael. 'I need the shine off it. Any spin bowler would.'

Michael just caught Bebington's reply.

'Too damned particular.'

He measured off his run up.

He wouldn't be too clever to start with.

In he came. One-two-three – four five.

The ball flew wildly out of his hand and landed level with the stumps and at least twelve yards from them. The most enormous wide. It trickled to the canvas surround.

'Ha,' laughed Bebington. 'Bloody marvellous.'

Ben retrieved the ball and tossed it back to Michael. It was slippery now with wet.

He walked slowly back to his mark.

He concentrated like mad.

He came in to bowl. One-two-three – four five.

This was better.

It pitched a yard outside the leg stump. Ivor left it. It bit into the soft wicket and turned sharply.

Ames stood mesmerised.

The ball flicked the leg stump and removed the bail.

Hughes looked horrified.

'As you say, Bebington,' said Kerr. 'Ha, bloody marvellous.'

Michael knew he could do it. He could do it on this grass wicket. He could do it even with a damp ball.

He bowled three overs and had Hughes out once more, clean bowled.

The outstanding feature was the number of balls that beat both Hughes and Ames and would have gone for four byes. They had no pre-knowledge of which way the ball was going and Peter Ames' pads were filthy from last minute dives to try and get to the ball. He really enjoyed it and was laughing loudly.

Kerr walked across to Michael.

'Would you go and pad up? We'd better see if your batting levels with your bowling.'

'You'll be disappointed, I'm afraid.'

'Don't worry. It's just to see what you can or can't do.'

Michael slipped out of the canvas flap and made for the pavilion.

'What do you think?' asked Ben, as the six of them moved together.

'Very interesting,' said Kerr. 'Very interesting indeed.'

'That's an understatement,' said Tom Lipton. 'I'm sorry to sound rude Sir, it's not just interesting, it's fantastic.'

'Hear, hear,' said Ames.

'We've seen him bowl three overs when he's fresh,' from Bebington. 'Can he do it when he's been in the field all day in a hot summer? I doubt it. He'd flake out at his age and with his physique.'

'He'd have to train up,' said Ben.

'It may be more than he can do,' Sir Maurice looked round the others. 'We may be asking too much of him. We ought to have a medical report.'

'I'd be prepared to carry him in the field,' said Tom. 'He's not completely useless, as we saw.'

'I'd back that,' from Ames. 'What do you say, Ivor?'

'I agree.'

'The point you seem to be missing,' said Bebington, 'is that you don't select the team.'

That shut them up.

Maurice Kerr and Ben Hendricks talked quietly, walking up and down. The others stood around waiting.

Michael came through the canvas flap.

He wasn't worrying about the batting. It didn't really matter if he made a crumbles of it, but he had been quite passable in his day and he knew his style would look good at least.

Lipton and Hughes didn't let him off lightly.

Tom's medium pace swingers were accurate and fast to Michael. Ivor's 'straight up and downers' were easier to play. He put his mind fully to the job. Bat and pad. Bat and pad. If you're going to put your foot out to the ball, put it right out to it. Get behind the ball. Behind it. Cover up. Bat and pad. Don't play back to the ball on this wicket. Leave that one alone.

For the first ten minutes Michael was madly out of touch. His timing all to hell. It was obvious that he knew what he was doing as a batsman but he was hardly effective. He turned an overpitched ball from Ivor Hughes into a yorker and was clean bowled middle stump. It wasn't a good ball – but he himself turned it into one. Lipton had him scratching at away swingers outside the off stump until he just touched one and sent what would have been a plum catch to second slip.

Then he got into his stride. He had a spell of some five minutes when his timing came back. He got a short one from the England Captain and timing it like a nut sent it high and deep over mid-wicket. It cleared the canvas, the out-field and nearly the whole ground. It gave him confidence. He cut and missed. Then cut again and cracked the ball hard and square into the canvas.

'Good shot,' said Hughes.

And then he went to pieces.

A dull pain in the back of his neck – really at the top of his right shoulder – developed. At first it was just uncomfortable but as the bowling went on it became sharper and affected his timing and his movements. He tried hard to show nothing. Suddenly his legs felt heavy. His feet like dead weights on the bottom of them. He knew he was overdoing it but he wasn't going to give up now.

He started taking longer rests between balls. He'd walk away from the crease and back again to gain relief. Sod my rotten body, he thought.

'Come on. Let's get on with it,' called Bebington. 'You're making a damned meal of it.'

Hughes had Horton L.B.W. clean as a whistle the next ball. He wished Bebington would shut up.

Michael finished the half hour's batting with a really good shot that fetched a ball outside the off stump from Lipton right round to square leg. It was a cheeky stroke but it came off.

'Right,' said Maurice Kerr, 'that's a good note to end on. Now get your gear off, Mr. Horton, and Ivor can pad up again. We think we ought to see half a dozen overs from you now that you've taken a bit of exercise. You agree?'

'Just as you like,' said Michael, as if it was an everyday affair. His heart was pumping pretty hard. His neck was most painful and he longed to be able to stretch and massage it. He thought the movement unwise. He tried to saunter to the canvas surround but his legs felt like lead and very weak.

He placed his bat carefully against an upright post. Took off his pads. Slipped out his box and removed his thigh pad. He laid the lot with his gloves on top on the ground. He took his time and breathed slowly and deeply. He wondered what the devil he was doing. Was he really capable of carrying out his plan? Physically capable. Or would his bloody old body let him down?

Again he took his time. Thank God Hughes was taking a long time padding up. Michael wondered if the Glamorgan player knew he needed a breathing space.

Sir Maurice and Ben stood still and waited.

Bebington paced up and down.

When it came to it Michael's first ball was as bad as the first one of the morning. A howling wide from one that slipped out of his fingers and landed near Ben Hendricks' feet.

His neck was giving him gyp.

He tried two simple balls to help find a length and Hughes dealt severely with both. Then he forgot his neck and his legs. He put aside his leaden feet. He concentrated every ounce of his power on his bowling. One-two-three – four five. The ball was a maximum back spinner. Ivor Hughes played forward. The ball popped up off the face of the bat and Michael took the easiest of catches.

'Damn and blast.'

'You're out, Ivor. Walk,' smiled Ames.

'Well done,' came from Ben.

'Well bowled,' said Lipton.

Bebington and Kerr were silent.

Somehow, he couldn't think how afterwards, Michael bowled seven overs. They would have been forty-two balls of agony had he not blanked out everything but pitching and spinning that ball accurately. As it was he was at his best. Even at the end of such a session, neither Hughes nor Ames were reading his spin. In some ways the batsman and the wicket keeper were a shambles. There were moments when they didn't know what they could do to control this wildly flicking ball. Hughes was even playing cross bat shots in desperation while Ames tried standing back which only improved things for him a little and was quite the wrong technique for a slow spin bowler.

They admitted defeat.

Michael Horton had almost done what he liked. He put Tom Lipton at leg slip and four balls later had Hughes caught there. He'd bowl short with tremendous top spin and the batsman having decided to hook found himself scrapping away to avoid being yorked! Michael almost did what he liked.

Maurice Kerr called a halt.

'I think we've seen enough. You chaps go and have a shower and change. Perhaps you'd spare me a few minutes in my care in about twenty minutes, Mr. Horton.'

'Of course. I'll be as quick as possible.'

They all slipped out of the canvas surround and made their way slowly to the pavilion. Michael was out front, carrying his gear and trying to walk lithely. His shoulder was aching like hell. Right up his neck and into his hair.

Meg sat in Mary Ware's small office which was just off Michael's. Opposite her was Mary behind a low sleek I.B.M. typewriter. There were papers on the roller. It was Mary's busiest time of the day.

They both had cups of tea. Meg smoking a cigarette. She'd been there for over ten minutes and said little except the expected platitudes. Mary knew there must be more to the now rare visit than this and she waited patiently.

'Have you noticed anything . . . well, . . . different about Michael these last weeks?' Meg at last came out.

'How do you mean, Mrs. Horton, different?'

'Well, pre-occupied. Something on his mind.'

'I've never known Mr. Horton when he hadn't got a million things on his mind. Yes, he's very pre-occupied.'

'What with?'

'Oh, there's a problem of our being too seasonal. We sell much more in the Spring than the Autumn . . .'

'I didn't mean like that,' interrupted Meg. 'He's always got that sort of thing on his mind. I mean some particular thing that's . . . really . . . well, pre-occupying him. To the exclusion of all else.'

Mary Ware was an intelligent woman. She could have gone to London and held down a really top flight job there. She preferred to work locally in a less dramatic way and have more time with her husband who was a Director of a small Surrey group of wine stores. She was small and thin. Not slim. That was too kind a word. Her face like her hair was rather neutral. Her saving grace were her eyes. Almost violent blue, people were quite surprised to see such lovely eyes in such an ordinary face. At thirty-five, Mary Ware was childless. One of the great sadnesses of her life. She was an incredibly kind and sincere person.

She guessed at once what Meg Horton was worried about.

Knowing Michael really well, she thought Meg was wrong. At least she felt fairly certain there wasn't another woman in the picture. Pre-occupied beyond reason? Yes that was possible. He'd often get wholly involved in something to the extent that everything else took second place. But Meg Horton must know that. There was nothing new about it.

Mary Ware put it carefully.

'There are no new people in his life at the moment,' she rushed on, 'he is terribly busy but it's with things and problems – not people.'

'You know that?'

'Well I think I would know. We work pretty closely together. I know most of what goes on.'

'But not all.'

'No. No I couldn't know all. But I've worked with him for five years – you get to know the man in a job like this.'

Just for a moment a flicker of suspicion went through Meg's mind. Could Mary Ware . . .? No. She rejected it. But why should she? Reject it. It was quite possible. Or was it? She threw out the thought as quickly as it had come.

They sat silent for a moment.

'What are you worried about, Mrs. Horton?' Mary Ware wondered if direct action were not the best thing.

Meg drew in hard on her cigarette.

'I thought he might be having an affair.'

Mary Ware looked down on the papers in her typewriter.

'I don't think you're right.'

'You only don't think it. You don't know.'

'No.'

'Then why shouldn't he be?'

'Because,' said Mary, 'I think you are wrong. Quite wrong.'

'I'd want better proof than your guess. I think he is . . .'

'Aren't *you* guessing? You don't seem to have much proof – or do you?'

'No. No I haven't proof,' Meg replied. 'I must be honest and say I've tried to get it but I haven't. Got it, I mean.'

'Then what makes you think ...'

'He does. His attitude.'

'Oh, Mrs. Horton, I do think you're wrong. Michael may be in love with an idea but I don't believe it's with a girl. I'm sure I too would notice that. Honestly I do. I tell you what. Now I know your worry I'll let you know if there's anything in it. Goodness knows, I'm fond enough of you both. I'd hate to see anything go wrong. He gets obsessions. He's on to one now. I don't know what it is. I've no idea. But he spends a lot of what he calls "Development Time" in the old drying shop behind the factory. He's got a bug on something – and I promise you it's work. You know him, Mrs. Horton. He's got ... involved – but it's not a girl. I think you can be pretty sure of that.'

'I may be wrong.' Meg stubbed out a cigarette. 'Thanks for being so understanding. I shouldn't worry you I know. But well ...'

They both stood up.

'I'll tell you if you're right. I promise that,' said Mary. She felt pretty sure it was a promise she wouldn't have to keep.

Meg Horton walked down the office stairs and out onto the car park. She walked round the building to the very rear. There was a long, high structure with a door but no windows. She tried to see in at the door. The keyhole was blocked up. The door fitted too well. It had a large Chubb lock that she fingered.

Michael Horton threw his cricket bag in the back of the Rover. On the seat. He walked slowly with approaching stiffness towards Maurice Kerr's Daimler, parked by the flagpole next to the pavilion. He opened the nearside door, smiled at Kerr, and eased himself in. He couldn't see Bebington or Ben Hendricks anywhere.

Maurice Kerr offered Michael a cigarette. He said 'No thanks' just in time. He'd got to start behaving like an athlete. He'd better begin now.

'You have, without doubt,' said Kerr, drawing on his short

cigar, 'a phenomenal control over a cricket ball. You wouldn't like to tell me how you do it, I suppose?'

'No.'

'Quite. Well leaving that aside it seems you can master the best batting we can put up to you and there's no doubt in my mind that makes for Test Match material. If any of our regular cricket boys could do what you've done today they'd get a Test place. No doubt about it. I suppose on those grounds you think we ought to play you?'

'Yes.'

Kerr paused.

'Look here Horton. You must see the jam we're in. We can't try you out in a County game – that would give the show away – and yet can you see yourself playing a hard five day game and not breaking down?'

'Yes – if I'm nursed a bit.'

'Damn it. Even with nursing you'd have to be fit and alert as hell for seven hours with minimum breaks.'

'Not when we're batting.'

'No. But you could spend up to two days running in the field.'

'Not if I'm as good as you so kindly seem to think,' said Michael.

'Again in theory, I agree. But what if you crack up? That leaves us ten men and one good cricketer gets left out.'

'Bebington's attitude.'

'Yes,' said Maurice Kerr. 'Bebington's attitude. We've got to select the twelve men likely to play in the First Test at Birmingham on June 3rd by Sunday week and I'm buggered if I know what to recommend. You've certainly caused us some bother.'

'O'K.' Michael sat up and put his hand on the door lever. 'If that's the angle I'd better go.'

'Don't be a bloody fool, Horton. Stay where you are. Surely you can see this causes some concern?'

'It seems to me I'm a problem you'd prefer not to be faced with. I don't blame you. You don't see it the way I do. Why should you? I'm not the sort of choice you have to make normally. You have a few hundred men from which you choose a balanced eleven. Well, now you've got a few hundred and one. And that one could go through the Australians like butter. I'm not being bumptious – merely practical. You know it. I know it. Those young chaps in the pavilion know it. Even Bebington knows it. We haven't held the ashes for years. This Australian team has beaten the West Indies – at home. Nine of them were in the team that beat us in three straight Tests in Australia. One. Two. Three. Just like that! And you've nothing really new to put into the field against them.

'Or have you?

'You think about that, Sir Maurice, and get Bebington thinking about it too.

'There! I've said enough. Too much. You'll probably tell me to get the hell out of it.'

Kerr listened quietly to every word. At the end he sat. Thinking. Pulling on his cigar. He looked tired and old. His brown face creased.

'See here, Horton. If it were up to young Lipton and myself I think you'd be on the short list of twelve on Sunday week. Can't say more than that. But there are ways this thing of selection are done and Bob Bebington is one of us and we accept his opinion. Since I've been President we've all ended up in full agreement with the teams chosen. We stand or fall by it – together.'

'Very cosy!' said Michael. Then 'Sorry! That was unwarranted.'

'No. I see your point of view. But you know that. I've told you I'll take the risk. I'll try and work on Bebington. He wants those Ashes just as much as you and I do. Make no mistake about it. But he's very conventional, Bob Bebington, and he's also bloody stubborn.' He sighed. 'Leave it with me. I'll keep in touch through Hendricks. I know he's your man. Salt of the earth. Often wish he was on the Selectors. Don't worry too much, Horton. And keep in training! You might let me know if that incredible ability of yours disappears.'

The incredible ability left Michael Horton as he drove back to Horsham. He had a cracking great migraine.

He knew he was pent up. Mostly with frustration. He was certainly tired. Physically exhausted. Add to that the hopes and the despairs and you have good migrainal material.

As he passed Cranleigh it hit him. Dizzy, jagged lines across his sight. A blank space at the point he concentrated his eyes. A funny sense of relief and welcome that it had happened. Almost pleasure.

He pulled up by the tennis courts on the edge of the green. He turned off the engine and sighed deeply. He couldn't see the clock on the dash properly but he knew it was almost one-thirty. He laid back with his head on the seat rest. The car was three-quarters off the road.

Michael's eyes were shut so he never saw the Police car drive past and pull in across his bonnet. The two young men got out. One walked slowly round the Rover, inspecting it. The other approached the driver's door. He rapped on the closed window.

Horton sat up with a start. He stared, unseeing properly, at the blur of the policeman's face close to the window.

He knew what the man was. He took a deep breath and lowered the window.

'Yes, Officer?'

'This your car?'

'Yes.'

'Can you tell me the number of it, please?'

'NNJ 7L.'

'I see. Do you have a licence?'

'Yes. Of course.'

'May I see it?'

For once Michael had a wallet on him. It was normally in his business briefcase. He fiddled about. Trying to make his eyes behave. He forgot a licence was no longer a pale brown booklet. He knew he'd got it but couldn't fine the bloody thing.

'May I?' The policeman put a hand carefully in and took the green and white paper. He didn't look at it. He looked hard at Michael instead.

'You feeling alright, are you?'

'Yes. I'm alright, thank you. Just a headache.'

'Um!' He looked towards his partner, who was standing by the wheel in front of the Rover. He nodded slightly. The other man moved off to the Police car.

Michael felt irritated by their attitude. Cold, inhuman lot, he thought. In the old days they'd have been respectful – and have been proud to be so. Not today. All that had gone.

'Mr. Morton, is it?'

'No.' Suddenly Michael was at that point of a really bad migraine when the mind back-fires. He knew bloody well his name wasn't Morton. It was Horton. Wasn't it? Damn it, he *knew* it was! Surely.

'No' he repeated. 'It's Horton – with an aitch.'

'I see, Mr. Horton. And where do you live?'

Michael concentrated hard. He knew it was at Deighton but what was the bloody house called? Sod this migraine! He looked up at the policeman.

'It's in my licence thing, isn't it?' he asked.

'Yes. But I'd like to hear it from you.'

Michael Horton knew the house was Keystones – or was it? Was that somewhere else? Keystones was a house alright. But was it his or someone else's? God, he was so tired!

'Keystones, Deighton, near Horsham,' he said clearly.

'Thank you.' The policeman handed the licence back through the window. He turned to his smaller partner, who had joined him. Took something from him. He leant in on Michael.

'I'd like you to blow into this device, if you would. Have you done this before, Mr. Horton?'

'No I have not. And the last drink I had was last night. A weak whisky and soda.'

'I see. Well, it's very simple. All you do is this,' and he explained the process to Horton.

Michael half took it in. He blew when he had to and felt the actual ache of the migraine come on viciously in the top right side of his skull.

The tall policeman took the balloon. He studied it. Turned to his junior partner. 'Negative.' He looked back at Horton.

'May I see what you have in that bag in the back?'

'Whatever for?'

'I'd just like to see, please.'

'The door's open. – No, not that one. The other side.'

The policeman sorted through his cricket gear.

'Playing a match today?'

'No. Yes. That is, no. I'm not.'

'I see.' The man slammed the door and took out a notebook. 'Do you have your Insurance Certificate and Ministry of Transport Form VT20 with you?'

'No. No, I don't,' said Michael. 'I'll take them to Horsham Police Station in five days. Will that be alright?'

'Yes. Just take this slip to remind you. You won't forget, will you?'

'No. Of course not. Thanks.'

'Now you pull right off the road onto the Green, Mr. Horton. You're committing an offence. Obstructing the road. We'll just give a warning, but don't do it again. Understand?'

'Yes. Yes, I understand.' Michael started the Rover. He had trouble finding first gear. The two policemen stood and watched, expressionless. He jumped the clutch and pulled onto the grass, just missing the Police car.

He sat while they took off and then closed his eyes for twenty minutes.

He drove slowly and carefully home.

Much earlier that Thursday morning, Geoff Middleton was driving down the A3. He had been on the Daily News for nearly two years. He called himself a 'leg man' and hadn't yet dropped into any particular niche within the Fleet Street paper. He was at the beck and call of the News Editor and found himself involved, one moment in some side issue of a murder hunt, and the next interviewing a New York musical star who had come to take over the Palladium. It was bloody good experience. He knew McCormack, the News Editor, liked him, and when he did get slotted he guessed it would be a good position.

On that Thursday morning he was driving from London down to Portsmouth to attend a Local Government Hearing on some condemned Council houses and he was due to be bored to death at half-past two that afternoon.

As he went down the A3 he found he was out of cigarettes and, cursing, pulled off at Guildford to find some. As he passed the Guildford Cricket Club Ground he noticed – in the way that all good newspaper men should notice – that something damn peculiar was going on. Three men were just completing erecting a large canvas screen all round the wicket area.

Jesus! he thought, looks like an exhumation's going on. He stopped and watched the men put the last pegs into the ground. They sauntered off towards the pavilion. In his twenty-one years Middleton had never seen anything like it. He couldn't think of the reason for it. That alone made him think it worthwhile reporting back to the paper.

He stopped at a red phone box. Heaved his way into it. Got his money out and was ready to make the call before he saw the phone was useless. It had been rifled. He cursed the bloody vandals and drove on through Guildford till he found another booth. He rang the News Desk at the Daily News and asked for Sarah Playdell. She was on in ten seconds and in crisp, short sentences he explained the oddity.

'Sounds weird,' she said. 'Okay. I'll come down. Can you wait till I get there in case something happens?'

'Sure.'

'Where will we meet?'

'I'll be about 100 yards north of the main entrance to the ground. I'm in the blue Victor, RBY.'

'Right,' the girl said. 'I'll be about an hour. Keep your eyes skinned, won't you?'

'Don't be bloody stupid! What do you think?'

'Sorry!' She rang off.

Middleton parked the Vauxhall where he said he'd be. Laid a morning paper on the steering wheel as if absorbed in it. Pulled an old cap down over his eyes and prepared for his observation vigil.

Absolutely nothing happened for an hour and ten minutes. Nobody went near the canvas screen and he thought maybe he'd started a wild goose chase and there might be some perfectly logical explanation.

A car pulled up behind him and a small, dark girl got out. Her hair, which had a touch of auburn, was cut short and wavy. She wore a green denim flared skirt and a low V-cut white, short-sleeved cotton shirt. She was only about five foot three and had a figure that was the envy of Fleet Street. A very attractive girl indeed was Miss Playdell, the Cricket Correspondent of the Daily News.

Sarah Playdell sat in her car near to the entrance to the Guildford Cricket Ground. Geoff Middleton had been gone for nearly an hour and nothing had happened.

Sarah had studied the canvas screening with her small opera glasses but was really none the wiser. She was just giving up hope when a car coming from Guildford town slowed down and flashed to turn into the Ground. She saw at once that it was driven by Tom Lipton, the England Captain. Sitting next to him was Ivor Hughes and the small figure in the back she thought, in the flash that she had of him, was Peter Ames, the England and Kent wicket keeper. They drove in and parked near the pavilion, disappearing inside. They carried heavy bags that they had collected from the boot.

So there is something going on, she thought. Geoff was right.

Even more surprising was the next car. A Daimler which entered the car park beside the ground. Sarah instantly recognised Sir Maurice Kerr, the Chairman of the M.C.C. Selection Committee, and sitting next to him none other than Bob Bebington.

This gets more and more interesting, she thought, and then suddenly realised that the whole of the Selection Committee of the England Test XI was present here today at Guildford.

Almost immediately a third car, a Rover 3500, drove in the gate and parked behind the others. She couldn't see the man properly as he got out, but she got a good look at him as he went into the pavilion, carrying a bag. He was tall and very bulky. Almost fat. He seemed to have a slight stoop. The bag seemed too heavy for him. He disappeared into the pavilion. A moment later Bob Hendricks, whom she immediately recognised, arrived and joined the others inside.

Now she was excited. She felt absolutely certain that she had happened on something that was important. Having got hold of this thing she must hang on at all events.

She waited, and saw them all walk out to the canvas screen. Ivor Hughes padded up. The other cricketers and the tall, fat, stooped man in flannels and heavy sweaters.

She knew nothing of what went on behind the canvas, except for the occasional crack of bat against ball. She desperately wanted to know more.

Then she saw MacTavish, and it gave her an idea.

MacTavish was cocking his leg on the Ground's railing. He was a near West Highland – though not too near.

Sarah grabbed a length of string from the dashboard pocket and leapt after MacTavish. She caught him easily. He immediately came up to her with his head, shoulders and front legs rigid and his stern waving from side to side with glee. She slipped the cord through his collar and they both trotted through the gate and onto the Ground.

Sarah had no plan, except to get somewhere near the canvas screen at the opposite end to where the men had entered it.

She walked slowly round the ground, talking quietly to MacTavish the whole time, with MacTavish talking back to her. When she reached the end, she turned casually and walked towards the canvas screen as if she were exercising the dog. MacTavish jumped ahead as if he were exercising the girl.

The crack of leather on wood continued to come intermittently from inside the screening. As she got nearer, Sarah could hear the occasional murmur of voices. Her heart was going like the devil. She didn't want to be caught eavesdropping but she desperately wanted to know what was going on.

She reached the pegs holding the canvas in position and MacTavish knew he had reached Shangri La of leg-cocking bliss. He went to work madly.

It suddenly occurred to Sarah that MacTavish might bark. He hadn't yet. But suppose he did? They'd certainly come and look. She kept her fingers crossed and eased up close to the green canvas surround. She kept one eye open for the Groundsmen who must be about.

Sarah suddenly heard uproarious laughter coming from the wicket. She'd know that laugh anywhere. It was Peter Ames. A voice confirmed it.

'Well I'm buggered, I can't see the blessed thing at all! It's fabulous!'

Another voice suddenly intervened.

'Would you go and pad up? We'd better see if your batting levels with your bowling.'

A deep, pleasant voice replied.

'You'll be rather disappointed, I'm afraid.'

'Don't worry,' said the number one voice. 'It's just to see what you can do.'

There was a pause.

'What do you think?' asked another man.

'Very interesting' said number one. 'Very interesting indeed.'

'That's an understatement,' said Tom Lipton. Sarah knew it was Lipton's voice. 'I'm sorry to sound rude, Sir, but it's not just interesting, it's fantastic!'

'Hear, hear!' from young Peter Ames.

'We've seen him bowl three overs when he's fresh', said a voice she didn't recognise. 'Can he do it when he's been in the field all day in a hot summer? I doubt it. He'd flake out at his age and with his physique.'

'He'd have to train up,' said another.

The number one voice replied again.

'It may be more than he can do. We may be asking too much of him. We ought to have a medical report.'

Tom Lipton flashed back.

'I'd be prepared to carry him in the field. He's not completely useless, as we saw.'

'I'd back that', said Peter Ames. 'What do you say, Ivor?'

For the first time she heard Ivor Hughes' voice.

'I agree.'

The unknown voice again intruded.

'The point you seem to be missing is that you don't select the team.'

Silence followed.

Sarah heard the flap of the canvas being opened and felt that she'd pushed her luck far enough.

She hauled MacTavish off one of the bigger tent pegs. Got her string lead caught in the rope. Somehow extricated herself and walked smartly away towards the boundary. She had plenty of time, she felt.

She strolled slowly round the edge of the field and came upon a groundsman scraping the heavy roller.

'What's going on out there in the middle?' she asked.

'No idea,' said the man. 'Some sort of nonsense. We was just told to put it up.'

'I see. Thank you.'

She walked across in front of the pavilion into the car park and back through the gates, where she had parked the Fiat.

Sarah took up position in her car, having paid off MacTavish with a fivepenny bar of chocolate.

She awaited the next move.

Sarah Playdell began to put two and two together. It seemed to her that she came up with all sorts of different answers. Surely they couldn't be thinking of bringing Ben Hendricks back into the England Team after all these years? And in any case, no, it was a bowler not a batsman that they were talking about. Could it be one of the younger men, who had devised some new bowling technique? That seemed hardly likely, since they were obviously in good training. No, the only explanation was that the unknown man – the heavy, bulky man with the stoop – had got something they were interested in.

Sarah found it very galling, knowing a little but not much.

Whatever it was, she realised she was on to something big.

About an hour later they all came out from behind the canvas screen. The bulky man was in front, carrying some gear and striding out purposefully. Even so, he didn't look very athletic. The rest followed.

Sarah realised she'd have to take a decision shortly. What to do next?

In a way that decision was taken for her. She saw Sir Maurice Kerr, whom she had met on numerous occasions and seen even more often, slip into his Daimler behind the wheel and wait.

Twenty minutes later 'Bulky' came out, talked to Sir Maurice through the co-driver's window and then climbed in beside him. They sat together talking, looking straight ahead out of the Daimler's windscreen towards where Sarah was parked. At one moment the conversation seemed to get heated and then cooled down. 'Bulky' got out and obviously said good-bye to Sir Maurice. He walked off behind and got into the Rover 3500.

Sarah knew the right decision was to follow 'Bulky'. Her news sense instinctively told her this.

The Rover pulled out in front of a huge furniture lorry and Sarah only just caught the letters NNJ on the number plate. She didn't worry. The Rover was there and she'd overtake the pantechnicon when she was ready.

The three vehicles moved towards the town. There were no hold-ups. They entered the High Street and turned onto the Cranleigh Road.

Sarah glanced at her petrol gauge. Half full.

On the Madison Straight she put her foot down to overtake the furniture lorry. Now she'd see the full number of the Rover.

Nothing happened.

There was no response.

The Fiat gradually slowed down and, cursing, Sarah drew into the side.

The engine wasn't even firing.

The pantechnicon with the Rover in front pulled away and out of sight.

For five minutes Sarah sat fuming. God, what a bloody thing to happen! What a bitch luck was.

She never noticed the Police Panda car pull up behind.

The driver got out and came to the Fiat's window.

'In trouble? – Oh, it's you, Miss Playdell. What's up?'

She looked round at the man in the peaked cap.

'Oh, Harry! It's you! Yes. I'm in trouble. Car's packed up on me. Are you going down the Cranleigh Road?'

'That's right.'

'Oh, Harry, can you help? I was tailing a Rover 3500, first three letters NNJ. Could you try and catch it for me and check the whole number? Please, Harry!'

'Alright, Miss. Seeing as how it's you. Where'll you be?'

'The King's Head. How's that?'

'Fine. If I find it I'll ring you. If not . . .'

'Harry, there's just one man driving alone.'

'You'll get me suspended, Miss! But I've said I'll do it.'

He smiled at her and trotted back to the Panda car. A moment later it swung past her and accelerated down Madison Straight.

Sarah locked the car and walked back towards Guildford town and the King's Head. She thought the Rover would have gone too fast and too far. She was depressed.

Sarah Playdell finished her second gin and tonic. There were half a dozen people in the bar.

The telephone rang.

' 'Ullo', said the barman. 'Miss 'Oo? – Wait a minute. 'Ow do I know?' He leant into the saloon.

' 'Ave we a Miss Plading 'ere?' he called out.

'Playdell. That's me,' said Sarah, jumping up.

She took the telephone.

'Hallo!'

'Harry here, Miss. We found your party.'

'Oh, well done, Harry! What's the full number?'

'I can do better than that', said the policeman. 'I can give you his name and address.'

'It's a Mr. Michael Vincent Horton of Keystones, K-E-Y stones,

Deighton. That's spelt D-E-I-G-H-T-O-N. Near Horsham. I've looked up the telephone number in the book and it's 04155. How's that for you?'

'Harry, you're wonderful! I am grateful. Next time you're on duty at the Oval come up to the box and see me. You really are marvellous!'

'It's a pleasure, Miss.'

And the line went dead.

Meg Horton was no longer the loving, adoring girl who Michael had married. She was equally not the devoted, ever-ready to support woman who had helped so much in the hard days in the Midlands and the early stages of the Horton Company.

All that had gone.

For too long she had lived a life of comparative luxury with damn-all useful to do.

She could at one time have done anything. She had the intellect. But now it was too late. Her life was taken up with bridge parties and the idle chatter that went with them. She was the central pivot of the Deighton useless women group. They did good works if it suited them. They tore each other, and outsiders, to verbal pieces. They drank and ate and played together. A Club without a purpose.

This is what Meg had become. She'd apparently done so willingly – having nothing better in life offered to her.

Michael saw it happening and tried half-heartedly to stop it. That caused dissension and he gave it up. Let her have her small, idle life if that was what she really wanted – but don't include him!

Meg was pouring coffee for herself and Alison Dunbar. The Hortons and the Dunbars had been friends for six years.

Meg knew that Michael thought Alison a rather stupid, spoiled bitch, but he liked Clive Dunbar enough.

Clive was a senior partner of Deloitte, Fergus, McLagan and commuted daily to the palatial offices in New Bowater House in Knightsbridge.

The four of them occasionally spent a long week-end in Dieppe, where the men played golf and the wives talked unendingly over hot chocolate and creamy cakes. Meg could eat anything and get away with it. Alison couldn't.

As Meg poured the coffee, she was glad she'd asked Alison over. Michael might easily have told Clive if he was involved with another woman, as Meg knew he must be. And Clive could have let it slip to Alison, though certainly Alison had kept it to herself if so.

'I'm worried about Michael.' Meg played a low card.

'Overworking?'

Meg hesitated. Pushed the sugar forward.

'No-o. Not more than usual.'

'He's not ill, is he, poor lamb?'

'Oh, no!' Meg stopped. 'He's ...' She paused. 'Well, I rather think ... that is, it's possible ... Alison, if I tell you will you keep it entirely to yourself?'

'Darling! You know me.'

'Well, I think there's another ...' She hesitated yet again. 'I think he's having an affair. There!'

'Who with?' Avidly.

'I don't know. Honestly, darling, I don't know.'

Alison looked supremely sympathetic.

Meg came out with all her suspicions and beliefs. No one had told her that Alison was known as 'Horsham Independent Radio' throughout the town. It probably wouldn't have stopped her had she known. Meg couldn't even keep her own innermost secrets. Somehow they oozed out.

Half an hour and some tears later they were consoling each other with brandy and ginger ale.

'I promise you, darling', said Alison. 'Promise you, that if Clive knows I'll find out for you.'

'Oh, Alison, you're so sweet. I don't know what the hell I'd do without you.'

'You don't have to, lovey. I'm here.'

My God! thought Alison, I can't wait to tell Dierdre.

Michael Horton sat alone in his office. He felt slightly sick. The girl had only been gone about fifteen minutes – no, less than that.

He pressed the buzzer for his temporary secretary, who had come in while Mary Ware was on holiday. She came in at once. A tall, rather angular woman with rimless glasses. Unattractive.

'Ah, Miss Fletching. Would you mind putting my "Do Not Disturb" notice on the door? You'll find it on the windowsill in your office. Just hang it on the knob, please.'

'Very well.' The door shut quietly.

What the hell was he going to do?

The girl – what was her name? – oh, yes, Playdell. Sarah Playdell. That was it – was a threat to all his plans.

He wondered if she knew a good deal more than she had given away. Even if she didn't, she certainly knew enough. Extraordinary thing. She'd promised that she hadn't got her information as a result of a give-away by any of the others involved. Horton was quite certain that she hadn't got it from him.

It sounded as if the wicket at Guildford had been bugged in some way, but he couldn't really believe that. In any case, that side of it didn't really matter. It was what she knew that affected things – not how she'd found out.

She'd sat there, cool as a cucumber, and told him that she knew he was being considered for the England Test Team. What did he propose to do about it? Would he give her the whole story, or was he not going to co-operate? If he wasn't, then she'd have to write it in her own words and in her own way.

He remembered how at first he'd tried to deny that there was anything at all in her fantastic story. But as it became clear to him that she knew a devil of a lot more than she had revealed, he knew the position was hopeless.

He'd either got to meet her terms, or take the risk of the whole plan being spoiled before it began.

'What exactly do you want?' he'd asked.

'It's quite simple, Mr. Horton. I just want the whole story, from beginning to end, in your words. Publish when it has most effect on the public and least effect on you and your ideas – in that order.'

'And how do you propose to do that?'

'It's very easy,' she'd said. 'Because I trust you, you see. I believe that if you come to an agreement with me you'll stand by it.'

'Go on.'

'I want you to write a good, honest description of everything that's happened so far. Everything. I want you to deposit it in a Bank – yours, if you like – and have it released to me either on your say-so or at the end of the first Test, whichever is the sooner. Now you must agree that's pretty reasonable.'

'I wouldn't know', he'd said. 'I don't like the idea much. God knows what Maurice Kerr would think.'

She'd gone on to explain to him in a nice, gentle, simple way, that her job was to get news. Cricket news. And if she wasn't given it willingly then she had to extract it as best she could.

Michael had looked at her. She seemed young to be so vicious. Extremely pretty. More than pretty, really. He'd looked her over. As much as he could see above the curved desk. She'd blushed slightly. Hardly enough to notice.

'And from here on?' he'd asked her.

'Leave that up to me. If I want information from you I'll ask you for it. You must know your wicket is sticky. You must expect to find it difficult, I'm afraid.'

Michael Horton had drawn an horrific-looking doodle on the pad by his hand.

'Tell me,' he'd said, 'who else knows about this?'

She didn't hesitate.

'No-one, as far as I know. One of our reporters nearly caught you out but I promise you he hasn't a clue.' She'd flicked her auburn hair back. 'Mind you, you've been pretty careless, haven't you?'

'No.'

'I think so.'

'You would!'

They'd paused and stared at each other. Michael's eyes dropped first.

'Won't you tell me', he'd pleaded, 'how you discovered all this?'

She'd refused to even discuss it. For her the interview was nearly over.

'I want you to write your statement at once. We shall meet in London at the Oak Club in Albemarle Street on Thursday and deposit it at any Bank you like. They announce the Squad for the First Test on Sunday and I want it all fixed up well before then. What time shall we meet?'

'I'll come up late morning.' Michael had thought like lightning. If I'm going to stop this girl I'd better get close to her. 'Suppose we have lunch at this Oak Club? Can we?'

'Yes.'

'Then we'll meet there at one.'

And she'd left. Elegant, poised and the complete mistress of the situation.

Michael had considered ringing the others – or at least Ben Hendricks. But what could they do? Nothing.

In the end he'd shovelled some loose papers on his desk into a drawer and stood up. Pensive. He'd go for a drive and think this bloody thing out.

'I'm going off,' he told Miss Fletching. 'I won't be back.'

Miss Fletching had a suspicious mind and had already heard of Mr. Horton's 'affair' in Horsham.

Maurice Kerr turned to Bebington.

'Have you written to Horton asking if he's available for the 3rd June?'

'Yes. Of course.'

'He's replied?'

'Yes. Immediately. Of course, he's free.'

'Naturally.'

Bebington looked uncomfortable. He rose from behind his desk and walked over to the window. It was raining on the green grass. A wicket was covered. He swung round.

'Look, Sir Maurice. I know you will want to play this chap Horton when we select on Saturday. Tom Lipton feels the same way. I'm the odd one out. It's difficult. Damned difficult!' He looked apologetic. 'It's just that I think we might make blasted fools of ourselves. It's a hell of a gamble, and pretty poor odds. It'll be the end of the selectors if we pick him and the whole thing flops.'

'My grandfather had an expression,' Kerr said. 'How did it go? ... Oh, yes. "Without that you stick out your neck no-one will place a decoration round it, else". That was it, I think.'

Bebington laughed.

'We come from different worlds, Sir Maurice. I expect my grandfather would only have stuck his neck out to get some soup poured down it.'

'It's not our grandfathers who have to make this decision, Bob. We have to – and by Saturday evening.'

'If we do choose Horton in the twelve then we must be very delicate in the way we put him forward.' Bebington moved from the window to his desk. 'I don't say I'm agreeing, but God knows we need to win the Ashes. Let's say I'm on your side at this moment, but I may change back by Saturday.'

Mary Horton answered the telephone at Keystones.

'Hallo, Mr. Hendricks. Do you want Daddy?'

'Please.'

'He's not back yet. Can he call you later?'

'I'm going out in a few minutes. Won't be back till tomorrow. I think I'd ...'

'Wait a minute, Mr. Hendricks, I believe he's coming now. I heard the car.'

Mary put the telephone down and ran for the door. She opened it right on her father. He looked so tired.

'Ben Hendricks wants you on the telephone. He's in a hurry.'

'Hallo, darling', and Michael Horton dropped his briefcase and ran.

'Ben.' Rather breathlessly.

'Evening, Mike. How are you?'

'Fine. What news?'

'None.'

'Then why ring?'

'You got Bebington's letter asking if you were available for the First Test?'

'Yes.'

'You replied?'

'Of course, you damned fool!'

'Good.'

'Was that all you wanted to know?'

'Yes. Really.'

'Oh, my God! I thought you had some news.' Horton sounded frustrated.

'There won't be news until Sunday morning at the earliest. They pick the twelve on Saturday night.'

'Do you think it's a good sign?' said Michael, grasping at straws. 'That Bebington wrote asking if I was free? I mean, he's the man against me.'

'No. He wrote as Secretary to the Committee. That's all. Are you in training, Mike?'

'Of course. Every day. Three or four hours.'

Horton heard a noise in the hall.

'If you haven't anything more to say, Ben, just tell me how I find out the decision.'

'Listen in to the early news on Sunday. You won't hear before then, officially or unofficially. With the problems they've got it may come out later on Sunday, but you'd better listen in early or you'll go mad.'

'Yes I will.'

'Try not to worry, Mike. I think you'll make it.'

Michael Horton travelled down from London on a late train on the Thursday evening after his meeting with Sarah Playdell at the Oak Tree Club.

He bumped into Clive Dunbar on the platform. They waited together and found an empty carriage to themselves. Michael thought Clive was rather withdrawn. Not his usual extrovert self.

For a few minutes they read their papers, or just sat. Michael Horton was tired.

Then they talked general pleasantries in a most artificial way for both of them.

They became silent. Michael broke it.

'What's up, Clive? You look as though you'd eaten a rotten egg!'

'Perhaps I have.'

'What on earth do you mean?'

'You.'

'Me?'

'Yes. You should know why.'

'What the hell are you talking about?'

Clive Dunbar looked embarrassed. His face even reddened up a bit.

'I think.' He paused. 'I think you're being bloody unfair to Meg.' He dodged looking at Horton and stared out of the window. He went on.

'You don't deny it, I suppose?'

'Deny what?' Michael was already angry.

'That you've . . . well, that you're having an extra-marital affair.'

Michael couldn't help laughing.

'Extra-marital affair? God, how pompous!'

'You admit it?'

'No, I don't! And if you weren't such a fucking idiot you'd know it wasn't true.'

'I'm sorry, Mike, but I know.'

'Do you?'

'Yes. I suppose it's your age. Fifty-five is a dangerous time.'

'Fifty-three.'

'What?'

'I'm fifty-three.'

'What the hell!'

'Yes. What the hell indeed!'

'It's no good, Mike. Everyone knows. And you've been seen with the girl.'

'Have I?' Michael was seething. 'And how does everyone know?'

'Look, Mike. I'm your friend. I'm fond of Meg, too. I'd like to help.'

'Naturally! You're being a great help.' The sarcasm was biting. 'What I want to find out is how you know, as you call it.'

'I heard first from Alison.'

'I'm not surprised!'

'There's no need to be funny. It didn't only come from her. Henry Ross told me several days ago. He said it was all over Horsham.'

'How nice!'

'Then your secretary . . .'

'Mary?'

'No. The temporary, Miss Fetching . . .'

'Fletching.'

'Alright, Fletching. She met Greg Masters. In the pub or somewhere. She's seen the girl. Been to your office.'

'Oh, yes?'

'Yes. And to cap it, "Daddy" Carstairs rang me this afternoon. He'd seen you both lunching in a Club in Dover Street today. She's got auburn hair, is small and slim. Attractive, of course.'

'Albemarle Street.'

'What?'

'The Club was in Albemarle Street. Not Dover.'

'Are you making a joke of it, Mike?'

'Yes.'

Horton wondered about Sarah Playdell. She certainly was attractive – in lots of ways. Was he attracted, though? Yes, of course. He'd be a bloody eunuch not to be. He'd enjoyed lunch. She hadn't even mentioned his statement until after the coffee came – and only then in the most friendly way. They'd talked cricket and about her life on the Daily News. He explained a little about his Company and she'd been fascinated with his new lightweight defence equipment. They'd touched on people in the Trade they both knew, like Max Salm of Roseblacks. It was like a pleasant business lunch. But did she appeal to him as a woman? Of course. He wondered what she'd be like. Rather good, probably.

'It's a pretty poor joke,' Clive Dunbar said. 'I'd have thought you'd have had more respect for Meg.'

'Me too.'

'Oh, you're bloody impossible!'

The train arrived in Horsham.

Michael had left the car at home. Dunbar offered a lift but Horton would sooner have walked. He waited a few minutes and got a taxi.

When Michael Horton got home, the house seemed empty. There were no sounds.

He looked in the study and walked across to the drawing room. Nothing. The kitchen was empty too. He called out 'Hallo, there!' but no-one replied.

He shrugged his shoulders and went to collect the mail from the hall table. Bill, bill, bill, bill. All bloody bills! No. The bottom one was a plain envelope without a stamp. Just the word 'Michael' in Meg's writing. He took it with him to the dining room. He made a long weak whisky and soda. The note from Meg was probably to say she was out at some blasted function or other. It was only nine. She may not get back till after eleven. There'd be some cold dinner for him in the larder or fridge. He'd wait a bit.

It was only on his second whisky that he remembered Meg's note. He slit the envelope open.

'I am going away', he read. (No 'Darling Michael', as was usual).
'If you want to know why, it's because I refuse to share you with some other woman.
I'm not waiting here to tell you because you'd only try denying it again and I wouldn't believe you.
You needn't try and find me, because you won't succeed. I've taken the Rover. You can use the Renault.
Mary will be quite alright with the servants to look after her and as for you I'm sure you'll do very well with your mistress.
When I'm ready I'll write to you. Not before then.
If this comes as a shock to you, you've only brought it on yourself.'

It was signed 'M'. She'd never signed a letter to him 'M' in her life.

Half an hour later, Horton went upstairs. He'd had a piece of veal and ham pie and some crisps. Washed them down with a mug of milk. He felt rather disconnected.

He knocked on Mary's bedroom door.

'Come in!' She looked up. 'Oh, hallo Daddy! I didn't hear you.'

'Hallo, love. How are you?'

'Tired. That's why I came to bed early. I've had a stack of homework.'

'Have you?' Michael sat on the edge of the bed. 'I got a note from Mummy.'

'I know. She told me.'

'When did she go?'

'About five-thirty. She took your car.'

'So she said in the note. Why?'

'There wasn't petrol in the Renault.'

'She could have got some. Anyway. It doesn't matter. Did she tell you why she was going?'

'Yes.'

'And do you believe it?'

Mary looked down at the floor. She paused for fully half a minute. She turned her head and looked her father straight in the eye.

'Yes. Unless you tell me differently.'

'I do. There's not a grain of truth in it.'

Mary smiled.

'I am relieved. I'd hoped you weren't . . . mixed up with someone else. I believe you, of course.'

'Your mother doesn't.'

'No. She doesn't Where can she have gone?'

'I don't know, darling.' Michael Horton got up and paced the small room. 'When I read the note I nearly made an ass of myself by ringing up likely people. Thank God I didn't! She won't have gone anywhere obvious. She says she'll write. I'm going to wait. Meanwhile we'd better get on as well as we can. Shall you manage?'

'Of course. Mrs. Pritchard and Amy come in every day. We're spoiled, really. Shall you be alright?'

'Oh yes! Don't worry. I've got a lot on. That will help.'

'Daddy.'

'Yes?'

'You've been – well – very occupied lately. What is it? Is there trouble with the business?'

'No, lovely.' Michael laughed. 'It's fine. But I have got something big on, yes. Don't want to talk about it yet. Understand?'

'Yes. But of course, Mummy doesn't. You have been a bit peculiar.'

'I know. But that doesn't mean I'm having an affair.'

'Why didn't you explain it all to Mummy?'

'I couldn't, darling. I just couldn't.'

'So she's gone away for nothing?'

He sighed and got up from the bed. Leaned over and kissed Mary.

'That's right. She's gone away for nothing.'

A few minutes after eight o'clock on Sunday morning 27th May, Michael Horton turned on the news. He listened to the depressing headlines and the boring follow-up. There was no mention of the team for the First Test. He switched off.

He'd got through Saturday by spending hours in his sanctum bowling over after over of gigantic spinners. He was able to bowl fourteen overs on the trot and his legs felt less heavy and cumbersome. Even his flannels could do with taking in an inch or so. He was fitter and less fat.

The nine o'clock news had no mention of the cricket, either.

At eleven he rang Hendricks in desperation – but he was out.

He missed the beginning of the one o'clock programme and came in half way.

'...Minister in the Commons refused to say anything further about diplomatic relations with Uganda.
Both Opposition and Government Back Benchers pressed for a full statement to no avail.

The team for the First Test against Australia at Edgebaston, Birmingham starting next Thursday has been announced. Our Correspondent, Basil Brook, reports...

Cricket circles are this morning thrown into some confusion. Firstly, thirteen Players have been selected in place of the usual twelve. While there are not many suprirses in the M.C.C. choice, the inclusion of "A. N. Other" is a complete mystery. This use of the expression "A. N. Other" indicates that the Selectors have chosen a Player who they will not reveal at this time. There is wide speculation about who it could be. The other twelve are, as I say, not surprising.
The Captain, already announced, is Tom Lipton and those selected – in alphabetical order – are Anders (of Northants.), Ames, the Wicket Keeper (of Kent), Bolte (of Surrey) Forsyth (of Yorkshire), Frost (of Sussex), Hughes (Glamorgan), Overton (Kent), Porthead (of Surrey), Sheddons (of Yorkshire), Trump (of Lancs.), Young (Hampshire) and the mysterious A. N. Other. It is thought that Lowe of Derbyshire would have been included but he did not pass a fitness test on Friday for his pulled hamstring.

With Frost being the only true fast bowler included, England will be at a distinct disadvantage. Young and Anders can only be considered as medium paced swing bowlers, who will both need an ideal wicket to achieve their best. It is likely that Trump will be left out on the day and the position of A. N. Other is quite unknown.

Sir Maurice Kerr, Chairman of the Selectors, refused to be drawn on the question of A. N. Other and we shall have to wait with patience to discover who the Player is.

A family of four died in a fire in Glasgow during the night. The husband and wife and their two daughters of five and three were sleeping in. . . .'

Horton flicked off the radio.

'A. N. Other'. Why?

It must be him! Of course it was! But why 'A. N. Other' and not M. V. Horton? What the devil was Kerr up to?

He rang Ben Hendricks but he was still out.

He tried to get hold of Maurice Kerr and Bebington. He failed.

He hung about the house, not knowing what to do.

At three-thirty Sarah Playdell rang him.

'Congratulations, Mr. Other!' Her voice was laughing.

'Sarah, why have they done this?'

'Keeping you under wraps, I suppose. It's rather clever.'

'Clever be damned! I want to know!'

'I expect they'll tell you soon enough. Don't worry, Mike. I think you're doing very well. I'm delighted.'

They talked for some time without Michael Horton finding any consolation.

As he replaced the telephone it rang almost immediately again.

He picked it up.

'Michael Horton.'

'Maurice Kerr here. You're well?'

'Indeed yes. Just impatient!'

'I'm not surprised. Sorry about the A. N. Other technique but we're not decided yet and it seemed the best answer. I've had all hell from the Press about this. It looks as though they'll be around the three of us all week trying to find out who you are.'

'Why not announce it, then?'

'I tell you, we're not certain. We need more time.'

'Oh, my God!'

'Yes, Horton, I know it's difficult for you, but it's not easy up here. Look, I want you to stay at a different hotel in Birmingham to the Team. Go up on Tuesday and wait unobtrusively until I contact you. It's the Royal Hagley in Launceston Avenue, near the Ground. Have you got that?'

'Yes.'

'Then take your kit, but keep it out of sight. Just behave as if you had a few days off. Hang around. Either Bebington or I will be in touch – most likely me. You're booked in and everything.'

'I hope it's not a wild goose chase.'

'So do I. But I can't say at the moment. Just lie low. Do you think you can do it?'

'Of course! I wasn't born yesterday.'

'I know.'

Mary had heard the conversation. Michael knew he had said nothing to give the show away. It might have been any business call.

He spent the rest of the day with a migraine. They were getting far more frequent than he liked or was used to. He supposed it was the strain and worry.

He tried two pain-killers, and went to bed.

The hotel was both Royal and in Hagley. It was extremely comfortable.

Michael Horton had left his cricket gear in the Renault under a rug and moved in for his few days 'rest'.

He had left the Works in good hands and driven up as fast as the car would go on the M1. The Renault was not as comfy or as good to drive as the Rover, but Horton had gone like hell in case good news waited for him at the hotel. It hadn't. No word at all.

He settled in, trying hard not to look impatient.

The hotel was full of cricket people. The Press and visitors. He began to feel real enthusiasm for the first time. He was nearly a part of this wonderful machine. He had time, as never before, to reflect on what he had done and what he was going to do.

Michael Horton consulted his version of God about the situation. He found the results satisfying. He was far from a religious man, but he realised he had needed some help to reach this stage of the affair and he was grateful for it. He had a strong feeling that all was going to be right.

A telephone call from Bebington was brief, and merely asked if he was settled in alright. He was.

Ben Hendricks, to whom he had given his address, also rang and was equally brief.

'See you on Thursday,' he said. And then rang off.

Horton spoke to his daughter, Mary, to see if all was well at home. It was.

He rang the office twice. All was well there.

His spirits rose through Wednesday and at tea he had a telegram merely reading 'Good luck – Sarah.' He hadn't a clue how she'd got his address.

At six-thirty he had a note by hand to say that 'MK' would be over in half an hour and would he wait. As if he'd been doing anything else!

An hour later another note to say 'MK' was held up.

Maurice Kerr eventually turned up at nine.

Horton was wondering how the hell he could get to know the other Players, let alone the Team's plans, in the few hours available.

He and Kerr walked slowly up to Michael's room.

They sat down. One on a chair, the other on the bed.

Maurice Kerr looked him straight in the eye.

'We're not playing you, I'm afraid.'

There was a pause. A rather nasty pause.

'What!'

'You've not been chosen. I know it's a disappointment, but there it is.'

'Why?'

'We think we can beat them with the existing Team on this wicket.'

'And can you?'

Kerr looked away for the first time.

'I don't know.'

'You know it's the wrong decision. Don't you?'

'It may be, Horton. We'll never find out.'

'I'm sorry if I'm angry, but I banked on this.'

'You shouldn't have.'

'Obviously. Now what?'

'I hope you stay up and see the match. You can have a good Stand seat.'

'Forgive me, but not likely! If I'm not playing, I've got plenty to do.'

'As you like.'

Michael drove slowly home in the Renault on cross-country roads. He took most of Thursday about it. He stopped at several pubs, having more beer than was strictly advisable. He dodged the cricket news, and it was not until he had been back at Keystones for half an hour that he could bring himself to listen to the Third Programme.

He switched on and tuned in. He heard George Allot's voice at once. The Gloucestershire burr unkiddable.

'. . . poor light but surely not too bad. Seems Umpires Fish and Derby are agreed as they both lift off the bails and walk in. The

Australian batsmen are already on the way, of course, but Tom Lipton is looking as though play should go on. He's shading his eyes against the light.

'All to no avail. They're coming off.

'Trevor.'

'Well, of course, this is ridiculous,' said Trevor Bridge, doing between-over summaries. 'We see far too much of this. Young and Anders are certainly not fast. Military medium at most. There's no danger and they shouldn't come off in this light.'

'So there we are,' Allot came in again. 'Australia's day. 351 for 2 on a wicket that was thought to favour the bowlers.

'There'll be a full scorecard given in just – what is it? – twelve minutes, but this will tell listeners coming in that bad light stopped play at six-fourteen, when Australia had batted all day for only two wickets.

'Oliver scored a beautiful, faultless 207 against an England attack that was never more than containing.

'An opening partnership of...'

Michael Horton had heard enough. He pressed the 'off' button. He sat and thought. 351 for 2. They're going to make a mammoth first innings score. The bloody idiots!

He felt guilty when he went to bed feeling rather pleased.

It was a week since Meg had gone. There was no word, and Michael still held his hand.

People who enquired were told she was on holiday. There was no trouble.

On Friday he went to the office and worked like a black. Nothing was too much trouble for him and except for paying off Miss Fletching and packing her off, everything he did was progressive.

He was told by a member of the staff when Australia were 468 for 4 at lunch. He heard again during the early evening that they were 550 for 6, with Prout scoring a hundred in forty-one minutes.

At five-fifty they declared at 638 for 8 and left England half an hour to bat.

Ivor Hughes and Porthead had occupied the wicket for twenty minutes for 8 runs before Hughes had hooked at Fleetfoot-Jones and been caught behind. The ball was a bouncer and should have been ignored.

Overton had come in as the night watchman and at the close England had replied with 10 for 1 wicket.

Mary wanted to talk about the cricket that she'd watched on television.

'The Australians were marvellous, Daddy! We're just hopeless!'

But Michael didn't want to talk. He was tired. He went to bed early.

At eleven-thirty Sarah rang.

'Were you asleep?'

'No. Reading. Or trying to.'

'I wanted to say how sorry I was. I didn't have a minute.'

'It didn't matter. There's not much point now.'

'Why?'

'Well, my statement is hardly worth much. You may as well have it.'

'Look, Mike. Don't talk such rubbish! I'll get your thing from the Bank after this Test, as agreed. I don't give in so easily, even if you do!'

'I don't normally.'

'Well, don't now!'

'If you say so.'

'I do.'

The First Test at Edgebaston followed its inevitable way, providing the weather held good. It did.

In reply to Australia's 638 for 8 declared England scored 271 on the Saturday and followed on 367 behind. It was merely a matter of when.

Before Tea on the Monday England were all out for the second time for 194. They didn't just lose, they were taken for a complete hiding by an innings and 173 runs.

The Selectors came in for a caning, too. Everyone knew a better Eleven Team to face up to the Australian fast bowlers. And everyone knew who could seam, or spin, or pace the Australian batsmen out. Everyone except the Selectors, that is.

One down and four Tests to go. A bad start.

Michael half followed the match. He was still stunned at being dropped at the last minute. He'd conditioned his mind to play and he was left in a limbo.

A letter came from meg. Posted at London Airport. By her? Or someone else? Michael hardly cared. She gave no address. Merely that she was well. Wouldn't be coming back yet. Had a lot more thinking to do. Hoped that Mary was alright. She just signed it 'Meg'.

Michael threw it on his dressing table. It stayed there for ten days.

The work at the office seemed to build up.

Mary Ware was back, which was a help, but Michael was at it flat out from eight-thirty until after six. He then put in two hours of bowling practice and got home to a late supper.

Sarah came down on the Friday after the first Test.

She arrived at noon and Michael took her over to Brencham for lunch. The pub was old, comfortable and had good food. There was no-one likely to recognise them there.

'Any word from Meg?' Sarah asked.

'A note, yes. She's still not coming back.'

'Is she rather a – well, silly woman?'

Michael thought.

'I suppose she is, poor girl. She's her own worst enemy nowadays. She used to be so solid. So dependable. Now she's – oh, I don't know! She's got no purpose in life.'

'I'm sorry, Mike. I shouldn't criticise.'

'I don't mind. You're not – unpleasant about it. Tell me, did you collect my statement?'

'I did. Yes. As we agreed.'

'What did you make of it, Sarah?'

'I didn't. I haven't read it yet.'

'Why the hell not?'

'I just haven't. I can't use it now, anyhow.'

'Why?'

'Because, my dear man, you're not news. If you'd played at Edgbaston, fine. It would have been great. As it is, Mike, you're just nothing cricketwise at the moment.'

Michael felt slighted. He knew, of course, it was true, but he wished Sarah had had the interest to read it. He thought about this.

The days came and went.

A week before the Second Test at Headingly, he got a letter from Bebington. Would he be available if selected? Of course he would, you bloody idiot! He'd been ready for weeks.

He doubled his training periods. If only he wasn't so fucking fat! He'd lost little or no weight, really.

All day Saturday, the day before the twelve Players were announced, he chased Ben Hendricks, Tom Lipton and Maurice Kerr. Michael put on all the pressure he could to be selected.

'They're bound to play me now, after the fiasco of the First Test,' he told himself. 'Even Bebington must see that.'

On Sunday he slept late. He missed the early news and took in Mid News on the television at one o'clock. The newsreader read.

'The twelve Players for the Second Test at Leeds, starting on Thursday, have been announced.'

The names came up on the screen.

Lipton	Caldecott	Hughes
Ames	Forsyth	Overton
Benning	Frost	Porthead

They were alphabetical after Lipton.

Where was Horton?

He wasn't!

. . .
Sheddons
Trump
Young

God damn it! He wasn't there!

Michael was angrier than he'd ever been before.

They'd ignored him.

Alright!

If they didn't know a bloody good thing when they saw it – too bad for them!

He wouldn't play now if they crawled to him.

He rang Sarah at her flat.

'You seen the Team?'

'Yes, Mike. I had it last night.'

'Why didn't you ruddy well ring me?'

'I – I didn't know how to tell you.'

'Well, they've had it now! I'll tell you that for free.'

'Look. You're upset, Mike. I know that. Certainly I understand. I know they need you. So do you. If it takes them longer to find out, it just does. Don't do anything silly, like letting the cat out of the bag. You'd regret it.'

'I've half a mind to turn out for Horsham next week. They'd have me.'

'Shut up that nonsense, Michael Horton, and listen to me!' Sarah tore a vicious, painful but realistic strip off him. She put him in his place, more as a man would have done than a young girl.

He felt rather small at the end of it.

She'd meant him to.

'You can come up on Tuesday and take me to the theatre,' she finished.

'Is that a consolation prize?'

'I don't ask everyone, I can tell you!'

'I'm sorry. That was unfair. I'd love to come. What time?'

'Seven-thirty at the Berkeley. I'll do the tickets.'

*

The Second Test at Headingly is in the record books.

England won the toss and batted on what was to be considered later as a perfect Test wicket.

For the first hour the seamers got movement and then an excellent batting wicket was revealed. The outfield was fast. The wicket took spin on the third day. The wicket wasn't the ogre. It was Australia's fast bowlers.

The first record went when O'Rory took three wickets with his first three balls. All clean bowled. A golden hat-trick!

Hughes, Berring and Caldecott were all back in the pavilion with nought on the board.

The commentators hadn't even settled in properly. The T.V. producers was stunned. So were the vast crowd still filing into their seats. So was O'Rory. The ball that got Hughes was a beauty and worth a wicket any time. The others hardly moved at all. Just up and down on a good length.

George Allot ran out of adjectives.

The pressure was on the next man in, Tom Lipton.

The whole journey out to the wicket he tried to out-think O'Rory.

He would certainly try to hit the wicket. That ruled out a bouncer. If he, Lipton, was in O'Rory's place he'd either throw up a beamer or a yorker right on the crease. Lipton favoured a beamer with a bit of in-swing.

He was absolutely right.

The ball curved in from the off at bail height, never touching the ground.

Lipton moved like lightning. Right forward, left back – and he hooked the ball high over mid-wicket up into the crowds. The only reply a man like O'Rory would understand. A glorious six.

Things were hardly even – but at least they were back in perspective.

England turned in a first innings total of 289, of which Lipton got 110. It could have been worse.

The wicket was beautiful by now. The Australians took advantage of it.

All day Friday and most of Saturday the English bowlers kept at it. There were times when it looked as though they'd never get a wicket. Even the Australian tail wagged madly. Both the eighth and ninth wicket records for Australia against England in England went, and a massive 617 faced the M.C.C. on Saturday night.

Again the end was but a matter of time.

If only the weather would break. A draw was then possible. It never happened.

England held on on Monday with some slow, dour, batting that would have been boring but for the position of the game.

Lipton got his second hundred of the match. 103.

At last on Tuesday morning England overhauled Australia's 617, with only two wickets standing. It was the last over before lunch.

Overton went for 27 the first ball of the new session. Frost and Young struck out valiantly till England had a lead of 53. Young was then caught on the boundary fetching Mallor from outside the off stump over mid-on's head.

Now it was done.

Graypath and Oliver played immaculate cricket to score 54 in forty-seven minutes.

England		Australia	
First Innings	289	First Innings	617
Second Innings	381	Second Innings	54 for 0

Australia won by ten wickets.

Two up and three to go.

A supremely strong position.

On the Sunday evening of the Leeds Test, Roseblacks, London's – and probably the country's – largest sports store had its 150th Anniversary party at the Savoy.

A century and a half of serving the nation's sports needs.

The magnificent shop on the curve of Regent Street had been running a special Anniversary Sale for two weeks. The party at the Riverside Room in the Savoy was the culmination of the Sale.

Suppliers and competitors from both home and abroad had been invited.

Famous sports and T.V. stars mingled with Roseblacks' directors and staff. It was a highlight indeed of the sports arena.

A plane had been chartered to bring down the Press and television people from Leeds and fly them back the next morning in time for play.

It was one hell of a party!

Sarah had arrived at eight.

She'd looked round quietly for Mike Horton.

For a moment she thought he hadn't come, in spite of her pressuring him.

'You damn well ought to go, Mike! They're your biggest customer, aren't they?' she'd said.

'Yes. Oh, yes. But I can't be bothered.'

'Don't be a bloody fool! You owe it to the business, if not yourself. I order you to go!'

'Do you, my God! That's rich!'

'Well, will you?'

'Suppose I'll have to. Ruddy bore!'

'It won't be, it'll be fun.'

'Well, I presume you'll be there?'

'I will.'

'Then I'll come. No other reason.'

And there he was. Over in the corner with Max Salm, the Roseblacks' equipment buyer, and three or four others. He looked a bit odd.

Sarah threaded her way through the crowd. She picked up champagne on the way.

Michael was talking – very loud.

'Whad'you mean, the besht Team pozible? Lot of balls! Could'n win a bloody village match, let alone a Tesht.'

Oh, God, he was tight! Right at the beginning of the party and Mike was as tight as a drum.

'Well, what's your answer, Horton?' asked a voice.

Michael started vaguely at the questioner and swayed forward. He put out a hand to a table.

'I.' He came upright. 'I could tell you a shtory.' He spoke slowly, but hardly clearly.

'I.' Another pause. 'I will tell you a shtory. Very remar..., rekam, rekarmable shtory.'

Christ, I must stop this! thought Sarah. Now.

She barged in.

'Hello, Max darling. How are you? Lovely to see.' She kissed Max Salm on both cheeks. She'd never kissed Max Salm in her life before. 'Hi, Mike. Just the person I want! Felix has got to see you.'

Michael looked vague.

'Who the hell'sh Felix?' he asked.

'You know Felix.' She took him by the arm. 'He's over there.' She began to propel him.

Max looked astounded. The others gazed away.

'I wash jusht going to tell these chaps abou' my wrisht. Can't Felix wait a minute? Whoever th'hell he ish!'

'No, he can't. And I know just what you were going to do.' She'd got him by the window overlooking the Embankment.

'Wanna wisky.'

'You've had enough.'

'Oh, bloody women! I' fed up with 'em.'

He wandered off towards a bar.

She got him back but he'd captured a huge glass of what looked very neat.

'We've got to go, Mike. Finish that drink.'

'Balls! We've only jusht come. Look! Over there! Thatsh Bebington, the little shod. I'm going to have a word or three with him. Bebin'ton, you little twirp! Come 'ere!'

Bob Bebington heard.

So did a crowd round about.

Bebington turned away.

Michael took a step forward.

'Oh, Mike!' Sarah pulled at him.

Michael was almost shouting now.

'Well, Bebington, looksh like you made a cock-up again! Doeshend it?'

Bebington looked over his shoulder.

'No, Mr. Horton. It doesn't. And you're tight.'

'Too true! But I'm a bloody shite better bowler than you!'

'That wouldn't be hard.'

'And bedder than Overton and Frosht and tha' lot! In fac' I'm practical . . . pracital . . . pracitality the besht bloody bowler of the lot!'

Michael waved his wrist at Bebington.

Sarah started to cry.

'What'sh up with you?'

'Mike. Can we go?'

'No' likely. I wanna nother drink. That one was piss.'

'I'm not feeling well, Mike. Please take me!'

'Oh, Chrisht! Jus' beginning to enjoy it. Bloody women! One more drin' and we'll go.'

He had two more and got more and more morose.

Sarah got him outside on the verandah. Far from doing him good, the air seemed to make him tighter still.

He swayed about next to Sarah, spilling his drink.

'How did you come up, Mike?'

'Drove. Tha' remindsh me. Where'sh the bloody car?'

'It doesn't matter.'

'Corse it does! I'm going back in it after th'party.'

'We'll see.'

'Like hell we'll she! Where's that bastard Kerr? He mus' be here.'

Michael wandered back towards the door.

Sarah blocked him. He pushed her aside.

'I'm going to tell Billy Hargreavesh abou' my bowling. He'll undershtand.'

'Mike, stop! Please take me home! I feel awful.'

'Have a drink, ole girl! Do wonders! Where's Billy gone?'

'He's left, like we ought to.'

'Chrisht, I feel sick!'

'Well, go! Can you go alone?'

'Don't know. May not have t-time.'

She took him firmly by the arm. She felt her nails bite into his skin. She pushed hard.

'Get a grip on yourself, Michael Horton! We're leaving.'

Sarah walked Michael fast through the lovely room. Out and up the passageway. She was fighting against time.

They weaved across the foyer and out of the luggage door.

A blessed taxi was waiting.

They got in somehow.

She gave the address of her flat.

Michael was slumped in a corner, looking green.

The taxi driver looked dubious.

' 'E orl right, Miss?'

'Yes, fine. Let's go!'

Michael was sick on the floor of the cab.

Sarah was uncomfortable. The sofa was too short. It was alright with two people sitting on it, but even for her height it was too narrow to sleep on.

She'd tried on both sides and her back. She couldn't sleep properly. She gave up.

She walked into the bedroom – her bedroom, and looked at Michael again. He looked better now. He had been a dreadful sight when she at last got him to bed. Very yellow. Almost jaundiced, and lying on his back, breathing heavily. Now he was on his right side. A better colour and his greying dark hair hanging over his forehead. He was still out to the world.

'What am I going to do with you, Mr. Horton?' Sarah asked out loud. Michael never moved. 'You're quite a responsibility,' she went on. 'What on earth makes me love you I just don't know. I must be out of my tiny mind! You're damned good-looking, but you're fat and fifty-three! Old enough to be my father without even being precocious. Damn you, Mike! And you have to be sick all over the place. Why can't you get your wife to look after you?'

Sarah went back to the sitting room. She collected the blanket and returned to Michael. she lay down on the double bed beside him and threw the blanket over herself.

She turned to Michael and kissed him gently above the ear. He stirred slightly.

Sarah flicked out the light. She went to sleep.

Sarah made a face at the telephone.

'Look, Mac. I'm not flying back to Leeds, and that's final!'

———

'No. I don't care if God's playing against the Devil, I tell you something more important has turned up.'

———

'No, I can't say what. I . . .'

———

'Mac. When I can tell you, I will.'

———

'Of course.'

———

'Yes.'

———

'Don't be stupid! I tell you it's . . .'

———

'No, Mac. Of course I won't. I'm sending Barry up on the charter flight.'

———

'Well I think he's better than me.'

———

'What?'

———

'Don't be bloody stupid! You know me better than that!'

———

'Yes you do.'

———

'Yes. Alright, I promise.'

———

'Yes.'

———

'Yes. Yes.'

———

'Of course not.'

———

'O.K., Mac. See you Wednesday. Thanks.'

———

'What's that?'

———

'You damned idiot! Go to hell!'

———

' 'Bye, Mac. Thanks again.'

Sarah replaced the telephone.

So! She would miss the last two days of the Second Test. Barry would cover that. It would be under her by-line. Barry knew what to do.

It was just seven-thirty. She'd got the News Editor at home. Now to lay on Barry Masters.

She rang his number and briefed him.

Michael was still asleep. Peacefully now. Sarah tucked him in more comfortably and made herself tea. She drank it in the sitting room by the window looking over the gardens. She wondered what would happen with her and Mike now. She decided to blank that off.

She dressed and boiled herself a couple of eggs.

At nine-thirty Michael was still asleep. Sarah tidied the rest of the flat and made a huge jug of very strong coffee.

It was past eleven when she heard movements from the bedroom. She went in.

Michael was lying on his back with one eye open.

'Oh, God! Where am I?'

'In my flat. In my bed, to be exact.'

'How very compromising! I think I may die here. Would you mind?'

'Yes, I would! How do you feel?'

'Quite appalling.'

'Got a head?'

'About six of them. Who are you?'

She laughed.

'Sarah.'

'Oh, Christ! What a thing to do!'

'You know what you did?'

'Very vaguely.'

'Do you want the details?'

'Not yet, thanks. Just tell me if I gave the show away – about my bowling, I mean.'

'Damned nearly! If I hadn't been there you certainly would. You tried to several times. As it is you've alienated Bebington. You called him a little sod to his face.'

'Oh Christ! That's the end. Why didn't you tell me to belt up?'

'You must be joking! You were absolutely plastered.'

'Hell, I'm sorry! Don't think too badly of me. I got a fair skinful before going to the party.'

'You're telling me! Do you want some coffee?'

'I suppose we'd better begin. Yes, please.'

All morning he dozed and drank coffee. Slept a little and had more coffee.

By three o'clock he felt better. He had poached eggs on toast. His head began to clear.

At four he got up. He was just in his pants.

'Where are my clothes, Sarah?' he called out.

'They're drying, Mike. I had to sponge your suit and wash your shirt. They're nearly dry. Another hour.'

'Oh, how ghastly of me! I am sorry. I don't know what to say!'

'Then say nothing. You can thank me later.'

'How?'

'Oh, I don't know. You'll think up something.'

He went back to bed. Sarah sat with him and talked. They were very close.

At seven he got up and shaved with Sarah's razor. He dressed. He felt much better. Well, really. He rang Mary, who was staying with the Honnimans for ten days, to let her know he was away from home.

They went out to dinner at a Pizza House round the corner.

Michael stayed at Sarah's flat on the Monday and Tuesday nights.

The circumstances were very different from his first night in the flat.

'My dear Mike, you are a bloody idiot!'

Ben Hendricks leaned forward urgently on the edge of his chair in Michael's office.

'I tell you they'll pick you this time! They're bound to! They're in a hell of a mess. Not only two down and three to go but those two losses were disasters. There's no gleam of hope for England in either of them. I tell you they'll play you!'

Michael looked cynical.

'After I called Bebington a little sod in public?'

'That was damned stupid, of course, but it's not the end of the affair.'

'D'you want to bet?'

'Yes, I do. I'll take a tenner at evens.'

'You'll lose!'

'Not if you try.'

'Why should I?'

'Because, you fat oaf, this time you can make it! I know you can! I know how these selectors think. They do damn-all till they're really in a corner – then they fight like the very devil! Well, they're in a corner alright now!'

'I'm tempted to try!'

'Thank God! Look, Mike, you must keep up the training. It won't help a lot, but it may a bit. Most important of all, you must develop the bowling as far as you can. The Australians aren't fools, you know.' He stared hard at Michael. 'And I want to be able to tell Kerr in all honesty that you're as fit as possible.'

It was the 30th June. Eight days to the start of the Third Test at Lords and only four days to announcing the twelve Players for selection.

There had been no further word from Meg and Mary was still staying happily with the Honnimans.

The house was empty and quiet.

Michael felt depressed there, for all that Ben Hendricks had impressed on him.

He rang Sarah.

'Can I come up for a few days, darling?'

'Of course.'

'I've got the hump down here. I'll have to come back each day for training and a bit of work – but I'd love to be with you.'

'Oh yes, Mike, that would be heavenly! When?'

'Now. I'll just drive up.'

'Mind if we go out to eat? I've nothing in the flat.'

'No. That's fine. I'll be about two hours. Alright, Sarah?'

'Oh yes, darling! Wonderful!'

Michael stayed with Sarah, commuting daily to Horsham.

After a couple of hours work in the office he'd put in long stints on his wicket. He was afraid he would get stale, but saw no sign of it.

The letter had come from Bebington asking if he was free if selected. Michael had replied simply and politely.

His time with Sarah was wonderful. He couldn't for the life of him see what she saw in a fat, middle-aged married man. He seemed to himself to have no attractions at all. Oh, he had a good enough looking face and he didn't squint, but compared to thirty years ago! Then he had been a man!

They woke early on Sunday. Michael was up at five-thirty, playing with the radio.

Sarah had tried the M.C.C. for news the evening before. There was none.

They picked up the six o'clock news.

The President of the United States was still in Peking.

All the escapees from Parkhurst had been rounded up.

The Queen had a slight infection and would be missing certain engagements.

It was thought that the earthquake in Turkey may not be as severe as was first thought and many lives had been saved by people moving out of the town at the first tremors.

The Pound had dropped five cents since last week on the Foreign Exchange Market.

The England Team for the third Test at Lords next Thursday has been announced. Over to our reporter, Basil Brook.

'Who can say that cricket is not an exciting game? Having lost the first two Tests to Australia as decisively as you can lose a cricket match, the Selectors now pull a magic wand out of the bag. Among those named in England's twelve is a man not playing County or League cricket. Indeed, from researches made he is not playing cricket at all at this time. His age is given as 53. No doubt more will come to light in the next few days but meanwhile we can only give you the Team details, which show no other real surprises, unless you include Brian Farr returning to the England side after ten years in the doldrums. Farr is afraid of nothing and it is felt that he will stand square to the Australians quick bowlers, taking whatever comes and giving a lead to the younger members of the Team.

Now for the twelve.

The Captain is, of course, Tom Lipton (Sussex).

Then, in alphabetical order.

Peter Ames (Kent). Tony Bolte (Surrey). Geoff Caldecotte (Lancs.) Brian Farr (Yorkshire). Pete Frost (Sussex). M. V. Horton (Unattached) – and unknown. Ivor Hughes (Glamorgan). Brian Overton (Kent). John Porthead (Surrey). Tom Sheddons (Yorkshire). Greg Young (Hampshire).

We hope to have more information about M. V. Horton in our next bulletins.'

The London businessman arrested in Hong Kong yesterday is reported . . .'

Michael turned the radio off.

He stood mesmerised for a minute.

Suddenly, Sarah was clinging to him from behind.

'You made it!' she squealed. 'You actually made it!'

Michael drew a deep breath. He felt rather faint.

He stroked the girl behind him.

'They still could drop me and play the other eleven.'

'Not a chance!'

They walked hand in hand back to the bedroom.

Five minutes later Michael suddenly sat up.

'Bugger it! I owe Ben Hendricks ten quid!'

'Thank you for coming up so quickly,' said Maurice Kerr.

Michael smiled at him.

'I happened to be staying in London. It was no trouble.'

'Good. Now look here, I want you to get together with Peter Ames. Peter says keeping wicket to you is impossible without a code between you. Scratching your left ear for an off-break. Touching your heel for a top spinner, and so on. I want you and Ames to spend all day Tuesday on this code. He's free then. Are you?'

'Of course. Why don't we meet down at Horsham, then we can try out the code on my wicket.'

'Fine. Here's Ames' number. You'd better ring him about eight this evening. I'm leaving this entirely up to you two. You know what to do?'

'Yes. Perfectly. Does this mean you're going to play me on Thursday?.

'Almost certainly, yes. We're all agreed.'

'Even Bebington?'

Kerr gave a guffaw.

'Yes – even Bebington, the little sod!'

On the Tuesday evening Michael said good-bye to Sarah. He was moving to the Team's hotel.

The Press had got on to the factory. Mary Ware was fighting off reporters from every paper in the country. She and the staff were giving the agreed 'No comment'. It did little good. Everyone was cornered by persistent men from The Times, The Express, The Telegraph, The Guardian, The Mirror, The Sundays and the Provincials. Photographers lurked around the office, shooting anything that moved.

Only the Daily News kept away and other reporters wondered why. Where was Sarah Playdell?

B.B.C. Sound and Television had men out looking for a lead. So did I.T.V.

The 'No comment' held good up to Tuesday night.

Michael had spent all Tuesday with Peter Ames. They'd got a first-rate code going. They were both delighted. They'd dodged all the reporters.

Michael came on up to London with his gear and collected a suitcase from Sarah's flat. As he got into a taxi to drive to the Team's hotel, a London City Broadcasting reporter stopped him.

'Mr. Horton?'

'Yes.' Michael turned back from the cab.

'I'm Bill Hank of London City Broadcasting.'

'No comment, I'm afraid. How did you find me?'

'Just a hunch. Luck really. I don't want to talk cricket.'

'Oh?'

'No. I wondered if you were too young to have served in the war?'

'Of course I wasn't too young.'

'In the R.A.F., were you?'

'No. The Army, Durham Light Infantry.'

'In Europe, I suppose?. Hank mused.

'No.'

'Stuck in England all the time?'

'No, I was not. I was in the Far East, if it matters.'

'Played on matting wickets, I expect.'

'No comment,' said Michael firmly.

'I thought they were all matting wickets in India.'

'Of course they're not.'

'They have grass?'

'Damned good ones. Yes. Now that's all I'm saying.'

'Thanks a lot, Mr. Horton. I didn't want to trouble you.'

Michael got in the taxi. He waited till he was out of earshot of the reporter before giving the driver his destination.

Bill Hank was a real grafter. Once he got a lead on a story he never let go.

All Tuesday night he worked through the first-class cricket matches played in India from 1943 onwards. There were a hell of a lot more of them than he expected. By three in the morning, he thought he was on to a dead duck.

Then he struck oil.

Early in March, 1945, a Captain M. V. Horton turned out for the Army in India versus the Combined Universities.

It must be him.

He'd opened the batting and scored 43 and 19 and taken 4 wickets for 41 in the second innings. He'd made two catches. Just those bare facts. The match was at Poona.

That information was pretty limited.

Hank looked at the other details of the match.

His eye flicked over a name – and back again.

'Lieutenant C. Freer.'

That must be Chris Freer. The writer.

He'd been out in India at that time. He'd been a damned good cricketer, too.

Freer had done several broadcasts on London City and Hank had interviewed him down at his home near Dartmouth once. He knew Freer. Well enough to contact him.

At eight on Wednesday morning Hank had got Freer on the line.

'Chris. Do you know a chap called M. V. Horton?'

'You mean this bloke selected to play for the M.C.C.?'
'Yes. You know him?'
'I don't, Bill. I'm sorry.'
'Yes, you do. You played at Poona with him in forty-five. Against the Combined Universities.'
'Good God! That Horton! Mike Horton. Of course I knew him. A very good chap. Wonderful fielder. You mean it's the same man?'
'I'm pretty certain. Yes.'
'Well, I'm damned!'
'Can you tell me about him?'
'I'm sorry, Bill. I really know very little. He might have been good enough for a minor Counties side at that time, but certainly no better. Most of us were about that standard. Good Lord, he must be well over fifty now! How come he's still playing cricket at all?'
'We don't think he is, Chris. That's the extraordinary thing. Was he in any way outstanding? You say he was a damned good fielder but that wouldn't get him into a Test side. What was his bowling like?'
'Oh, Bill, I hardly remember! Military Medium, I'd say. He took some good wickets at Poona. Steady rather than flamboyant. Old Mike Horton! I wouldn't have believed this chap was him! Sorry I can't help more.'
Gradually people like Bill Hanks and the other Press people built up a picture of Michael Horton. Everything was printed or went over the air. Some of it the truth – some highly imaginative. One of the more scurrilous Dailies came out with the fact that M. V. Horton was separated from his wife and lived with a 'friend' in London.
On Wednesday the Times printed a picture of Michael arriving at the Roseblacks 150th Anniversary at the Savoy. When Michael Horton saw it he felt like suing for defamation of character.
At the Team's hotel Horton had a room to himself. The others shared. He rather wished he were in with Ivor Hughes or even this chap Brian Farr who, at thirty-eight, had been brought back

into the Team to strengthen the batting. Michael liked him. He was blunt to the point of rudeness, but really solid. When Bebington told Farr he was wanted up at the nets at nine-thirty on the Wednesday, the answer was a simple 'Fuck that! Tom tells me what to do.'

That really went to Michael's heart.

On Wednesday morning the Team loosened up at the nets. Michael was kept in the hotel. Stuck in his room, reading a book. He wasn't to be released on either the public or the Australians until the final moment. He was bored. He could hear the Press reporters gathered in the foyer. Bebington kept him protected.

In the afternoon there was a planning session at the hotel. Michael was again left out. Even the England Team were being kept in the dark.

Only after dinner – again in his room – was he taken to a special planning meeting.

Maurice Kerr was there. Bebington and Tom Lipton were sitting side by side. Ivor Hughes and Peter Ames were on a sofa. All the people who were in on the Horton scheme.

'Firstly,' said Kerr, 'I must tell Horton that he is playing tomorrow. The Selectors are unanimously agreed on that.'

Michael felt sick. Now the moment he had planned and striven for had come, and all he could think of was that he might throw up! He took deep breaths.

'Surprise is the main weapon we've got and if we field first we'll get that. The snag is that we want to bat tomorrow. If Tom wins the toss he'd be a fool not to bat. If Horton goes in number eleven then we give away the fact that he's a bowler. Surprise gone. Anyone got any ideas?'

They looked at each other. No-one spoke.

'Well?' said Maurice Kerr.

Michael looked around. There were no glimmers.

'How would it be,' he muttered, 'if I went in lower down in

the order? Say four or five? I'll make damn-all runs anyway but it would kid them that I was in as a batsman. Since we know we're going to lose my wicket for nothing, it won't affect us.'

'That's it!' said Lipton. 'A double bluff. We look as though we're looking to Mike for runs, when we don't give a bugger whether he stays or not.'

'Yes, it's good,' Bebington joined in. 'It's very good indeed. I suggest number five, between Brian Farr and Tom here.'

'Why not?' asked Kerr.

'No reason,' said Tom Lipton. 'Furthermore, they'll rule him out as a serious bowling threat to them, although he might be an all-rounder. It's a damn fine plan.'

'Right.' Maurice Kerr turned to Bebington. 'We leave Caldecotte out as twelfth. Announce the Team at ten in the morning and list Horton at number five. The others slide down a number.' He turned to Michael. 'I've no idea how you'll get on, Horton. You're taking just as much of a gamble as we are. All I can say is that you're giving us the devil of a lot of excitement! As an old man I say thank you for that!'

After the meeting Michael rang Sarah. Mainly to thank her for the easy, sensible, constructive way the Daily News had handled his selection.

'I'm getting my story later.' She smiled into the telephone.

'So you are.'

'Mike, darling. I've been busy.'

'You always are.'

'This time it's with Mary. Your Mary.'

'My daughter?'

'Yes, you idiot! Your daughter. Who else?'

My secretary's Mary, too. Mary Ware.'

'Yes. I've been busy with her, too.'

'What an extraordinary person you are!'

'Yes. Mary – your Mary – is coming up tomorrow for five

days. She's staying with me and I've got her and Stephen decent seats in the Mound Stand.'

'How the hell have you done all this?'

'Well – well, Mary Ware and I got to work and Mr. Honniman was marvellous and your father doesn't play every day for England at the age of fifty-three and – well, Mike, I thought you'd like it.'

'You are an angel.'

'Naturally!'

Ten minutes later he rang off.

He tried to sleep.

He failed.

The Team doctor looked in.

'How are you, Horton?'

'Too tired.'

'Of course. Try two of these.'

He took them. He slept till nine-thirty on the day of the Third Test at Lords.

THE THIRD TEST 1st DAY

The B.B.C. Radio 3 commentators eased themselves into their positions in the box high up above the pavilion.

Trevor Bridge, who was to do the comments between the overs, had already started talking to the millions of listeners.

The time was eleven-thirty exactly.

'Well, there it is then. Lipton won the toss for England, using his famous Churchill gold crown – the first toss he's won in this series – and I think probably quite rightly they've decided to bat on what should become, after the first couple of hours, an easy wicket.

'The umpires of this Third Test – Umpires Fox and Derby – are already in the middle and the Australians are taking up their positions under the eagle eye of Ian Church, who is playing in his twenty-seventh Test match and his eighth as Captain of Australia.

'The English opening batsmen are coming out. The tall Ivor Hughes on the left – Ted, how tall is Ivor? He must be, what . . . ?'

'He's six foot three, Trevor.'

'Six foot three. Yes, he's a huge man, of course. And the diminutive – or he looks diminutive alongside Hughes – Porthead, the left-hand opener for Surrey. I think I'm right in saying that Porthead is playing in his forty-seventh Test for England. Ted, is that right?'

'Forty-eighth, actually.'

'Right. Forty-eighth. I won't argue. His forty-eighth Test match. And he has a highest score of 234 against the Australians at Adelaide two years ago. Yes. Two years ago. And I think that was a "not out" innings as well.

'O'Rory is opening from the Nursery End. He's marked out his long run which curves in as he approaches the wicket and he's bowling to four slips and a gully. No. It's really three slips and two gullies. A third man. Cover. Mid Off – which is Fleetfoot-Jones, who will probably open the bowling at the pavilion end. Then a wide Mid On fairly close and a Short Square Leg just fine of square and four yards from the bat.

'Prout is standing right back, perhaps a pace in front of First Slip. He taps his gloves together rather nervously.

'They're settled. The third Test Match here at Lords is about to begin.

'Your commentator for the first session is George Allot. Good morning, George.'

'Good morning, Trevor. Good morning, everyone.

'The Ground is full. The gates are closed. The sun is shining. England are two Tests down. If you're half as excited as me, you'll be looking forward to enjoying yourselves.'

The rich Gloucestershire voice started to wrap itself round the cricket. It could convey so clearly the whole atmosphere of a match. Rising and falling. Slowing and speeding up. Giving the very heartbeat of a game as it occurred.

'And Umpire Fox drops his hand and O'Rory sets off from the far distance. He really has got a remarkable run this man. Increasing in pace the whole time as he comes in and it's outside the off stump and goes straight through to Prout. And Ivor Hughes just stands and looks. He glares at O'Rory. And O'Rory glares back, turns and starts his walk off to the distance. As he goes he winds up his right shirt-sleeve and he'll do exactly the same several hundred times more before this match is done. I often wonder, Trevor, why he doesn't have it cut off. Then he wouldn't have to wind it up.'

'Quite a good idea, George. Actually they make shirts like that now.'

'Short sleeved you mean? Yes. That's right.

'And he comes in again, increasing his speed. Past Umpire Fox – and he bowls. This one's straight. Moved a little in the air and Hughes played it out towards Cover. No run. Trevor, do you think they'll move the ball in this atmosphere early in the day?'

'I should think quite possibly. Yes ... there's generally a little damp in the air here in the mornings and although O'Rory is not a great swinger of the ball – not as much as, as, ... Fleetfoot-Jones for example, and certainly not as much as Frost, he should be able to move the ball – and in fact that last one did move slightly. Hughes had to go across to play it. Not a lot but quite a bit.'

'He did so very competently,' Allot went on. 'O'Rory turns and he comes in again. The slips go down. Prout chooses to put his cap straight. This is on the leg stump – and it's runs – Hughes turned it round to leg just clear of short square and they're running through for one, they'll come back for a second. That's two to England and Hughes has opened his account. The score board starts what all Englishmen hope will be a very long journey.

'Trevor, used you feel better when you got off the mark? Make a big difference, I mean.'

'Well yes of course it does. When you're there looking at the scoreboard and there's a big Nought against your name then ...

it makes you feel pretty low. You've only got to get one and you begin to realise that you can move. Yes, it does make a big difference. I was once stuck on nought for, I think, seventy-two minutes. Ted here will confirm it but ... O'Rory's coming in again. I'll tell you in a minute.'

'Indeed he does,' took up George Allot, 'and he bowls. It's a bumper. Hughes goes down. It goes over his head – not very far over. It didn't seem to get a lot of life out of the wicket that one. Prout took it fairly high up all the same, just above his cap and Hughes has walked down the wicket. He's walked an excessively long way – past where the ball bounced – and he's patting in the ground sarcastically. Sarcastically near to O'Rory's feet. Of course he's a character, this fellow Hughes. And now that we've got Brian Farr back in the England side if they should get batting together, I think it might be quite hilarious.'

The commentary kept going on its almost ceaseless way.

Hughes played out the over and Fleetfoot-Jones opened for Australia from the pavilion end.

Porthead was never a quick starter but he took three off Fleetfoot-Jones' fifth ball and the partnership got under way.

Michael Horton sat on the verandah outside the England changing room biting his nails.

Sir Maurice Kerr stood by the closed window in Bebington's office.

He could only hear the background murmur of the crowd surging when runs were scored. The click of the cricket was inaudible.

He was alone watching England's opening pair. They were on twenty-two. Hughes thirteen and Porthead nine.

He lit a cigar, twiddling the burned out match in his fingers. The black carbon fell on the carpet. He tore the wood into thin, uneven strips.

Fleetfoot-Jones was bowling away from him to Porthead. Extraordinary how we couldn't produce bowlers of this pace in England

– and the Australians had three. Not all as fast as O'Rory, but only a yard shorter – if that.

The ball was short. Rising outside the off stump. Porthead got on top. He cut majestically downwards. The ball flew between Cover and Extra. Beautifully imed. Beautifully placed. Four runs. God, Porthead was attractive when in full swing! That was a perfect shot. Timing – everything. Umpire Derby signalled the boundary with a flourish. The scoreboard moved up to twenty six. Both batsmen on thirteen.

'We need a decent start this time,' said Kerr aloud to the room.

Fleetfoot-Jones bowled. Straight, pitching on the line of the stumps. Porthead played forward – missed. The ball hit his back leg.

Maurice Kerr couldn't hear the appeal. He saw Fleetfoot-Jones change direction in mid air and throw an arm out towards Umpire Derby. He saw the three slips rise as one with wicket keeper Prout and spreadeagle themselves like four flying X's two feet off the ground.

Umpire Derby raised a finger. Porthead walked. L.B.W. bowled Fleetfoot-Jones for thirteen. England twenty-six for one.

Kerr turned away from the window.

'Damn.'

'Stop picking your nose.'

'I weren't our Dad.'

'Yer were. I sor yer. Yer little liar.'

'Oh.'

Terry and his father sat on the grass in front of the Tavern. The white boundary board was right in front of them. The grass was crowded.

Terry, eight, wore a pair of green shorts and a T shirt left over from one of his older sisters and printed rather weakly 'I love Ringo'.

'Our Dad.'

‘ ’allo.’

‘Will the ball come ’ere?’

‘No.’

‘Why?’

‘Becos.’

‘Why becos?’

‘Becos it’s three ’undred and sixty to one says it won’t come ’ere.’

‘Why?’

‘Shut up.’

O’Rory tore in past the umpire and his arm hurled the ball at Skeddons who had replaced Porthead. He played and missed. The crowds at either end of the ground looking down the wicket groaned.

‘Our Dad.’

‘Wot.’

‘Wot ’appened?’

‘ ’e missed.’

‘Why?’

‘Cos ’e’s no mucking good.’ Terry’s father turned to the man on his left. ‘I’m tellin’ my son ’ere that Skeddons’ no mucking good.’

‘I don’t agree.’

‘Oh. Sorry I’m sure.’

Terry was silent for a moment.

O’Rory thundered down again. Good length outside the leg stump. Skeddons played a leg glance. Even as he played the shot he realised his mistake and tried to withdraw his bat. Too late. There was a loud click and a clear deflection and Prout, diving to his left collected the catch just above the grass level.

The whole field and the Australians in the crowd appealed

OWAZATOWZATAWAZAT!

Skeddons didn’t even wait to be given out. He turned and walked. The Australians gathered in groups. Elated. England twenty-nine for two. They’d got them on the run again. Skeddons out for nought. Only this giant Hughes looking a problem on sixteen.

'Our Dad.'

' 'allo.'

'I seed that. I seed it all.'

'Well stop picking your nose.'

'I weren't.'

'I sor yer.'

'Oh.'

Terry's father slapped at his son halfheartedly.

'Yer missed our Dad.'

'Shut up.' He turned to the man on his left. 'So Skeddons is good, eh?'

The man looked away.

'My son 'ere could do better.'

'Wot our Dad?'

'Shut up.' He turned back to the man. 'Well?'

'I've nothing to say.'

'Skeddons couldn't hit a fucking football.'

The square figure of Brian Farr arrived at the crease. Hughes met him. Farr waved him aside with his bat. He took guard and read the field. He pulled his cap slightly over his left eye. He gave the impression he was here to stay. As if to endorse this he cut the last ball of O'Rory's over for two, square of third man and walked home.

'Our Dad.'

'Wot.'

'I wont to wee.'

'You wot?'

'I wont to wee.'

'Oh hell no. Can't you wite?'

'I bin witing.'

' 'ow long?'

'Ever so long.'

'Well wite till the end of the next over.'

'I can't.'

Silence.

'Stop picking yer nose.'

'I weren't.'

'You wos. I seed yer.'

'I wont to wee.'

'Oh muckin' 'ell then. Come on.'

Michael Horton's thumb nail on his right hand was nearly down to the quick. It had reached the point of being painful.

He sat on the verandah in the sun to acclimatise his eyes.

Oh God. I'm in next. If one of these chaps goes, I'm on. It's mad. What the devil am I even doing here?

He got up and took off the sleeveless sweater he'd thought he'd bat in. It might be better without. He was sweating too much anyway.

A moment later he felt cold. Took the sweater and pulled it over his head again.

He looked at the England players. All so calm and cool. But they weren't in next. Not like he was.

For the fourteenth time he went to the loo. He stood there – doing nothing now. He'd done it all. He slipped his box back into the jock-strap and returned to the verandah. Hughes and Farr were still there.

Every ball he winced – sure that a wicket was bound to fall and the longer it went on the worse it was.

Hughes went for the runs while Farr played sheet anchor. For thirty minutes Farr stuck on five. A few ignorant hand claps came from the crowd. They took the score from twenty-nine to fifty without incident. Then Hughes on thirty-one cut a possible – but really difficult chance to Mallor in the gully. He juggled it and dropped it. A sigh went up. Michael felt the sick in his mouth. He got a glass of water. It didn't help much.

Overton had to speak twice before Michael realised he was being talked to.

'See you've got those fantastic new pads.'

'Yes. . . .' Michael hesitated. 'My firm makes them.'

'Aren't they incredibly light or something?'

'Yep. About half normal weight.'

'What are they stuffed with?'

Michael realised that Overton was trying to distract him. He went along.

'Material called Proflex. Weighs damn all. Strong as hell.'

'Can you get me a pair?'

'Surely.'

'I'll pay of course.'

'Don't be silly. My pleasure. You can have a pair of Supreme Protecta gloves too if you like.' Michael threw a glove to the Kent player. 'All one piece protection but with finger ends. Better than the single block type.'

'God they're light.'

'Same stuff as the pads.'

'Thanks.'

Michael appreciated the few moments of respite from intense fear. He's a nice young man, this Overton, he thought.

Then his mind was back on Hughes and Farr.

He gnawed at his thumb. He put his right glove on so that he couldn't. Then started on his left.

The England score crept to sixty.

One o'clock came and went.

At twenty past, with the socre on eighty-one, Farr called 'Yes, come one' and ran. He was seven yards down the wicket when Hughes screamed 'Get back – No. Get back.' Farr turned. He tried to run. His bat dropped from his hand. The ball flew from extra cover towards Prout. Farr scrambled. The throw was near the base of the stumps. Farr's studs tore at the earth. Prout fumbled. He knocked down the stumps but hadn't gathered the ball.

A red faced, heavy breathing Farr made his ground.

Ivor Hughes and Brian Farr played out time to lunch at one-thirty. Eighty-four for two wickets.

Michael couldn't eat a thing.

*

'... and it will be Jock McGillery giving us the ball by ball commentary for the first session after lunch on the first day of the Third Test here at Lords.' Trevor Bridge was so at ease. 'We remember Jock mainly for his wonderful three hundred and thirty at Nottingham in the first Test after the war.'

'A little before your time, Trevor,' laughed the Australian, with the strong Australian accent.

'Only a little, Jock. I played against you in fifty-three.'

'I was past my prime then, son.'

'Jock. Are the players better than in our day?'

'I don't think so. No. They're more professional. They train more than we did. I don't think we were so fit as they are. Now. Take young O'Rory there. He's bowled fourteen overs this morning on the trot at one hell of a pace – and he came in looking as fresh as a daisy. You've got to be in prime nick to do that.'

'Well, he's not bowling now because Rose has come on at the Nursery end and is bowling to Farr.

'Jock McGillery.'

'Rose has a shorter run up than O'Rory. He's a "square on" bowler. Doesn't shove his left shoulder at the batsman on delivery. Practically face on.

'And he comes in. Arms working. He hammers down his left foot as he bowls. It's short and wide. My goodness me, that's almost to second slip! And it *is* a wide. Umpire Fox signals.

'Is that the first sundry, Trevor?'

'No. Fleetfoot-Jones bowled two No Balls just before lunch. He lost his run up.'

'I know there've been very few so far.

'Trevor, I see this man Horton's in next. Perhaps you'd tell us a bit about him at the end of the over. He's quite fresh to us.'

'And to me, Jock. We really know nothing about him at all ... but more on that later.'

'Rose comes in,' McGillery took over. 'Twelve, thirteen, fourteen paces – and he bowls. My, but that's a fast one! A yorker, right on the stumps and Farr comes down hard at the last moment.

That was a much better ball. Nearly as quick as O'Rory. Perhaps half a yard slower.'

The commentary went on with jokes and side talk to keep the listeners' interest. The voices and the techniques changed. Phillip East took over from McGillery and George Allot from him.

The score mounted.

It was East who was commentating when the hundred came up.

'Well, there it is. A hundred and one for two with Hughes on sixty-seven and Farr playing the much junior role on seventeen. These two have done England well. They've been slow. The hundred took ... a hundred and fifty-seven minutes – is that right, Ted? Thank you, yes. Two hours and thirty-seven minutes. But of course that doesn't matter at this stage. They need a really solid base for Horton, Lipton, Young and Ames to build on ... and Fleetfoot-Jones comes in. This man must be tiring. He's bowled at each end all day with only a three over break. He thuds in past Umpire Derby. Bowls to Farr – who pushes out between Cover and Extra and they take one. Farr eighteen. Hughes with the bowling on sixty-seven. He's really played beautifully. Playing the better balls with immense respect and hitting anything loose really hard. The partnership now worth seventy-two.

'Fleetfoot-Jones again. Short. A bumper. Hughes hooks. He mistimes it. High up on the splice. Oh dear, oh dear – Graham Church takes the easiest of easy catches at Mid Wicket – and Hughes goes. What a pity. Trevor, I think that was meant to be a six over square leg, wasn't it?'

'I think so – yes. Hughes can hook magnificently. It's a favourite move of his. That ball was short. Very short. It asked to be hit and Hughes accepted the challenge. He mistimed it – that's all. Very sad for England. almost the first mistake he made – and he paid for it.'

'There it is, then,' said East. 'Even a bad ball can take wickets. England a hundred and two for three. Farr on eighteen and obviously intense excitement as this unknown man, Horton, is due to come out. He didn't cross with Hughes going off and I wonder why.'

Michael got to his jellied legs. Now it had come.

Somehow he'd got to do this thing.

Lipton said, 'You're on Mike.' No 'Good luck' or 'take it easy.' Lipton had too much respect for Horton to say anything more than – 'You're on Mike.'

Michael walked across the dressing room. Through the passage and down the stair. His studs made it difficult. Out into the air and along behind the Members' heads. A few looked round.

He must have passed Hughes but he couldn't remember it.

Down the steps, back into the sun.

The gate was opened automatically for him.

Oh God help me.

He put his feet on the Lords' turf. He wondered if that would make him feel any different.

He looked up. It was a mistake.

He saw a bowl of thirty thousand pairs of eyes concentrating on him. It was an overwhelming experience. The ground didn't matter. The wicket with the fourteen men in white waiting for him were unimportant. The domination was the arena full of people – shrinking him.

This was really serious.

He looked down at his firm's gloves with his name on them in bold letters. 'Horton'. Somehow it gave him confidence.

He felt like the focal point of thirty thousand pairs of pins pointed at him. They mesmerised him in their three-dimensional circle.

The other cricketers came closer. The umpires. Suddenly there was Brian Farr standing before him, slightly away from the Australians.

'Welcome Mike,' he said. 'I'm not going to tell you what to do. You just do it yourself. Do it your way. The only thing to watch is not to run each other out. Let's concentrate on that.' He turned and walked back to the bowlers end.

Michael found himself at the batsman's wicket.

He couldn't look up at the people. He must either look at the ground or at the sky. The blue sky above. He must not look at the people. He must not allow them to sway his concentration.

God he'd never been in such a jam in his life before. Forced in to bat at number five for England when number eleven was the only place suitable for him. All part of a kid-the-Australians policy of which he himself had been the main contributor.

He suddenly found he had taken guard without any memory of having done so.

He marked the crease with his foot. He hammered his bat in to recognise his own patch.

The beautifully cut wicket looked incredibly rough out here. He wondered if he should do some gardening and then thought better about it.

He looked round and tried hard to memorise the position of the field. It wasn't going to help him much. He doubted that he had the ability to steer the ball even if he hit it.

He might be out first ball.

It suddenly occurred to him for the first time that he might be out first ball. In fact the odds were that he would. All this paraphernalia – all this batting number five, this kidding of the Australians – none of that mattered a damn. It was what the people – those thirty thousand people around the ground – were expecting, that worried him.

Michael would have been surprised indeed if he had known what was going through Ian Church's mind. 'This old chap looks a cool cove,' said the Australian Captain to himself. 'He's not taking a damned notice of anything.' And then because he realised he wasn't doing his job he called up Graypath into a Silly Mid Off position and moved Cornwall into the Fourth Slip Slot. He called in the leg field about ten yards to save the one and to act as more of a threat to the incoming batsman.

Michael just accepted all these moves without concern. It hardly seemed to be anything to do with him.

He saw Fleetfoot-Jones standing a million miles away tossing the ball from hand to hand.

He took up his stance and patted the ground with the end of the bat.

Here it came.

Fleetfoot-Jones came thundering in, increasing his pace as he passed Umpire Fox and thudded his right and then his left foot hard down on the ground.

The ball came with quite incredible speed.

Had it been straight Michael was convinced it would have knocked the bat out of his hands. As it was, it was just outside the off stump moving away slightly towards First Slip.

Michael found himself with his bat cocked up about a foot, standing leaving the ball go by.

Christ. This was even worse than he'd imagined.

He looked up and caught Farr's eye.

Farr was laughing.

Suddenly Michael got it in perspective.

He wasn't meant to do anything. If he was out this next ball it wouldn't matter a damn. That wasn't what he was here for. He was here to give the impression that he was a number five batsman for England. Well he'd give an impression. He'd bloody well make something of it. Yes. That was it. None of this mattered. He was being worried by something which was . . . well, . . . quite irrelevent really. He was in this team to bowl and bowl he would. But, by God, at the moment it didn't matter what happened.

He took up his stance and patted the ground – quite differently this time.

Fleetfoot-Jones came in. He came in with his electrifying run and thudded down on the ground. This time the ball was straight. Still moving slightly away to the off. Michael put his left foot and the bat forward together forming a defence. The ball hit the bat with a crack, bounced onto his leg and went back down the wicket slowly to meet Fleetfoot-Jones' follow-up.

That wasn't so bad.

He actually saw that one.

He even did what he'd intended doing.

Of course he was right. This didn't matter.

Well, see what this chap bowls as the next one.

But there wasn't a next one. It was the end of the over and Michael suddenly found himself disappointed that he wasn't going to face this fast, lightning bowler again for a few minutes.

He walked out slowly towards Square Leg. He passed Umpire Derby as he came in. Michael looked up and smiled. Derby nodded.

Good heavens. He felt quite at ease.

O'Rory bowled to Farr. It was an eye opener to Michael. This massive Australian was faster than Fleetfoot-Jones. For a moment he had another pang of fear. Then it went.

Farr drove the fourth ball hard between Extra and Mid Off. 'Come two.' Michael was backing up well. He accelerated. His heart hammered as he tore down the wicket, touched and turned. Farr was half way back. Oh God. He set off. He saw the fielder throw. His legs pumped harder. He got home as the ball arrived. This wasn't funny.

Michael Horton leant on his bat. He needed some support. He looked up at Farr and shook his head. Brian Farr smiled back.

Then it was Fleetfoot-Jones to Horton again.

An erratic over.

Michael only had to play two. Both defensively. The rest were off the wicket.

He was beginning to see the ball.

He felt a surge of confidence.

He turned to Prout as the Australian wicket keeper passed. 'Is he always as bad as that?'

'Just for two overs to aged new batsmen. That's all cobber.'

On the second ball from O'Rory, Farr turned it to leg and called for one. Michael went like hell. The lightweight pads were marvellous. If only he were not so heavy himself.

He took guard. Studied the field and settled in.

The ball fizzed. He swung at it. Got an outside edge. It flew between Slip and Gully down to Third Man. Farr called 'Yes'. They ran. The scoreboard under five moved up to one. Michael stared at it. Great God he'd scored. Off O'Rory.

He felt ten metres tall.

He smiled at Farr. Farr grinned back.

The first two balls of Fleetfoot-Jones' next over to Horton were 'No Balled'. He'd lost his smooth run up again. Michael played out the over quite easily. The Australian was obviously having desperate trouble with his approach.

O'Rory bowled a maiden from the pavilion end to Farr. A hundred and eight for three. The time was two fifty.

Rose came back on for Fleetfoot-Jones at the Nursery end.

Michael calculatedly made up his mind to swing at the first ball. He was only still here now by the grace of luck. He'd put it to the test.

Rose tore in. He bowled face on. It was a good one on the off stump. Perfect length. Moving in off the seam. Michael lunged forward with his left foot – swung the bat across the ball to leg. Right on the drive. He felt the colossal power of the shot through his arms. The crowd roared. The ball flew over Mid Wicket – one bounce into the spectators. Four lovely abandoned runs. A bit more adrenalin and it would have been a six.

Only Michael knew he was going to play the shot before Rose bowled.

The scoreboard read number five – five.

Stan Rose was not used to a perfect ball being punched away contemptuously. He didn't like it much. In fact he didn't like it one little bit.

He made up his mind on the way back to his disc.

He turned and powered in. Flung his left foot down and delivered a wicked bouncer on the line of Horton's legs. It bit the wicket short and climbed sharply. Michael saw it too late. He turned and tried to duck. Too late again, the ball thudded angrily into the muscle between his left shoulder blade and his armpit.

He gave a loud gasp of pain. Dropped his bat. Swayed towards the stumps. He was bound to fall on them. By some chance he didn't.

He doubled up clutching his back with his right hand. The pain was awful.

Graham Church reached him first. He pushed Michael's head down between his padded knees.

It worked.

Umpire Derby felt his back carefully. They'd nearly all gathered round.

Michael was white. He found taking a full breath painful.

'Christ,' he said, 'I'm still alive.'

He stood upright and took off his gloves, massaging his agonised back.

'Want to go off Mike?' asked Farr.

'Yes. But I'm not going. I'll be O.K. in a minute. Just give me a moment. God that hurt. What'd he do with it? Fire it from a rifle?'

They laughed.

Michael picked up his bat. Bardman handed him one glove. Oliver had the other. He put them on still stretching and trying to ease his painful body.

'Give me a minute will you?'

'Of course.'

Umpire Fox spoke to Ian Church. 'I warn you officially to advise your bowlers not to play aggressively. Understood?'

'Yes.' Ian Church walked over to Rose and spoke with him.

Michael took up his stance. He patted the crease. One, two, three, four, five times.

Rose flew in past Umpire Fox, both shoulders facing Horton. He bowled. Michael swung partly in anger, partly in frustration. He got an outside edge. The ball flew high again – but with no power. It seemed to hang over Bardman's head at Cover. Michael called 'Yes' decisively. They ran. Bardman moved back. He turned and lunged for the ball. It dropped harmlessly two feet from his outstretched hands and rolled on.

'Come again' called Farr and Michael pounded down beside the wicket and ended by walking the last five yards.

God his shoulder ached. He kept trying to ease it. He shook his left arm. Nothing seemed to help.

Should he go off? Hell no. Yet 'Retired Hurt' would be quite presentable. He'd think about it.

Rose came in. It was a beauty. Dead on a length. Six inches outside the off stump and moving in. It was half a yard faster than he'd been bowling all day. Michael played defensively. In a millionth of a second he sensed he was too late. He never felt the ball on the bat when he should have. He heard a racket behind him, a groan from twenty-five thousand throats and he saw Rose leap in the air.

He looked round. There were only two stumps. Prout was picking up the third.

Agonising disappointment.

Engulfing relief.

He turned and walked.

'Oh dear, oh dear,' said George Allot to the listeners. 'But *what* a good ball that was. It had wicket written all over it from the moment it left Rose's hand. An absolute peach of a ball.' His voice rose and fell. 'Trevor, you have the glasses on that I think.'

'Yes, I did. It was a very good ball indeed but Horton was far too late to stand a chance. I'm very surprised at this man Horton being selected. He's obviously in as a batsman. I don't think there's any doubt about that. But his timing was really quite dreadful. He's got the shots, of course, but he never looked right.

'Anyway, there it is,' he went on, 'England are a hundred and fourteen for four and Horton's gone for seven. They're in some trouble again. When you lose Hughes, Porthead, Skeddons and your mystery star for just over one hundred runs in forty three overs, you can hardly be satisfied.'

'But Trevor, it's not the wicket is it?'

'Great heavens no. The wicket has been really plum all day. There was a little damp for the first hour but it's a perfect batting wicket. No. It's a cross between the current English Batsmans'

Disease and very, very fast bowling. Hughes played a good innings. Sixty-seven out of a hundred and two. That sums it up. I don't really think that...'

'...sorry to interrupt Trevor but Tom Lipton has come out to a standing ovation. They really love this man. He's not very big and he's not very pretty but he's a real fighter and the crowd knows it. He needs seventeen runs for his three thousand in Test Cricket and I'm sure half the spectators here are aware of it. They've cheered him nearly all the way to the wicket.

'I'm sorry Trevor. You were saying?'

'I've rather forgot now. I think I wanted to make the point that in county cricket we have no really fast bowlers so that batsmen get little or no practice. Then they have to face up to O'Rory and Rose – and even Fleetfoot-Jones – and it's too much for them.'

'Very true,' Allot pondered. 'Ah well. Let's see what England's captain can do to improve the situation.

'Rose comes in full of a wicket and full of fire. He bowls. Overpitched. Lipton drives. He beats Mid Off. This is runs. They'll get two. Oliver's going for the ball. My goodness me he's moving. They take one. Turn for the second. This is good running. They're going for a third for the throw. They'll make it. A hundred and seventeen for four. Lipton three. Farr on twenty one.

'Trevor, that was good running.'

'Very good.'

'Funny how Tom Lipton can put spark into a game.'

George Allot's commentary went on.

Later Lipton took a two off the last ball of Rose's over. He glanced delicately to leg and the ball flew along the grass fine of Cornwall down to Graypath at Long Leg on the boundary. They ran two. Lipton five. Farr twenty-one. England a hundred and nineteen for four.

Fleetfoot-Jones bowled a maiden to Brian Farr who obviously intended continuing his role of sheet anchor, leaving the run getting to his captain.

Lipton had a devil of an over from Rose who was on top of the world having secured Horton's wicket. It was another maiden.

The game had gone quiet.

Ian Church told Fleetfoot-Jones that this was his last over unless he got a wicket. He intended putting Mallor on against Lipton. He wasn't so good on spin. The Australian fast bowler was angry. He didn't want to come off. He re-doubled his effort. He concentrated on Farr's off stump.

The third ball was short but on line.

Farr leant back and cut it hard. He got a top edge. The ball flew to Second Slip's left hand. it was Graham Church. He grabbed. The ball hit his fingers and dropped. His cousin, Ian, was crouched on the ground. He collected the falling ball inches off the grass.

Farr was out. Bowled Fleetfoot-Jones caught Ian Church for twenty-one. He smiled grimly at Lipton as he passed.

'Clever catch,' said the Captain.

'Too bloody clever,' and Farr passed on.

'So that's the end of Brian Farr for twenty-one,' George Allot was in full flood. 'He was there while ninety runs were added and he was very slow. Very slow indeed but *what* a useful innings. In a way he's justified his return to the England team. He's done his job and he's done it well.

'But goodness me, a hundred and nineteen for five. It's just not good enough.

'Trevor. Your comments.'

'As you say, it's not good enough. On this wicket England needed at least three hundred and fifty and at the way they're going they'll be lucky to pick up two hundred.

'No, it's disastrous. These Australians are too good and that's all there is to it. They won easily at Edgbaston and again at Leeds and I think they'll settle the Ashes problem here. Very disappointing.'

'And now,' said Allot, 'it's Greg Young of Hampshire. The last of the accredited batsmen coming in to join his captain.

'Oh. He's stopped half way. He's coming back. That's strange. Perhaps he's found he's forgotten a piece of his equipment. Or he doesn't fancy Fleetfoot-Jones with his tail up.

'He's been handed something at the gate. It's very small. Did you see what it was Trevor?'

'No. I can only think he left his chewing gum in the dressing room.'

'You're probably right. He'll take more than the two minutes allowed if he's not careful.

'All seems well with Young's world and he joins Lipton.

'A hundred and nineteen for five. Lipton on five and Young nought.'

'Harry.'

'Yes.'

'Are you coming?'

'Yes. In a minute.'

'What are you doing?'

'I'm watching the cricket. That's why I took this flat. It overlooks Lords. I can see when there's a Test – like now.'

'You mean you brought me back here this afternoon from the office and you're watching cricket?'

'Yes. It's very exciting.'

'Harry, I think you're the bloody bottom.'

'Oh, come on Margot. Don't be a spoil sport.'

'Spoil sport! Here am I lying in your wife's bed stark naked – and you call me a spoil sport!'

'I didn't mean it like that.'

'I should ruddy hope so. Are you coming?'

'Not for a second. Look here, we've got three hours before Daphne's back. Give me a bit of time.'

'Why does this damned Test have to be on a Thursday – our day?'

'Margot darling, it's only one Thursday in the whole year of Thursdays. God what a good throw. If Daphne didn't go to her mother every Thursday we'd have no time at all.'

'Well let's use it Harry.' Wistfully, 'Come on.'

'Just a minute. Young's done a classic Downside drive.'

'What's that?'

‘He made to hit Rose like hell to the off and the ball come off the inside edge down to Long Leg.’

‘Is that clever?’

‘No.’

‘What’s the score?’

‘A hundred and thirty-two for five.’

‘That’s pretty rotten, isn’t it?’

‘Yes. Pretty rotten.’

‘Why are we so bad?’

‘God knows.’

‘Too many people watching the game instead of romping in bed I should think.’

‘Lipton’s doing well.’

‘Bully for Lipton. Harry.’

‘Yes.’

‘Are you coming?’

‘No. Oh my God. Young’s been bowled.’

‘I’m not surprised.’

‘Why not?’

‘Doing Downside drives or whatever. At least he can go for his romp now. Harry, will you come?’

‘That was a damned good ball by Fleetfoot-Jones.’

‘Who?’

‘Fleetfoot-Jones.’

‘I don’t believe it.’

‘Don’t believe what?’

‘Fleetfoot-Jones. No one has a name like that. Certainly not an Australian.’

‘That’s his name you ass. His uncle played before the war.’

‘As Fleetfoot-Jones?’

‘Yes.’

‘It’s impossible. You made it up.’

‘Oh have a sleep.’

‘No. Who’s in now?’

‘I can’t see. The pavilion’s in the way. You’ll have to wait ’til he gets out on the field. We could turn on the radio.’

'Harry.'

'Yes.'

'If you turn on the radio, I'm going.'

'It's Ames.'

'What's aims?'

'He's in. Peter Ames. The wicket keeper. He can make runs. He's scored a hundred in a Test before.'

'Let's hope he won't do it now.'

'Why?'

'Because I'm fed up.'

'Don't be stupid.'

Pause.

'Harry.' Breathlessly.

'Yes?'

'Come here a minute.'

Harry dropped his binoculars to his side. He moved from the window. Margot was half sitting up on one elbow. The sheet had fallen below her knees.

'Coming Harry?'

'Oh bloody hell. Yes.' He put the binoculars on the window sill. Perhaps England would still be batting later.

' 'core Card. 'core card. You want a Score Card Mister?'

'Yes.'

'1op.'

'Good heavens.'

'Don't cost exactly nothing to print.'

'Here you are.'

'Ta Mister.' The little man moved on.

' 'core Card. 'core Card. Want a Score Card, Lady?'

The man looked at the slim pasteboard.

He knew most of it. But it was nice to have. He'd show it to Lilian later.

England 1st Innings.

I.A.R. Hughes	ct Church, G. b Fleetfoot-Jones	67
J.R. Porthead	L.B.W. b Fleetfoot-Jones	13
L.A. Skeddons	ct Prout b O'Rory	0
B. Farr	ct Church, I. b Fleetfoot-Jones	21
M.V. Horton	b Rose	7
T.A.M. Lipton	Not Out	13
G. Young	b Fleetfoot-jones	3
P.E.G. Ames	Not Out	0
Extras		8
	Total for 6 wkts.	132

1 for 26. 2 for 29. 3 for 102. 4 for 114. 5 for 119. 6 for 132.

The man tucked the Score Card in his lunch bag.

He'd buy another one later. For his son, who was only three. But he could have it as a momento when he grew up.

Michael Horton sat on the massage table in the small First Aid room behind the England dressing room.

He looked a bit drawn.

'Sorry I took so long,' the doctor said. 'Emergency.'

'That's O.K. The Coach looked me over.'

'What'd he say?'

'Damn all.'

'That's Fred all right. Means there's nothing wrong with you. I'd better look though. Lie down on your stomach.' He rubbed his hands together. 'God you're overweight, aren't you?'

'Yes. So what.'

'You should lose two stone – mostly from around here.' He poked. 'Let's see this back now. Oh golly, you did stop one, didn't you? That's a beaut. It'll be even better tomorrow.'

'Thanks.'

The doctor pressed.

'Does that hurt?'

'No. Not much.'

'That?'

'No.'

'How about that?'

'Slightly. Not really.'

'There?'

'No.'

'Clench and unclench your left fist. Any pain?'

'No.'

'Fred's right. It's nothing major.'

Michael started to get up.

'No, stay there. I'm going to give you some treatment. Deal with the bruise – it's an ugly customer.'

The doctor dragged over an electrical looking box.

'We put these two pads, here – and here. Then we put small sandbags on top to hold them in place. Where are the bloody sandbags?. He searched around the room and returned with two cotton covered bags. 'They go like this. Now. I'm going to switch on the current and you'll feel a tickling sensation. It will become hot and sharper. I want you to say when you can't take any more.'

'Will I die?'

'I doubt it.'

'Christ!'

'What's the matter we've hardly started yet. Say when it's too much.'

Michael gritted his teeth. His shoulder was a red hot mass of vibrating needles. He took all he could.

'When!'

'O.K. That's not bad. We stay fifteen minutes like that.'

'Fifteen minutes! God help me. I thought it was just a oncer. You'll maim me.'

'No I won't. Don't be a baby!'

'Turn it down a bit. You deceived me.'

'All right then. Very little. How's that?'

‘I am dying.’

‘Well try not to go for fifteen minutes. I want the treatment to work first.’

‘Thanks a lot.’

‘I’ll send Hughes in to hold your hand. Don’t touch anything will you?’

‘Not bloody likely.’

The doctor went out.

Three minutes passed.

Ivor Hughes appeared by Michael’s head.

‘Hi Ivor. I’m being murdered.’

‘Good.’

‘Thanks. What’s the score, Ivor?’

‘A hundred and seventy-eight for six. Tom’s on forty-three, playing really well. Peter’s got sixteen. They’ve put on forty-six for the seventh wicket. It improves things quite a bit. If only they can stick it out. There’s not much batting to come.’

‘Go to the door and give me a commentary.’

‘I can’t you idiot. They’re taking Tea.’

‘How pathetic. A hundred and seventy-eight at Tea.’

‘It’s not good man.’

The doctor came in.

‘He dead yet?’

‘No. He’s fighting,’ said Hughes.

‘Turn me off. I’m done on this side.’

‘Two more minutes.’

‘Ivor, turn it off.’

‘I don’t know which way the switch works.’

‘Then don’t touch it! Doc, that’s enough. Really.’

The doctor flicked a switch. ‘Yellow.’

‘Oh God that’s better.’

The doctor removed the pads.

‘Holy David,’ said Hughes. ‘You’ve got a real peach there, haven’t you?’

‘How do I know? I can’t see it.’

'We ought to take a coloured photograph for you.'

'Oh go to hell – both of you.'

Maurice Kerr sat down in the seat in the Members' Stand provided for him. He was next to Freddy Barrington.

'Evening Maurice. See you came a cropper with this chap Horton.'

'I don't think so. Not yet.'

'You mean there's a second innings? Be too late for any genius by then, I should say.'

'Uh huh.'

'What's that meant to mean?'

'Nothing.'

'The Inscrutable Kerr. Good shot Sir. What a lovely hook. Young Ames can bat when he has the mind. Four very useful runs.'

Rose bowled again.

'And four more,' said Kerr. 'Leg byes or byes.' He looked for Umpire Fox's signal. 'Byes. It all helps.'

Rose finished his over from the Nursery End. The field changed. Mallor had been bowling since tea, presumably on the surmise that Lipton wasn't so happy against slow bowling. Mallor came to the pavilion end. Started rearranging his field with Ian Church. He was obviously going to concentrate on off-breaks. He'd only got one slip and a gully, with a cross between Extra and Cover. That was the off-side field. On the leg he had Cornwall deep at Mid-On, very deep Mid-Wicket. Bardman out on the Square-Leg boundary and three fielders close to the wicket. A Slip, Short-Square and Silly Mid-On. It was an attacking field with three brave men close to the batsman.

The first ball was loose. Well outside the off stump. It hardly moved off the wicket. Lipton cut square. He slightly mistimed it. They ran one. Came back for two. Only five to go for Lipton's fifty.

The second ball was good. On the middle stump. Well pitched

up. Lipton played bat and pad. The ball kicked to leg. Hit the bat – glanced onto his pad and flew upwards. Ian Church at Silly Mid-On flung himself flat. He caught the ball at grass level.

Lipton stayed. He made no move to go. The close Australians were patting Church on the back.

Lipton stayed.

There was an awed hush round the ground.

Ian Church asked quietly, 'How was he?'

Umpire Derby raised his finger without hesitation.

The crowd gasped.

Tom Lipton walked.

'Damnation,' said Maurice Kerr. 'What infernal luck.'

'Luck, nonsense. He was careless.'

'Maybe.'

'Well that's the end for sure. Overton, Frost and Bolte won't last ten minutes. They'll be all out for under two hundred. What are they now? A hundred and eighty-eight for seven. Hopeless.'

'Ames is still there. On twenty.'

'The Aussie's will get five hundred on this plum wicket.'

'Balls, Freddy.' Kerr took out a cigar and slowly lit it. 'They certainly wont get more than two hundred and fifty.'

'Want to bet?'

'Yes.'

'A fiver?'

'O.K. A fiver.'

'Done. Now watch Overton go.'

He did.

First ball from Mallor.

He lunged forward at a good length ball and mis-timed it. The stumps disintegrated and Prout caught a bail. Overton was on his way back within thirty seconds of taking guard.

'Told you so,' said Barrington.

'Hell,' said Kerr. He got up. Shook his head and went up to the England dressing room to have a campaign meeting with Lipton.

*

'What did you really think of Daddy?' asked Mary Horton. 'I mean honestly.'

'Well he got seven runs,' replied her brother.

'Oh Stephen I know that, you idiot. I mean ... well ... how did he play?'

Stephen thought.

'Well truthfully, I didn't think too much of him. He didn't look convincing if you know what I mean.'

'You said 'Jolly good shot' when he scored that four.'

'O.K. That was the exception. He looked just like Dad batting in the nets at home. Not an England number five.'

'Why on earth did they pick him?'

'I've no idea at all. Really I haven't.'

'Perhaps he'll do better in the second innings.'

'Let's hope so. If he doesn't I'll get hell from the chaps at school.'

'Me too.'

They sat and watched Ames and Frost push the score slowly along.

For four overs Ames kept the bowling by scoring one on the last ball. He protected Frost who took a two off the edge off Rose down to Long Leg.

Ames got two more and a one off the fifth ball of Mallor's next over. Frost played the sixth successfully.

Rose bowled Ames five maiden balls. The last one of the over Ames hit gently to Extra Cover. He called 'One' and went like hell. Frost was halfway down even as the ball was bowled. Cornwall tore in. He picked and flicked the ball with his wrist. It flew to the bowlers end where Ames was struggling to get home. The ball hit the single stump facing Cornwall. He roared. So did Rose and a half a dozen other Australians. Umpire Fox's hand shot up and Ames was out. He continued running in a wide arc and then walked off the field.

The scoreboard changed with remarkable speed.

A hundred and ninety nine for nine. Last Man twenty-seven.

*

‘Our Dad.’

‘Wot?’

‘Will the ball come ’ere?’

‘No it wont.’

‘Why?’

‘ ’Cos no fucking Englishman’s got the strength. That’s why.’

‘Why?’

‘ ’Cos.’

‘When Australia’s batting will it come ’ere?’

‘Might.’

‘Good. I’ll stop it.’

‘You won’t.’

‘I bloody will.’

‘Watch yo’r tongue you filthy little sod.’ He swung at the child.

‘Yer missed.’

‘Shut up.’

Bolte hit out. He scored a four off Mallor and after Frost took three from Rose, he got another two. For the first time for hours the batting came alive.

Frost ran a short quick run to Mallor. Bolte faced the slow bowler. The ball was short on the off stump. Bolte leant back and flashed wildly at the ball. The timing was perfect. It ripped through the close field and fine of Cover. It tore for the boundary in a curving track. Four heavenly runs down towards the Tavern.

‘Come ’ere you little bastard. Leave it be.’

Terry took no notice. The ball was coming. That was all that mattered. The other twenty boys around him were nothing. He was going to get the ball. He ran ten yards into the field.

‘Come ’ere damn you.’

The ball arrived.

Three of them fell in a heap on it.

Terry came up from underneath clutching the ball.

‘I dun it. I got it. Hey Mister,’ he yelled at Oliver. ‘It’s comin’ Mister. Catch it.’

He flung the heavy ball all of fifteen feet. Oliver walked in and picked it up. ‘Thanks son,’ he called, ‘you’re all right.’

Terry crimsoned with pride.

'Our Dad.'

'You little swine. Cum 'ere.'

'I caught it.'

'You never. You stopped it. You never caught it you little liar.'

'I dun it Our Dad.'

'Oh shut up.'

'Why?'

'Becos. That's why.'

Suddenly Terry's father saw the players going off the field.

'Wot 'appened?' He turned to the man beside him. 'Why they goin' orf?'

'Bolte was out. Caught and bowled Mallor. It was a lovely catch. They're all out for two hundred and seventeen. Not much good.'

'Much good! It's fuckin' awful.'

He looked round disbelieving.

'Stop pickin' yo'r nose.'

'I aint.'

'You are. I seed yer.'

'I worn't.'

'Oh shut up.'

The time was six thirty five.

Sarah Playdell was finishing off the rough of her story on the day's play.

For seven hours she'd watched every move and hammered away at her typewriter. Gradually the story took shape. The first day's happenings were condensed into the important and the chuck out. She'd scrapped a whole wastebasket of useless sheets. She was hot, tired and sometimes bored.

'England finally collapsed for two hundred and seventeen in three hundred and ten minutes.' Sarah's fingers clappered on the keys. 'Only Ivor Hughes (sixty-seven) and Tom Lipton (forty-five) kept the Union Jack on the Pavilion from fading to a dirty pink colour.

'The Australian innings opened with three fours by Martin Graypath off Frost's first over. This indicated the nature of the wicket which England had been wrestling with all day.

'Graypath and the small dynamo, Rob Oliver make a perfect team. They work together like Morecombe and Wise. Their timing is their success. They took the score to thirty-six for no wicket in thirty-six minutes playing like twins. They were even both on eighteen at the day's close. By six thirty Australia had given England the warning 'Beware of Friday'.

'In spite of the apparent domination by the Australians your Correspondent recommends that you drop everything on Friday and come to Lords. You may very well get the eye opener of the cricket decade. Your Correspondent has information that would lead her to bet her girdle to a lump of mud that sparks will fly in St. John Wood on the second day of this Test.

'Today's score was:

England. First Innings.

I.A.R. Hughes	Ct Church G. b Fleetfoot-Jones	67
J.R. Porthead	L.B.W. b Fleetfoot-Jones	13
L.A. Skeddons	Ct Prout b O'Rory	0
B. Farr	Ct Church I. b Fleetfoot-Jones	21
M.V. Horton	b Rose	7
T.A.M. Lipton	Ct Church I. b Mallor	45
G. Young	b Fleetfoot-Jones	3
P.E.G. Ames	Run Out	27
B. Overton	b Mallor	0
P.A.R. Frost	Not Out	6
A.L. Bolte	Ct and b Mallor	10
Extras		18
	TOTAL	217

1 for 26. 2 for 29. 3 for 102. 4 for 114. 5 for 119. 6 for 132. 7 for 188. 8 for 188. 9 for 199. 10 for 217.

Australia. First Innings.

Graypath	Not out	18
Oliver	Not Out	18
Extras		0
	TOTAL FOR NO WICKET	36"

Sarah straightened her papers and brush-cleaned the type on her machine. She put on the hard cover.

'Coming for a drink?' asked the man from the Express.

'God yes. I could do with one after that. I've never written so many words for a measly total of two hundred and fifty-three runs in a day.'

'Horton was a flop all right, wasn't he?'

'No. I thought he did rather well.'

'You're joking.'

'No I'm not,' said Sarah. 'If anyone can save this match for England then Horton is the boy.'

'Can I quote that?'

'If you mention that it came from the Daily News – yes.'

'Damn you.'

'Don't mention it.'

They got a cab in Mostyn Road and headed for Fleet Street.

Michael was lying on his bed.

If he had any sense he'd get undressed and get between the sheets.

His whole body ached. Partly from the bruise on his back and partly from the total tension of the day.

What a sensation to have. Playing cricket for England. Beyond his wildest dreams.

He thought about Meg for a moment. Then put her out of his mind.

The door knocked. And Ivor Hughes came in.

'May I?'

'Of course, Ivor. I was just resting before the major task of undressing.'

'You did bloody well today, man.' He sat down in the arm-chair.

'I did nothing.'

'I don't mean your results. I mean your overcoming the stress.'

'So you know it was mental hell?'

'Of course.'

'I don't think the others realise it.'

'No. They don't. But remember they don't know the background story yet. They're still in the dark. Only Tom and Peter and I really understand. They're a good bunch of lads though.'

'I like young Overton,' said Michael. 'He tried to help.'

'He would. He's sensitive – that one.'

'The batting was just a farce but I found the fielding rough. I hope I can stand it all day.'

'You did bloody well. Saved four off Oliver certainly.'

'It hit my arm. Didn't do a thing. Anyhow what could I do at First Slip half hiding behind Peter and the other half with your great bulk protecting me. I'm being carried too much.'

'You can't be carried too much,' said Hughes. 'Your job is to bowl these mucking Australians out tomorrow as soon as the ball is suitable for you.'

'I looked at it tonight. It's still bloody shiny. Need another sixty or seventy runs off it.'

'It'll get them. Time you went to sleep, I think.'

'Yeah. I've got one 'phone call to make.'

'Get into bed first. Then make it. I expect the Doc will be round in half an hour.' Hughes got up. 'I'm off. Well done Mike. You've really got through the worst of it – mentally. We're rather proud of you.'

Michael rang Sarah.

*

Frost continued bowling from the pavilion end on the Friday morning.

The ground was not full at eleven thirty but the crowds were flowing in. There must have been twenty thousand people to see Graypath cut Frost's last ball for four searing runs fine of Gully.

Michael walked crisply down beside the wicket to the other end.

Even allowing that it was the first over of the day, Frost was nowhere near the pace of the three Australian fast bowlers. He was quick – yes. But he lacked that extra punch and speed. Graypath had seemed to have all the time in the world cutting for four.

At the other end Young was only fast medium. He swung the ball effectively off the seam and Michael thought he looked the more dangerous of the England openers.

Young Overton had bowled the last over on Thursday night. Very tidy. He dropped onto a spot immediately with his slow left arm leg breaks to the right hander and he'd bowled a maiden to Graypath.

Michael was surprised. He wasn't too stiff this morning. His back ached a bit – but not on his right side thank God. He felt on top of the world. Almost too well – which was odd as he had only slept intermittently in spite of the doctor's pills.

'Slips' called Tom Lipton from Mid Off, 'come up half a yard will you?' He signalled with both hands. Michael, Ivor Hughes and Brian Farr took a half pace forward.

Graypath leant on his bat, chewing his gum and watched the three move nearer to him.

'That old cove is bloody fine. Wonder what he's doing hiding round the corner there.' Graypath mouthed to himself, 'Well if they want to waste a man why should I care.' He tickled the next ball down the leg side and took two runs to Skeddons on the Long Leg boundary.

Most of the Press correspondents were sitting idly watching the play and smoking. Only Srah Playdell was pounding her typewriter. She wrote, "M.V. Horton is wonderful at First Slip and I've no idea why but I love him to distraction.' She stopped and peeled the sheet out of the machine. She was going to drop it in the wastebasket – thought better of it and folded it neatly away in her bag. 'Damn him.'

Graypath and Oliver continued on their way from thirty-six for no wicket, that they had built in the evening before.

The fifty came up in a quarter of an hour and Frost and Young attacked as well as they could.

At twelve-thirty the score stood on eighty-four.

Tom Lipton walked over to Michael. He took him aside.

'What do you think? Can you handle the ball now?'

'I don't know,' said Michael, 'I haven't felt it.'

'John. Throw us that ball a minute.' The cherry came through the air. Lipton caught it. Handed it to Michael. 'What d'you say?'

Michael fingered the ball. He looked closely at it. Felt the seams. He rubbed it on the ground. Examined it again.

'Can you give it another half hour?'

'Yes if we must. You're quite sure?'

'I'd make a balls up with this as it is.' Michael looked at the ball yet again.

'O.K. We'll give it eight more overs.'

They returned to their places.

George Allot had been talking to the listeners.

'Now we seem to be taking a breather and Lipton and Horton are discussing the condition of the ball. Lovely sunny summer's day to be considering the spheric quality of the ball.

'Trevor, why on earth do the bowling team make a song and dance about a ball not being round? I should have thought the more egg shaped it could become the better.'

'It is strange, yes. There's been some problems with balls this season. I've seen this happen half a dozen times. However all seems in order and Young turns to come in.'

George Allot took over.

'He comes towards us. Long run for a medium pacer. He bowls. This is runs. My goodness four of them between Long on and

Mid Wicket. Graypath only leant on that ball. He seemed to stroke it quite gently and it flew to the boundary interrupting a conference between the Lords Pigeon Council taking place out on our far left. The ball returns and the Council settles down to its affairs again.'

The score was ninety when Oliver got his fifty. A quick run taken to Extra cover brought it up. The many Australian supporters were jubilant. Ninety for no wicket – and no sign of one.

At one o'clock Oliver brought up the hundred with a three that put him on sixty-one.

Lipton called on Horton.

For a moment Michael's knees buckled.

Supposing he couldn't? Supposing fear took away the ability?

He moved over to the pavilion end from where it was agreed he'd bowl.

He sensed the awe and surprise in the crowd.

Graypath turned to him.

'You bowl too?'

'A little.'

'Thought you were an all rounder.' He poked at Michael's middle with his bat, and laughed.

'Right arm over?' asked Umpire Derby.

'... what's that? ... oh yes. Right arm over.'

Michael took off his sleeveless sweater. Gave it to Derby. He paced off his short run. Tom gave him the marker disc.

'Thanks.' He footed it in. Turned round to face the wicket and swung his right arm, exercising it.

Tom Lipton was arranging his field as they'd agreed. Two Slips. Two Gullies, one of them really old fashioned point. Close Extra. And on the leg side a conventional Mid On, Mid Wicket, Short Square Leg and Leg Slip. An attacking field by any standard.

England settled.

'Right arm over,' called Derby. 'Play.'

Michael came in.

One, two, three, four-five. He bowled.

The ball went wild.

It fizzed out of his fingers and flew towards Gully. It landed five yards off the line of the stumps. It kicked sharply as if dropping on a bump on an old wicket. The Gully, Farr, dived for it.

He'd bowled the most enormous wide.

Oh God help me.

He felt the roaring silence of the crowd.

He walked back. Lipton flicked the ball to him. He came in. One, two, three, four-five.

This was identical. Miles off target. Further than the first if anything.

Oliver just stood and smiled.

Suddenly a voice came from the spectators down near the Tavern.

'Why don't you move the bloody stumps?'

It eased the tension.

People laughed. Others called 'Shut up.'

Michael tried to blot them all out.

He tried again.

The signal he gave to Ames was a leg break pitching off the wicket.

It was on the leg all right. It was off the wicket. Twenty yards off. Bolte at Square Leg retrieved it.

The crowd were laughing openly now. Someone clapped and a lot took it up.

Umpire Derby signalled Wide for the third time.

The score had gone up from a hundred and two to a hundred and five.

Michael came in.

One, two, three, four-five.

This was better.

It pitched well outside the off stump on the edge of the mown wicket. It kicked viciously right. Oliver just stood. The ball deflected in sharply. It flew past the static bat and clipped the top of the off stump.

He'd done it!

By God he'd done it!

There was a roar of approval and relief. The spectators went mad.

Oliver stood disbelieving. He went and examined where the ball had pitched. He shook his head and walked.

They gathered round Michael. They patted his back.

'What a trick,' said Overton. 'Never seen anything so cunning in my life. Three wides than a beauty. What an idea. Well done.'

Phillip East was trying to comment.

'Well after that quite remarkable exhibition of incompetent bowling we have what England have been searching for since last night at six o'clock. A wicket. Oliver bowled Horton with a sort of sideways Yorker for sixty-one. Australia a hundred and five for one in reply to England total of two hundred and seventeen.

'What do you make of that Trevor?'

'The ball moved all of two yards to the right after pitching. It must have landed in an old bowler's footmark on the next wicket. That's all I can think of. Still, it got a wicket and that was needed badly enough. Tough on Oliver though. Here comes Bardman playing in his first Test. He's a young man – twenty-one, Ted?'

'Yes. Twenty-one last month.'

'... and he's got a wonderful future. I think he's too alive to be kicked out as Oliver was.'

Phillip East took over. 'Bardman takes guard. It looks like leg stump from here. It'll be interesting to see what Horton does.'

Horton was rubbing the ball on the ground. It didn't help much but he'd got to get a better grip on it. That was all he needed.

He looked up. The batsman was a good looking young Australian with very fair hair. He looked unconcerned.

Michael glanced round the field. Gave Peter Ames the code for a heavy leg break and ran in to bowl. One, two, three, four-five. He bowled. The ball was well flighted. It landed a good length but four feet outside the leg stump. Bardman hardly moved. He'd let that go by as a wide. The ball snapped in sharply – passing only inches from the leg stump. Bardman jumped. At the last second he tried to make a stroke. Ames took the ball cleanly.

There was silence from the spectators. They couldn't understand what was going on. Then as the ball was returned to Michael round the ring a murmuring broke out. It was as if everyone were asking 'What is this?'

Horton walked back. He looked down at the ball in his hand. He couldn't see it! He blinked his eyes, disbelieving. It couldn't happen now. Now of all times. God Almighty make it a mistake.

But he knew it was no mistake.

He'd got a migraine.

A damned bad one.

A sod.

He looked at Lipton. Tom's head was a space. By shifting the line of his vision he could just see the England Captain looking at him. Waiting for him to start his run.

He couldn't.

Bardman and the stumps were a blank.

Everyone waited.

A minute went by.

Umpire Derby looked round at Horton. 'Play,' he called.

Michael stood frozen. About half vision available to him – and that moving dizzily from side to side.

He's got to do something. To bowl.

He ran in. Automatically. No spin now. Just to get the ball down.

It was a long hop. Slow and inviting. Bardman flashed at it. The ball rocketed between Silly Mid On and Short Square. Four runs.

Michael found difficulty in getting back to his marker.

It was no good. He couldn't bowl like this. Just at the critical moment – and this had to happen.

He called Lipton over.

'I've got a migraine,' he told him.

'Oh no.'

'Oh yes. A hell of a one.'

'You'd better stop.'

'No. I'm going to finish this over. I'll do it somehow. Then I'll go off. I'm sorry.'

'What a bloody nuisance. Are you sure it won't go?'

'Certain. I'm finished for half an hour at least.'

'It'll be lunch then. You've got over an hour. Can you get back after?'

'Yes. Sure. Let me finish these – what is it – three balls.'

'O.K. But don't make yourself worse.'

'I won't.'

Somehow Michael bowled. He never knew how. The first two were presentable and Bardman watched them go by. The last was a half volley on the off stump. If it hadn't been for some extraordinary acrobatics by Overton it was a certain four runs. As it was they only got one.

Michael turned away and walked off. He steered for the centre of the pavilion. He passed the twelfth man, Grant, one of the Lord's ground staff, coming out to replace him. By pure determination he got up the steps. He steered himself by touching the wall and arrived, sick and frustrated in the England dressing room.

He stood for a moment near to tears.

Then walked into the first aid room and collapsed on the massage table.

There were no flashing zigzag lights.

Where were they? He always had them.

Then he knew.

It was a new type of migraine to him.

Mary and Stephen Horton sat quietly in the Mound stand. They were each brooding on their own thoughts.

'Stephen.'

'Yep.'

'I can't really believe that it's Daddy playing here for England. It feels like ... like a dream.'

'More like a nightmare.'

'Oh. Don't be cruel. It's not as bad as that.'

'It is. It's awful. For some unknown reason Lipton puts Dad on to bowl and he throws up three of the most laughable wides Lords can ever have seen. It's a pure nightmare. Nothing less.'

'But,' said Mary defensively, 'he gets a wicket which is what counts.'

'And then goes off. It's ludicrous. It's insane.'

'I think he was jolly clever to have got Oliver. Clean bowled too.'

'Jolly lucky you mean. The ball pitched on the next wicket and hit a footmark. It must have. Wonder why he went off?'

'Perhaps he's not well.'

'After those wides, I'm not surprised.'

'You're being horrid.'

'I don't care. It's all so ridiculous.'

'You're wrong Stephen. There's some good reason behind Daddy playing. They've selected him for his bowling, I think. I'll bet that's it.'

'And a pretty big flop he's being.'

'Oh shut up being so beastly.'

They sat watching Bardman and Graypath taking the score along.

England was playing a containing game. Brian Overton at one end with his left arm over the wicket leg spinners pitching time and again on the spot. Difficult in the extreme to get away. At the other end Greg Young changing his medium fast for medium slow seamers and trying desperately to keep the score down.

For a quarter of an hour they succeeded. In that time Australia only went from a hundred and five for one to a hundred and twelve for one.

The field placing was containing. The whole attack in a low key. This was how Lipton intended playing it up to lunch.

The team doctor entered the first aid room.

'Saw you coming off Horton. Anything I can do?'

Michael looked at the man. He didn't recognise him. He said nothing. Just lay on the massage table.

'Horton is your back causing you trouble?'

No reply.

The doctor took his left arm. Felt the pulse.

'Here. Come onto this bed. You'll be more comfortable.' He half lifted Michael off the table. 'You're in a poor way, aren't you?'

Horton tried everything within his power to make a reply to the questions which he only half understood. He knew this man was being kind. He even knew he was a doctor but he couldn't find the word for doctor in his stricken brain.

He tried.

'Mienne.'

Even as he said the meaningless word he knew it wasn't the one he meant.

'Have you had an attack like this before?' asked the doctor gently.

Michael understood the question. He wasn't too sure of the answer. In any case he couldn't find the word. He made a supreme effort.

'Name Horton.'

'Yes. Quite right. Now you lie still. I'm going to check you over.'

He got Fred in. They undressed Michael which seemed to cause him distress. They put a blanket over him. The doctor tested his reflexes and examined his eyes. He tried out muscles and spent some time on Michael's fingers.

He stood up.

'This chap has a real cracker of a migraine.' Michael half nodded. 'Ah so you know it, do you?' The doctor smiled. 'Well it wont kill you but you'll feel pretty bloody in the head when it goes off. I wonder how long you usually last on this stage and if you take anything for it?'

He leant near Michael.

'Pills?' he asked.

Horton struggled. What the Devil were 'Pills'?

God he should know what 'Pills' were.

After a minute he gave up struggling. He just couldn't be bothered. He went to sleep.

The doctor pulled the blanket up round his neck. He'd have liked to give Horton an injection or some 'Q' but he wasn't sure if the man was on any drugs that they'd disagree with.

He pulled the blanket up over the exhausted man.

'... as you say, Jock, this is a very satisfactory lunch time score for Australia. A hundred and twenty seven for one with Graypath looking so very secure on forty nine and Bardman eighteen.' Trevor Bridge was talking as the England eleven left the field. 'They've been slow this morning largely owing to defensive bowling to a thoroughly defensive field. I think England have got to take a risk and go for wickets even at the expense of runs.

'The experiment with Horton was a pretty daring move but at least it got a desperately needed wicket.'

'Who would you put on, Trevor?' asked the Australian commentator.

'I'd certainly try Tony Bolte and possibly Hughes. He doesn't bowl for Glamorgan but he has taken timely wickets for England before and wickets now would be timely indeed.'

'I don't want to be depressing to you, Trevor, or to the listeners, but I see a very big score for Australia building up during this perfect day. So far they've put on ninety-one this morning for the loss of Oliver. That's a little slow but impressive.'

Trevor Bridge took over.

'That's it then 'til ten past two when we will be back with you for a ball by ball commentary of the second day here at Lords.'

'Well doctor,' said Tom Lipton, 'how is he?'

'Not too good ...'

'Oh hell.'

'... he's got a massive migraine and is going through a non-lucid stage.'

'What do you mean, non-lucid?'

'Well he hardly knows who he is. He's cut off from the world. Can't speak or express normal thoughts. It's not abnormal with his state.'

'What brought it on? The fact of having to bowl?'

'Not necessarily, Tom. Could have been anything, could have been nothing. Frankly we know damn all about it. I suppose you want to know when you can have him back?'

'Too true.'

'Well it wont be for another hour and it may be four hours. I gather he's a fairly determined bird and I think he'll be on as soon as the lucidity returns. He'll have a cracking headache though.'

'To hell with his headache. Will he be able to bowl?'

'Yes. I'm pretty sure about that. You had lunch yet?'

'No.'

'Well go and get some – or you'll flake out on us.'

'Come on Bill. They've started. For Christ sake sit down can't yer.'

The small man in an alpaca coat fumbled with a plastic bag. He was standing up and trying to sort himself out.

'Sit down there,' came from further up in the Grandstand.

The small man shrank and half sat on his seat.

'Got the beer?' asked his companion.

'No. I fergot.'

'You silly sod. Go and get it. Four tins.'

The small man dumped his bag and started down the row of seats.

'Not now you bloody idiot. Wait 'till the end of the over.'

The small man shrank to nothing. He wished he had come alone and not with Alf. Alone he'd have been all right. Stayed in his seat and eaten the sandwiches Pearl had made for him. With Alf he was just a delivery boy. 'Go for the beer.' 'Get me some fags.' 'Go buy a Score Card.'

He'd already missed this new chap Horton bowling huge wides and then getting Oliver. He was out buying Alf some matches.

He waited 'til Young bowled a maiden to Graypath and set off across other spectators' legs for the exit and the nearest bar.

When he got there he hadn't enough money.

He scratched his thin, dirty, greying hair and set off back to Alf again. Before he reached daylight he heard a roar of applause. He ran. No one was out. Overton was coming in to bowl.

He watched 'til it was over and set off down the row of legs again.

' 'scuse me. Sorry. Pardon Miss. Oh I'm so sorry.'

He got back to his seat.

'What 'appened?' he asked Alf.

'A six. Really lovely. By Bardman off Overton. Pity you missed it.'

'I'm sick of missing things.'

'Where's the beer?'

'I 'adn't got the money. It's in me bag.'

'Oh fuckin' 'ell. You're 'opeless. 'Ere. Take this quid and get it. I'm parched.'

The little man who missed things set off.

'Not now you silly bugger. At the end of the over.'

Bill waited. Crouching. He set off yet again.

Once more the legs were knocked and the feet trodden on. The owners complained bitterly.

'What's the matter with you? Can't you keep still?'

'Sorry mate.'

He dived for the bar.

'Four cans of beer.'

He heard a gasp from thirty thousand mouths and then a long 'Oohhh.'

He ran.

Knocked knees again.

Breathlessly.

'What was that Alf?'

'Bolte put Graypath down. Looked an easy catch at Mid Wicket.

'e ran back. Took it and it bounced out of his hands. You miss all the best bits don't you?'

The little man looked at his watch. Two thirty. Then at the scoreboard. A hundred and forty-three for one. Last man sixty-one.

Alf could do his own bloody leg work from now on. He was going to watch the cricket.

'Did you talk to Lipton during the interval?' Bob Bebington asked, easing himself into the armchair in his office.

'I did. Yes,' said Maurice Kerr. 'I suggested the use of Bolte but he wasn't keen.' He stood leaning with both hands on the windowsill. 'He seems determined to try and hold on 'til Horton gets back. Keep the runs down – that sort of approach.'

'And how is Horton?'

'Much the same. It seems he's asleep in the dressing room when he's needed on the field.'

'I said he was a poor gamble.'

'Oh don't let's start on that yet.'

'Well it's going to come to that.'

'We'll leave the inquest until the body is dead, if you don't mind.'

'Just as you like.'

Freddy Barrington turned to the Member on his left.

'This is ridiculous, Professor.'

'It's not very good. Is it?'

'Not very good be damned. It's hopeless. This chap Lipton seems to have lost his touch. He should be using speed and spin. Frost at one end and Bolte at the other. That'd shift them. Speed and spin. It worked in the old days and it'd work now. Overton's all right. Damned fine bowler on his day and his wicket but this is neither. Young is just closing it down. And not too effectively at that. Look there now!' Bardman took three down fine of square leg off Young who was beginning to tire and lose his length.

'I think,' said the professor, 'that Hughes might break up this pair. I saw him do it to the West Indians once or twice last year.'

'Hughes. He's not a bowler. Damn good batsman in a débacle – but he's not a bowler. Nonsense.'

'I can't agree.' The professor said meekly.

'Damn it he doesn't even bowl for his county.'

'It doesn't matter.'

'It bloody does.'

They sat disagreeing with each other in their silence.

For five minutes they sat and watched.

'Lipton's changing Young.' The professor broke the silence.

'Now we'll see. It'll be Frost and then Bolte at the other end.'

They sat and watched eagerly.

'My God,' said Barrington. 'It's Hughes.'

'There's the hundred and fifty,' George Allot told the listeners. 'A hundred and fifty-two for one. Graypath fifty nine and young Bardman in his first Test on twenty-eight. This chap Bardman is going to be a thorn in England's side for years to come, if I'm any judge. He seems to have all the strokes and beautiful timing. His straight six into the pavilion over Overton's head was a gem.

'Trevor, is there any news of Horton?'

'Yes. It's not very satisfactory as news. Phillip came back from the England dressing room a few minutes ago. They just say that Horton is incapacitated and will be back on the field as soon as possible. Make what you can of that.'

'I can only say poor chap,' sympathised Allot. 'He was only on for one over – a pretty long one I admit – but I'd like to see more of Mr. Horton. He's in this team for a purpose and I'd like to be able to tell you what it is.

'Now Hughes comes in his twelve pace run. Past Umpire Fox. He bowls. On the off stump. Good ball. Graypath plays defensively.

There's a lot of this defensive play by both the Australians, and Lipton has a field spread to save the four.

'It's not the most exciting way of playing cricket but if England want to slow the scoring rate at the expense of wickets – then it's working. Twenty five runs in forty minutes since lunch. I suppose once could say it's been England's threequarters of an hour.

'Here's Hughes again from the Nursery end. He comes in and bowls ...'

The Coach, Fred, was sitting on a hard arsed chair next to the bed. His hand was resting near Michael's arm as if to lend him strength in his battle.

The doctor came in.

'Any change Fred?'

'Nope. He's asleep but very restless. Can't we help him at all?'

'Not yet. I may be able to when he wakes up. I wouldn't like to now in case I did the wrong thing.'

'Was it worry that caused it?'

'I've no idea. Everyone's worried. I just saw Kerr downstairs. He looks worried to death. Bebington looks exhausted. Even the young fellow standing in as thirteenth man is sweating with fear in case he has to go on. He's only one of the lads. Seventeen I think.'

'He'll be all right. It's this chap Horton I'm concerned about.' Michael twitched and half turned under the blanket. 'What happens doc?'

'With a migraine?'

'Yep.'

'We don't really know. All the knowledge we have and yet this, one of the most widely spread of man's troubles, defies us. It's a blood shortage to the brain. A temporary one. The blood vessels seem to narrow and restrict the flow. Snap – a migraine.'

'Like a small stroke?'

'Loosely yes. Only temporary though. Just to muddle you some more, people who get it seem to be the more intelligent.'

'I needn't worry then.' Fred laughed.

Michael moved.

'Hold on doc. I think he may be coming round.'

Sarah was on one of the telephones at the back of the Press Box.

'Mac. Mac is that you?' she called her editor.

'. . . .'

'What do you mean, what do I want now? I cause you damn all trouble.'

'. . . .'

'That's bloody rude.'

'. . . .'

'O.K. I accept it. Look Mac. Any news on that person I want located?'

'. . . .'

'Hell, I've given you two days.'

'. . . .'

'All right. Take two more. But it's getting urgent.'

'. . . .'

'Of course you'll get the story. When I'm good and ready. Not before.'

'. . . .'

'Then sack me.'

'. . . .'

'You might at that.'

'. . . .'

'And my love to you. Goodbye.'

'. . . .'

'Say again.'

'. . . .'

'You're a good chap, Mac. Thanks a lot.'

'. . . .'

'Yes.'

'. . . .'

'Yes. Of course. O.K. Bye, Mac.'

Betty Barsleigh had finished preparing the dinner. The house was tidy. Everything would be just so for her Nick and this Mr. Carstairs the new Sales Manager.

Of course Nick should have had the job. Hadn't he been on the road for twenty two years? Didn't he know more about selling than anyone else in the firm? He was 'Good old Nick' to the customers and he deserved promotion. He was getting on now for doing twenty calls a day in a big area. Life was so unfair.

Mr. Carstairs was only twenty eight. A child. But Nick seemed to like him. Soft. That's what Nick was. He'd let anyone ride roughshod over him.

She'd listen to the afternoon play on radio. That's what she'd do.

She went upstairs and got her slippers. Came down and made a cup of tea. She'd missed the beginning – but that didn't matter. She'd pick up the story.

She switched the 'on' button.

There was a lot of static that turned into clapping.

'. . . and there's Bardman's fifty. A really faultless fifty two runs even if it was in slow time.'

Of course. This was the cricket. The Third programme. Nick had been listening when he got in last night. She didn't switch off. The voice of Phillip East went on.

'His first appearance for Australia and very impressive it's been too. Right Trevor?'

'Right. He's really got everything that's in the book. I'm most impressed.'

'So are the crowd I think,' continued East. 'They've given him a great reception on his fifty.

'So there we are. Bardman scored twenty-four out of the last thirty runs. He's had a good deal more of the bowling for the last half hour.

'Australia a hundred and eighty-two for one. Bardman fifty-two. Graypath sixty-five. These two have put on seventy-seven and look very solid indeed.'

Betty Barsleigh went on listening and sipping her tea. She tried to remember the details so she could tell Nick when he got back. It might impress Mr. Carstairs too.

The more she listened the more interested she became.

She knew something about cricket. You couldn't be married to Nick Barsleigh for twenty years and not.

She forgot the afternoon play on the Fourth programme. She got interested in the growing possibility that these two Australians might get their hundreds. She wanted the young one to get his specially. The commentators made him sound so nice and attractive.

The two hundred came up with a four from Graypath. He was seventy-six now.

Two hundred became two hundred and twenty and two hundred and thirty. Bardman seventy-four. Graypath ninety.

It was really quite exciting.

Half Betty's tea got cold and she tucked her feet up comfortably under her on the settee.

'No he's not waking yet,' said the doctor. 'Let him sleep. He'll come to the surface when he's ready. Do you mind sitting here, Freh?'

'Not a bit. I'd just like to be able to help the blighter.'

'You can't. He's on his own. Call me the minute he wakes.'

' 'course. What's the score, doc?'

'Two hundred and thirty-four.'

'Ta.'

'Hey Rob.' The Texan moved his gum from one cheek to the other. 'I still don't get what these guys are trying to achieve.'

'Keep your voice down a bit, Tex.'

'Sorry Rob.' He dropped to a loud whisper. 'Are those throwers trying to hit them sticks?'

'Yes. Roughly.'

'Wad do you mean 'roughly'? Either they are or they're not.'

'Well they are.'

'Then why bounce the bloody thing? That gives the hitter more chance.'

'It doesn't.'

'Doesn't it?'

'No.'

'Oh.'

'They can move it off the ground. Bend it.'

'Cute.'

The American sat mesmerised. He'd only been in the arena ten minutes and was already bored as all hell. Why did the hitters let so many balls go? And these other fellows ran about a mile before throwing the ball. Everyone else just stood about. Waiting. The crowd seemed happy but dead quiet. Oh well.

'How many have the hitters made, Rob?'

'Two hundred and thirty five. One man was out for sixty one.'

'Gee. Tough shit.'

'The fair haired chap's on seventy seven. The taller man, Graypath, is ninety two.'

'Are they trying to get to a hundred or something?'

'Yes. And beyond. Two hundred or more.'

'Hell. It'll take all week.'

'Not really. Keep your voice down a bit.'

'Oh, soory.'

For a moment the American was silent. But only for a moment.

'What're those guys in the fancy jackets?'

'Umpires.'

'Two of them!'

'Yes. Of course.'

'That must be confusing as all hell. What if they disagree?'

'They don't.'

'Why not for Chris'sake?'

'They're trained. Anyway they work different ends.'

'It would surely speed things up if the throwers always threw from the same end and everyone else stayed put. All same the umpire in his fancy jacket. Have they thought of that?'

'Don't be absurd, Tex.'

'Oh. Sorry, Rob.'

Bebington found Maurice Kerr in the entrance to the Long Room.

'I've just heard. Horton's come to.'

'When?'

'A moment ago. A lad came down for the doctor. Fred sent him.'

'I think I'll go up straight away,' said Kerr. 'The sooner Horton's back on the field the better.'

Frost stopped opposite Tom Lipton.

'Are you taking the new ball?' he asked hopefully.

'No. Sorry Pete. We're keeping this old one.'

'Why? It's not doing much good.'

'No. But I think it will.'

Frost moved off. Thoroughly disappointed.

Kerr entered the first aid room.

Horton was sitting up on the bed. His arms round his knees. His head bowed. He looked very drawn and old.

The doctor gave him two pills.

'Here, take these. They may help and they won't disagree with what you're having. Not even the Nardyl.'

'Thanks.'

Kerr sat down on the seat Fred had left.

'How are you Horton?'

'I'm not sure.'

'Headache?'

'Yes. A real cracker. Just on my left side. I'm not too bad otherwise. I haven't tried walking yet.'

'What's the normal pattern after one of these?'

'I've never had one nearly as bad as this. I've no idea. No idea at all. This is beyond anything I've been through.'

'You better take your time,' said Kerr.

'What's the score?'

'Two hundred and forty-six for one.'

'Oh no! God I can't stay here. What time is it?'

'They're coming in for tea. Four fifteen.'

'All that time. Hell.'

Michael started to get up. He moved quickly and suddenly felt sick and weak. He slowed down.

'I must go back with them. The two hours remaining should help. God we ought to be able to do something to them in that time. Where's Lipton?'

'He's just coming up now.'

'I must see him. Please Kerr. Straightaway.'

The umpires were out. The bails were on. England trooped onto the field. They were all there. Hughes brought up the rear with Horton.

Graypath and Bardman came down the steps.

The scoreboards screamed out two hundred and forty-six for one. Number one, ninety-eight. Number three, eighty. Last Man sixty-one. Extras seven.

The Australian position was dominating.

Graypath took guard again at the pavilion end. Only two runs off his century.

Half the spectators were hoping he'd get it. The other half praying he wouldn't. As a contrast they all hoped young Bardman would get his, in his first Test.

Hughes had come off at the Nursery end. Young replaced him. Bowling his slow medium seamers.

The game was set.

Umpire Fox called 'Play'.

In the slips Michael was guarded by Ames on his left and the small Porthead on his right. The ball would have to come through a very narrow gap to reach him.

He was feeling very shaky. His knees were weak and his leg muscles quivered. Oddly enough the bruise on his back gave him little trouble. He'd almost forgotten it. The other aches were much more positive. The one in his head the worst of all. He still felt detached and mentally adrift – as if he were floating on a raft after days without food. He felt lost. The only certainty he had was that he knew what he'd got to do and he was going to do it.

Young came in. He thudded his foot down into the crease. It was outside the off stump, moving towards Michael. Graypath tried to force the ball away into the Covers. He got an edge. It flew to Skeddons in the Gully. He misfielded. Bardman called 'Yes. One' and almost immediately 'No. Get Back.' Skeddons back flicked the ball to Ames. Graypath was in his ground. It all happened in a flash.

The Australians met in the middle of the wicket.

'Look Son,' said Greypath. 'Don't do that again.'

'I'm sorry. I thought there was one.'

'Well think fucking twice next time – and then don't do it.' He turned and walked back to the stumps.

The next two from Young were close outside the leg stump and Graypath had nothing to do with either of them. He was content to wait for a loose ball.

The fourth was good. A near Yorker on the stumps and Martin Graypath came down hard on it. The ball rolled back to Young who flicked it up with his right boot, caught it and set off for his mark.

He turned. Came in. Graypath tapped the ground. The ball was short. Outside the off stump. He leant back and cut crisply. The ball flashed fine of Gully. Overton at Cover ran. Got his left hand to it. Slowed it down but didn't field cleanly. They ran one. Then two. The clapping began. The Australian spectators howled with delight. They ran one for Overton's throw.

Australia two hundred and forty nine for one. Graypath a hundred and one not out.

He raised his bat. Acknowledging the crowd.

A red haired youth of about fourteen rushed onto the field. He dodged a policeman and ran for the middle. He reached Graypath. Patted him on the back and shook his hand massively. A moment later he was losing himself in the crowd again.

The field settled.

The last ball of the over from Young was deflected by Bardman to Fine Leg for no score.

The field crossed over.

Lipton carried the ball to Horton.

'What do you think of it now?'

Michael took the well worn ball. There was virtually no shine on it at all. The seam stood out and the surface was coarse.

'It's perfect.'

'It's all yours Mike. For God's sake make it work.' He moved off. 'Field for Horton.' He called out.

'Hey Rob. This is a new pitcher, ain't it?'

'He's not a pitcher, Tex. He's a bowler.'

'Thought that was some kind of hat.'

'It is. But this chap's the bowler. Don't you have Bowls in the States?'

'Surely we have boles.'

'Well, that's it. He bowls.'

'You can't say "he boles". It don't make sense. You can say "them boles" – but not "he boles".'

'Them bowls what?'

'What them boles what?'

'What the hell are we talking about?'

'Christ knows. Boles. Timber boles.'

'Who's Timber?'

'Anyone's fucking timber. Does it matter whose?'

Rob pondered this obscure problem.

'No I suppose not.'

'Jesus, this game makes bloody idiots of people. Those stump things are boles.'

'Of course they're not. How could you bowl with a ruddy long thin thing?'

'They are ruddy long thin things.'

'The stumps?'

'The boles.'

'Look Tex. I give in. Let's call him the pitcher.'

Michael paced his run and moved the white marker. He took off his short sleeved sweater. Handed it to Umpire Derby.

He made a dummy run up.

One, two, three, four-five.

It was all right.

He looked round his field.

He moved Mid On in six feet. The rest were O.K.

He looked to Tom Lipton. Lipton smiled.

He saw the Slips go down. The close leg field crouch.

'Play.'

He ran in.

The ball was a top spinner on the line of the stumps. Graypath played forward. The ball hardly rose at all. It fizzed through. Got the bat on the very bottom of the blade. Trickled out to Short Square. No score.

Graypath looked surprised. This wicket which had been playing perfectly, suddenly let a shooter through. He walked forward to where the ball landed. Swept with the blade of the bat. Then pounded with the toe like a roadmaker driving in stones. Bloody peculiar.

Horton signalled another top spinner to Ames.

He came in smoothly past Umpire Derby and bowled. Hell. Overpitched. The ball was a half volley. With perfect timing Graypath lifted it over Skeddons at Mid On. It flew high and far. It didn't seem he'd hit it as hard as all that. It arced down into the Mound Stand for a perfect six.

The ball landed by the man next to Mary Horton. He retrieved it.

'Dangerous game being a spectator when this chap Horton's bowling.' He laughed and chucked the ball onto the field.

Mary looked at Stephen. He glared back grimly.

Their father came in again. Pitched one two yards outside the off stump which whined back and only missed the off bail by three inches.

This time all the close fielders except Lipton joined Graypath in looking at the ground. Overton got down and felt it. He rose. 'There's nothing there.' They returned to their positions perplexed.

The crowd had gone 'ooooh.'

The third was equally good.

It pitched on the leg stump and cut across sharply towards where Fourth Slip would have been.

Graypath played and missed.

The two Gullies and Slips rose on their toes in consternation.

This time the crowd 'aaaah'd.'

They and the players were beginning to think these massive breaks were actually bowled by Horton. He no longer seemed a joke.

It was certainly something new.

He came in.

One, two, three, four-five.

Bowled.

A back spinner on middle stump. It pitched a good length and Graypath played forward. The ball sat up straight in front of him like a dog begging. His stroke was far too early. The ball popped up gently into Michael's hands waiting a few yards down the wicket.

There was a roar of cheering.

The spectators stood. Their hands joining their voices.

'What was that?' Bill shouted to Alf.

'Di'n't you see?'

'No. Dropped me scorecard. It were under me seat.'

'You bloody fool. You missed Horton catch and bowl Graypath.'

'Oh fuckin' 'ell. I miss 'em all.'

Australia two hundred and fifty-five for two. Bardman eighty. Ian Church nought. Last man Caught and Bowled Horton one hundred and seven.

Horton finished the over with two wicked balls which left Ian Church grovelling.

The crowd clapped the over as Michael limped to his position at Slip. His legs were still very shaky. They felt like half inflated rubber tyres.

Three uneventful overs followed – if you can call Horton's second over uneventful. He beat Church four times out of six and bowled a maiden. Bardman cut Young hard to Cover for no score and tried to run a cheeky one when Frost overthrew. The board still showed two hundred and fifty-five for two. Church on nought.

On the fourth ball of Michael's third over he pitched it miles outside leg stump. Off the mown wicket. It cut back viciously off the seam and he just knew it was heading for the stumps.

Church turned to deflect it between Short Square and Leg Slip. He only got an edge. The ball deflected sharply to Ames left. He threw himself flat out and landed with a thud that seemed to shake the ground. A goalkeeper couldn't have done better.

The ball was clasped in his left hand.

There were nine earcracking appeals from the field and ten thousand from the stands and on the grass.

Umpire Derby raised his finger. Church walked for nought.

Maurice Kerr sat down heavily next to the Bishop.

'This is better. Eh Tony?'

'Much better. Where'd you find this Horton chap?'

'We didn't. He found us. Came through Ben Hendricks. They do some business together or something. Ben approached me. Told me about this man with a quadruple jointed wrist. Didn't believe him at first. Did when I saw it. Incredible. – Good ball that. Young's bowling better. Getting a bit of movement off the wicket.'

'He's a bit old isn't he?'

'Who? Horton? Yes. Fifty-three.'

'Where's he been Maurice? I mean all these years.'

'God knows.'

'Naturally. Have you asked him?'

'God or Horton?'

'Either.'

'No. Don't even know him very well. Most of the contact has been about his availability to play for England and his physical state.'

'Did you know he had migraines?'

'No. How do you know about that?'

'The doc told me.'

'Forgot you were old friends.'

'I won't say a word. – Oh, good shot! This man Bardman is good isn't he? Classic stroke play.'

'Like most of these Australians – he's too good.'

'What do you think now?' Mary Horton asked Stephen.

'I certainly think differently. The old man is rather remarkable. How the devil did he develop this type of bowling? He's never done it before.'

'You owe him an apology.'

'Why?'

'You were jolly rude about him earlier.'

'So were you.'

'I know. I feel awful about it.'

'You needn't. He was pretty bad to begin with. He's only been so good since Tea.'

'It's too late isn't it? I mean two hundred and fifty-five for three is pretty formidable against England's two hundred and seventeen.'

'It was two hundred and fifty-five for one a few minutes ago.'

'You mean you think Daddy can go on getting wickets at this rate?'

'I've no idea. We'll just have to wait and see.'

Betty Barsleigh meant to switch off when Bardman got his century. She thought that would be the end of the interesting part. She was genuinely depressed when he seemed stuck on eighty but the commentators were so fascinating about this new man Horton that she went on listening eagerly.

Everything was ready for dinner. Nick and Mr. Carstairs would be in before seven.

She stayed on the settee and went on listening.

She clapped when Ian Church went to Horton for a duck and she caught some of the excitement from the crowd and from George Allot's commentary. She could have done without Trevor Bridge who, she felt, slowed the game up.

Ian's cousin Graham Church came in next.

It was two minutes to five.

Michael Horton bowled a loose one for the final ball of the over and Chruch let it go.

At the other end Donald Bardman was still on the eighty he'd taken in to tea.

Young was bowling better than he had all through the innings. His length and direction were perfect.

Bardman had to struggle to protect his wicket.

Young's over was an attacking maiden.

Lipton was setting fields to get wickets now. Not just to save runs.

Horton bowled three poor balls to Church. He was terribly tired. His legs felt like melted margarine. He wasn't sure he could go on.

The fourth ball was one of his mammoth wides. It was fielded by Leg Slip; He breathed deeply as he limped back to his mark.

Lipton moved over from Mid On.

'Are you O.K.?'

'So so. I've very tired.'

'Can you keep going?'

'For a bit. I'll need a rest though.'

'Let me know when.'

'Right.'

He came in. One, two, three, four-five. Damn. Another wide. Outside the leg again. Sod it.

Church looked amused.

The spectators were oddly silent.

The next one was a beauty. Pitched on a length on Middle Stump, it had colossal top spin. Church played over the top just catching the bottom of the bat. The ball rolled past the off stump by the thickness of another coat of varnish.

Church didn't look nearly so amused.

The fifth good ball was short and breaking from off to leg. Church hooked. Hard. It flew over Skeddons' head at Short Square for four.

Horton felt himself slipping. He hadn't the control over his body that he needed. His fingers and his wrist were O.K. It was the rest of him that let him down.

He mustered all his concentration.

He took as much time as Umpire Derby would give him before the next ball.

'Play.'

Horton bowled.

It looked almost as bad a ball as the previous one but it hugged the ground only rising three inches.

Church hooked hard. Got an edge. The ball curved fast and low to Young's left hand at Leg Slip. He dived and came up clasping the ball.

The spectators went mad.

Allot allowed himself to let down his hair.

Betty Barsleigh jumped off the settee screaming 'Oh well done. Well done.'

Two hundred and sixty-one for four with both the Church's out for a miserable four runs.

Two hundred and fifty-five for one to two hundred and sixty-one for four in fifteen minutes.

England began to hold its head up.

The Jack over the pavilion seemed to give an extra zip in the light breeze.

The television cameras swept the crowds standing and cheering.

Horton felt dreadful.

'Trevor,' said Phillip East. 'Do you see what I see? They're taking Horton off. How quite extraordinary.'

'Everything about M. V. Horton seems extraordinary.' replied Bridge. 'I've seldom found it so difficult to convey to the listeners the effect a player is having on a game. He comes out with England to field. Stays in the slips for twenty four overs and then bowls nine very mixed balls and takes a wicket. Darned if he doesn't go off 'til after tea, and then he comes back and takes three more wickets in quick time and then gets taken off. It's like a fairy story.

'Ted, he's taken the four wickets for ... what?'

'For twenty, Trevor. An average of five.'

'Incredible.

'Lipton's bringing back Overton at the pavilion end.

'Good heavens the crowd don't want Horton off. There's a chant coming from the Grandstand of "No. No. No." You can probably hear it on our effects microphone. I've never come across this before. They want Horton to go on. Lipton's shaking his head. Horton's giving the thumbs down sign. They won't stop. The play's held up by it. Umpire Fox is calling for quiet. I've never heard an English crowd behave like the West Indians.

'This is remarkable, Phillip.'

'I said Horton was extraordinary. The spectators think so too.'

'They're still going on. This is too much.'

'Look Trevor. Umpire Fox is walking towards them. Lipton's with him. They're asking the crowd to stop. I think it's going to work.'

Gradually peace was restored.

Poor Overton had to bowl knowing that a large number of the spectators didn't want him.

The 'No. No. No.' went on half heartedly by a few extremists.

Harry was back in the flat.

He hadn't seen Margot all day.

He passed Daphne as he came in. Pecked her and dropped his brief case, tore off his jacket and made for the bedroom window overlooking Lords.

He'd heard the up to date score as he got a lift home in a friend's car.

God this was good. He adjusted the binoculars.

Overton was bowling to Mallor. Bardman was at the other end on eighty. Two hundred and sixty-one for four.

The match went on.

Mallor opened his score with a pulled four and Bardman got off eighty at last with a straight drive off Young down to the sight screen.

Harry made himself a pink gin between overs.

Daphne was fussing about.

The Australians went on. Two hundred and seventy came up. Then two hundred and eighty. They were going at a run a minute.

Bardman was on eighty-nine. Mallor ten.

'Harry.'

'Um.'

'Have you been at the sheets?'

Harry blushed for a brief moment.

'What on earth do you mean?'

'Well I put new ones on the bed on Wednesday morning and I've just looked in the linen cupboard and two clean double sheets are missing.'

'You miscounted, old girl. Oh well bowled.'

'I didn't Harry. I know they were there and only you or I could have been at them. It wasn't me. So that leaves you.'

'Don't know what you're talking about.'

'Oh come off it Harry. We lost a pair in April. I don't understand it.'

'I'll buy you some on Saturday. Well fielded Hughes. My God he's good in the Gully.'

'Well I think it's most peculiar.'

'Shut up about it Old Thing. It doesn't matter a damn.'

'I think we should ask the Flats Porter.'

'No don't.'

'Whyever not?'

'Well . . . He might think we suspected him.'

'Don't we?'

'No. That's it. Yes. Oh hell I don't know. You probably got muddled. Forget it.'

'I'm not going to.'

On the last ball of Young's over Bardman edged the ball down to Third Man and they walked one easy run. He was on ninety. Within striking distance of his century in his first Test.

Overton, from the pavilion end had been bowling immaculately without any luck at all. He'd beaten Mallor four times and beaten the stumps too.

He floated a slower one in to Bardman. He read it correctly but played too slowly. The ball pitched and rapped him on the back leg.

ARAWAROWRAWAZAT!

came from the whole of the close field. Overton leapt high in the air. Both arms outstretched.

Umpire Derby stood rigid. He slowly turned and looked at the score box.

'Not out.'

Overton stood amazed.

'Oh no,' said Harry in the flat.

'Oh no,' said Overton.

'Brian!' Tom Lipton warned Overton.

He turned disconsolate and walked slowly back to his mark. He snatched at the ball as Skeddons tossed it to him. Dropped it and picked it up angrily.

He came in past Umpire Derby. A faster one. On the stumps again. It kept low. Bardman played a bad back stroke. The ball broke slightly to the off. Enough to beat the bat. Again it rapped Bardman's pads.

'Well then,' shouted Overton. 'How was that!'

Derby's hand flew up. The finger pointing straight at Bardman.

The crowd rose. The cheers took a moment to begin. It was only when Donalf Bardman walked that they fully realised that he was out.

Australia two hundred and eighty-one for five. Bardman out for ninety. Mallor, not, ten.

'I'm going down to see the Porter,' said Daphne.

'Don't.'

'Why not? What are you afraid of?'

'Nothing. Then bloody well go.'

''Core Card. 'Core Card. 'Core Card.' The little man went on his rounds. ''Core Card.'

'Yes,' called Stephen. 'Mary can you reach him? It's too far for me.'

'Could I have one too?'

'Why?'

'Well I'd like to keep one. In fact I'd like one of each print. Lend me a pound will you?'

'But it'll all be in the papers.'

'I want the Score Cards.'

‘Oh very well.’ He passed over the money. They got an up to date score card each.

England.	First Innings (Hughes 67. Lipton 45)	217
Australia	First Innings	
M. Graypath	ct and b Horton	107
R. E. Oliver	b Horton	61
D. Bardman	L.B.W. b Overton	90
I. R. Church	ct Ames b Horton	0
G. Church	ct Young b Horton	4
S. R. Mallor	Not out	10
W. Prout	Not out	0
Extras		9
	TOTAL	
	TOTAL (for 5 wkts)	281

1 for 105.	2 for 255.	3 for 255.	4 for 261.	5 for 281.
6 for	7 for	8 for	9 for	10 for

Mallor and Prout settled in and looked comfortable against Overton and Young.

Lipton brought on Hughes again in place of Young at the Nursery end. He gave Bolte three overs to rest Overton. It was not a success.

The score mounted to two hundred and ninety-five.

‘If you do that again I wont bring yer tomorrer.’

‘Yer will.’

'Wy?'

''Cos our Mum's away to her 'ome in Liverpool.'

'I'll lock yer in the 'ouse.'

'Yer won't. Will yer?'

'Oh shut up. I want ter watch.'

The woman beside Terry's father looked uncomfortable.

'Excuse me. But why do you keep striking that boy?.

''Cos he's a filthy little b-b-blighter.'

'What does he do?'

'Do? 'E keeps picking 'is nose.'

'Why?'

'Wot yer mean, wy? 'Cos he does. That's wy.'

'Nonesense. There must be a reason. Have you asked him?'

'Arsked 'im? Course not. Whot the 'ell would I arsk 'im? I tell 'im. That's wot. I tell 'im. And then I 'it 'im.'

'May I ask him?'

'Do as yer bloody like.'

'What's his name?'

'Terry.'

The woman leant over.

'Terry.'

'Yus Miss.'

'Your Daddy tells me you pick your nose.'

'Yus.'

'Why do you?'

'It itches.'

'I thought so.' She turned to Terry's father. 'Worms.'

'Wot?'

'Worms. He's got worms.'

'I ain't surprised. 'e's got everythink 'e 'as. Might as well 'ave worms.'

'You should do something about it.'

'I'm goin' ter. I'm goin' to 'it 'im again.'

*

At five thirty Michael told Lipton he was up to another short stint.

'Do you want the pavilion end?'

'Don't mind. Up to you.'

'I'll put you on in place of Hughes then. Next over unless he gets a wicket.'

Hughes didn't.

Overton was back on in place of Bolte.

Mallor and Bill Prout were getting dug in.

Australia were getting away again. They had a lead of eighty-two and five wickets in hand. Mallor on seventeen. Prout seven.

Maurice Kerr's enthusiasm was slipping away. Certainly things were a hell of a lot better than when they were two hundred and fifty five for one but they could bat down to number nine, Cornwall, and a total of four hundred was possible. Too much depended on Horton. Much too much.

Sidney Mallor senior was sitting close up to the radio set in the living room.

He had a dressing gown over his flannel pyjamas.

The stove was low. It had all but burned out in the night.

It was cold. It always was in Gavney, West Australia in winter.

Mrs. Mallor was still in bed. Half asleep – or half awake, as it seemed to her.

The time was 3.0 a.m.

'Come on Mother,' the man called. 'Come on out o' that bed. I'll have it in a minute.'

Mallor senior twiddled the knobs.

'Bloody British radio station. No fucking power.'

He turned up the sound control.

A crackly voice came through.

'... and he turns that square on the leg to Lipton. No score.' The friendly Australian voice of Jack McGillery came through.

'I got it Mother. Come on now.'

'Going to the loo.'

'Hell no. Not just as I get the station.'

'Nature calls.'

'Australia's batting still.'

'Young Sid in yet?'

'Don't know who's in. McGillery ain't said.'

'I'm going to the loo.'

'Well hurry.'

'You can't. Leastways I can't.'

The radio became clearer.

'Horton comes in on his short, stubby run. He bowls. On the stumps. Mallor moves right out. He takes it full toss. Gently back to Horton. No runs.'

Sidney Mallor senior ran to the toilet door.

'Come on Mother. Sid's in. He's batting now.'

'How many's he made?'

'I've no idea. Are you coming?'

'Fast as maybe. You listen.'

'Oh very well.' He shuffled in his woollen slippers back to the radio.

'... two hundred and ninety nine for five with Mallor on seventeen and Prout seven.'

'He's scored seventeen Mother,' shouted Mallor senior.

'What?' came a distant voice.

'Oh come on.'

'... Horton again. Well outside the off stump. A mile off. Breaks in sharply. Mallor reads it. Plays it carefully into the Gully. Trevor. It seems that Sid Mallor is beginning to understand Horton.'

'It does, Jack. Yes. He's the first Australian who seems to have time to play Horton's breaks. Of course if they can learn to read Mike Horton then they'll be a long way towards defeating him. Jock.'

'Horton bowls. On the stumps. Mallor leaves it. It goes over the top of the sticks. Horton got a lot of lift off that one. Mallor read it again. This Mallor Horton battle is becoming interesting.'

Mallor's father sat close to the loudspeaker.

The voice of McGillery came and went in a surge of static.

'. . . 'orton bowls. Well up. Outside the leg stump. Mallor jumps out. Drives hard on the half-volley. Gets an edge. Ball flies to Slips right. Oh and Farr takes a wonderful catch high up to his right. Oh dear me. What a pity, Horton beat Mallor all ends up that time.' He paused for breath. 'How very disappointing for Australia. Mallor seemed to be getting on top of Horton but he . . .'

'Mother! He's out.'

The lavatory flushed.

'Oh damn her.'

Mrs. Mallor came in wrapping her dressing gown round her.

'Well?'

'He's out. Just now. Seconds ago.'

'For how many?'

'Seventeen.'

'He wont be satisfied for that.'

'No. He won't.'

'Will he keep his place?'

'There's always the second innings.'

'Poor boy. He'll be worried.'

'Yes Mother. Write to him tomorrow will you?'

'Yes. Will you go on listening?'

'Um.'

'Then I'll go back to bed. Must be up at six.'

Young and Horton tore into the Australian tail.

One hundred percent attacking fields with the batsman surrounded.

Rose went to Young L.B.W. for three.

Michael Horton had Cornwall caught behind for one.

Only Prout seemed impregnable.

He played Horton and Young with great aplomb and his score moved to thirteen.

Australia were three hundred and eleven for eight at six fifteen.

A quarter of an hour to go.

Michael was near to dropping again.

He was determined to see out the last overs of the day.

By twenty past six Horton had clean bowled O'Rory, middle stump after the Australian fast bowler had hit him for four and two consecutively.

Three hundred and twenty-one for nine.

England struggled for the last wicket. They brought in all the outfield and ringed the batsman.

When Derby and Fox removed the bails Australia were three hundred and thirty for nine. Prout twenty-one not out. Fleetfoot-Jones, one.

Sarah had written most of her story of the day in the Press Box.

She returned to the flat with Mary Horton.

Now Mary was watching television.

Sarah finished the last lines of her story on the portable in her bedroom.

'I told you to come to Lords today. If you didn't – you should have.

'If a man called Mike Horton hadn't been ill for three hours Australia would have been out for under two hundred.

'As it was he took seven wickets for thirty-eight runs in an extraordinary exhibition of spin bowling.

'This portly, fifty three year old, selected out of the blue has endorsed the policy of the old firm of Kerr, Bebington and Lipton.

'With no classic English bowlers to put in the field, they have found an unknown worthy of the Battle of Britain pilots. Of Churchill's Britain. Of Land of Hope and Glory.

'He fought illness. Physical and mental distress and the whole Australian XI. If he bowled wides that nearly broke the windows of St. Paul's – and brought slow, derisive hand claps from the ignorami in the crowd, he also bowled fantastic balls that had some of the finest batting in the world groping. What a sight! What a man!

'England rose to the Horton occasion. The fielding was first class. I only remember two misfields all day – and only one catch go to ground. Overton bowled with his usual accuracy and enthusiasm while Young was better than I've ever seen him and would have done more than one for eighty six if Horton hadn't stolen the other wickets. Mike Horton even broke down the commentators of the B.B.C.!

'During the first overs he was 'Horton bowling some appalling stuff.' When he got O'Rory four and a half hours later George Allot merely exclaimed 'And Michael does it again.'

'Such was the day and the man of the day.

'He bowled himself into all our hearts and thirty thousand people were the happier for it.

'Were you there on this Crispin Day?'

Sarah banged the last key and tore out the paper.

The office would put in the score details that she always finished her piece with.

She was tired. Emotionally and physically.

'Bed?' she said to Mary.

'Bed.' The girl replied.

England.	First Innings.	217
	(Hughes 67.	
	Lipton	
45)		
Australia.	First Innings.	
M. Graypath	ct and b Horton	107
R. E. Oliver	b Horton	61
D. Bardman	L.B.W. b Overton	90

I. R. Church	ct Ames b Horton	0
G. Church	ct Young b Horton	4
S. R. Mallor	ct Farr b Horton	17
W. Prout	Not out	21
S. Rose	L.B.W. b Young	3
I. Cornwall	ct Ames b Horton	1
R. O'Rory	b Horton	6
M. Fleetfoot-Jones	Not out	1
Extras		19
	TOTAL (for 9 wkts)	330

Australia lead by 113 runs with one wicket standing.

THE THIRD TEST — 3rd DAY

'What're you going to do Teddy?'

'Get where there's a crowd. That's what.'

'Where the hell can we find a crowd round here?'

'It's not "we" it's "me".'

'I'm not going to leave you now.'

'And get caught up in a murder rap? Don't be soft. You're not in trouble. It's me.'

'I'm staying with you. I give you better cover. They're not looking for a couple. They just want a single man. I'm coming whatever you say.'

'O.K. We're going to a bloody Test match.'

'What's that?'

'Cricket.'

'Cricket! Where?'

'Lords. There'll be a ruddy great crowd there all right. It's only half a mile away.'

'Sure it'll be a big crowd.'

'You bet.'

*

The Saturday crowd was enormous.

They closed the gates to non ticket holders at ten forty five.

The sun was already hot. Not a cloud in the blue, blue sky.

The England team had been loosening up in the nets.

Even Michael Horton had bowled a few overs. He felt fine. Fit and eager.

He was one of the team now. No hanging about in his room alone. He was permitted to join the others and they had completely accepted him. The relationships varied from young Overton's open admiration for Horton to Brian Farr's level teammate to teammate bluntness.

At 11.29 a.m. Umpires Fox and Derby straightened the stumps and carefully placed the bails.

The England team were out on the field.

Prout on Twenty one and Fleetfoot-Jones, the last man, on one, reached the wicket.

Young was bowling to Prout.

Australia three hundred and thirty for nine.

'Play.'

The Australians wasted no time in playing themselves in.

Prout took one down to Long Leg off the first ball and Fleetfoot-Jones cut the next for three.

Horton opened at the other end and had six runs taken off him by the Australian number eleven.

They went for the runs off anything loose and were not troubled by either Young or even Horton's massive breaks.

Three hundred and forty-five was up on the board before the England bowlers began to get on top.

Young bowled four maidens running and Michael began beating the batsmen – and the stumps too. He tried everything he could but Fleetfoot-Jones somehow anticipated the deadlier balls and kept them out of his wicket.

It couldn't go on.

The three hundred and fifty came up and Prout took a single off the last ball of a Young over.

Horton bowled to him for the first time for nine overs.

His first ball pitched five feet outside the leg stump. Cut in low and hugely. Prout jabbed at the last moment and missed. The leg stump reeled back drunkenly.

Prout bowled Horton, twenty nine.

The Australian innings closed on three hundred and fifty one for first innings lead of a hundred and thirty four.

Fleetfoot-Jones not out twelve. Extras twenty one.

The time was 12.36 p.m.

At 12.37 p.m. Superintendent Roger Martin was closeted with Colonel Shrain, the Assistant Chief Commissioner, Crime, at Scotland Yard in Victoria Street.

They had been together for an hour.

'Then the odds are, it is Teddy Blackman we're after.'

'From the description of the witness, yes.'

'How many of your men know him by sight? I don't mean from pictures – I mean really know him.'

'About half a dozen. And myself of course.'

'Well we want to get all of you where he's likely to be. Any ideas?'

The Superintendent thought for a few moments.

'He lives in Battersea. But he wouldn't go there. In any case we've got that covered.'

'He might try to hide away in a crowd. Say the Underground – or Madame Tussaud's on a Saturday.'

'Where's this Motlam Street place?'

'On Primrose Hill Road. North of Regents Park.'

Shrain mused.

'What about the zoo?'

'Could be.'

'Where else?'

Martin walked over to the big map on the wall. He stood with his head level with the Marylebone Road.

'What about Lords? The Test,' he said eagerly.

'Good idea. Big problem though.'

'I like it. It's the sort of thing Blackman would try.'

Colonel Shrain looked uncertain. He was by nature cautious.

'How about half at Lords and the others at the zoo?'

'Splitting forces.'

'Covering more options.'

'Might miss him.'

'Might get him. Two to one.'

'Want me to split three ways and take in Tussaud's?'

'No. Too thin.'

'Lords and the zoo?'

'Yes.'

'I'll take Lords, Sir.'

'Just get him. That's all.'

'The time is 12.46,' said George Allot to the millions of Saturday listeners. 'And Fleetfoot-Jones, who has just had time to remove his pads and what-have-you and do whatever Australians do when they have ten minutes, is about to bowl to Hughes who looks massive and secure in his crease down at the Nursery end.

'The wicket's been swept. Had a light roller at Mr. Lipton's special request and the lines repainted a vivid white for the benefit of Messrs Fox and Derby and other partakers.

'Incidentally, Fox and Derby have, of course, swopped ends for the second half of the contest. Perhaps the view becomes boring and the umpires need a change of scene.

'Trevor, what is the origin of umpires changing ends?'

'I don't really know, George.'

'Well I'll have to ask Sir Maurice Kerr and tell you.

'Fleetfoot-Jones, as his name indicates comes in at an increasing pace.

'He bowls.

'This is runs straightaway.

'Hughes steers the ball down to very deep Third Man. It's one. No. They come skittling back for two as Cornwall throws.

'That was asking for trouble as Cornwall's throw was a beauty. Right into Prout's gloves above the stumps.

'England two. And a hundred and thirty-two needed to knock off the arrears. It's a lot of runs when you only scored two hundred and seventeen in the first innings.'

'What's the policy?' asked Freddy Barrington, sitting down next to Maurice Kerr.

'What you'd expect. I've asked Hughes and Porthead to go very easily, take their time and don't come back until they've knocked up the one hundred and thirty-four.'

'And Tom Lipton's instructions?'

'The same but cruder,' laughed Kerr.

'You sound happy?'

'Why not? If we can score three hundred and fifty we've got them. Horton can get them out for under two hundred.'

'If he's on the field.'

'He will be.'

Teddy Blackman climbed the concrete steps ahead of his girl.

He kept his head low.

They'd dodged two uniformed police in the ground and he'd been frightened to death.

'Ticket please, Sir.' The man in a peaked cap held out his hand.

Teddy felt for the stubs of paper he'd bought on entering Lords.

He produced them.
'Haven't you Stand Tickets, Sir?'
'What?'
'You need special Third Day Stand Tickets up here.'
'No. . . . oh no . . . I've got none.'
'Then I'm afraid you'll have to go elsewhere.'
'Can't I – well, buy some?' He felt the wad of money in his hip pocket.
'Good heavens no. These have been booked for months. Your best bet is to get down on the grass. There's still room there.'
Teddy turned away.
The girl followed.
They walked down the steps and stood – uncertain.
They moved left.
'No not this way. There's the fuzz.'
They turned round and walked fast towards the Nursery end.
Five minutes later they were sitting on the bare grass by the boundary board as near one of the exits as they could get.
Teddy looked round carefully.
There was a small boy beside him.
'What's happening?' Blackman asked.
' 'ughes 'as just 'it a four,' the boy replied eagerly.
'Which is Hughes?'
'The big chap,' said the boy. 'T'other Port'ead. Plays for Surrey. That's my county.'
'Oo yer talking to?' asked the boy's father.
'Me friend.'
'You 'aven't go' no friend.'
'I 'ave.'
' 'ughes never 'it a four.'
' 'e did.'
' 'e didn't.'
' 'e did.'
' 'e didn't.'
'Well they run four.'
'They never. They run two.'

'Well 'ughes run two and Port'ead run two. Ain't that four?'

'No you silly little bugger. That's two. Tell the man right.'

The small boy turned to Teddy Blackman.

'Our Dad says it's two 'ughes 'it. Not four. I don't understand but that's wot 'e says.'

'Never mind.' He had an idea. 'This here's Lucy. Like to sit between her and me?'

The small boy thought. He looked up at his father.

'No, ta.'

'Well, perhaps later.'

'Year. Per'aps later.'

They all watched the cricket.

Porthead got two down to Cornwall at Long Leg.

O'Rory came tearing in again.

'Stop pickin' yer bloody nose.'

'I worn't.'

'Yer were.'

'I worn't.'

'Yer were.'

'I worn't.'

O'Rory flung down a fast beamer on Porthead's off stump.

He dangled his bat. Hardly played a stroke at all.

It swung late. Sharply in.

The middle stump rocked back. The bails flew towards Prout. The stump followed.

There was a roar of disappointment from the crowd.

'That was your fault.'

'What wos?' asked the boy.

'Port'ead gettin' out.'

'Why?'

'You was pickin' yer fucking nose again wosn't yer?'

'P'raps.'

England eight for one wicket.

Porthead gone for three.

The start that Maurice Kerr and Lipton had asked for had disintegrated.

Skeddons came in.

He'd scored a duck in the first innings. He was on a pair.

Hughes met him at the pavilion end. They talked for half a minute.

Skeddons took guard and looked round the field. He knew that another failure would probably lose him his place in the England team. He tried to put the matter out of his mind.

O'Rory thundered towards him.

Skeddons played defensively.

He got an outside edge.

The ball flew between Third Slip and Gully.

'Come one,' called Hughes.

They went through.

Skeddons was off his pair.

He felt a different chap.

'Thank you God for that.'

The match went on.

A maiden from Fleetfoot-Jones was followed by a maiden from O'Rory.

Hughes got a single and went up to six.

Neither batsman looked comfortable.

On the fourth ball of his next over Fleetfoot-Jones dug in a short ball.

It rose outside the leg stump.

Skeddons hooked hard and high.

The ball hit the splice – much too far up the blade.

Instead of four runs it dollied to Bardman at backward Square Leg.

He didn't even have to move.

The ball dropped safely into his waiting hands.

'   ', said Maurice Kerr.

'What was that?' asked Freddy Barrington.

'I swore. That's what it was.'

'I don't blame you. What's that. Ten for two wickets. Enough to make anyone swear.'

'I'm going to have a word with Farr.' Sir Maurice got up and moved to the bottom of the stairs from the England dressing room.

'Brian.'

'Yes?'

'Tell Hughes to try and leave O'Rory to you. And tell him not to try and score for a few overs. Runs don't matter for a bit. Just keep the wickets intact.'

'Tom's just said the same.'

'Good. Good luck.'

'Thanks.' He moved off towards the pavilion steps.

At lunchtime England were thirty-one for two.

Hughes and Farr had dug in.

They'd both controlled their natural flowing cricket and adopted their batting to a debacle situation.

Michael Horton was able to both eat and enjoy lunch.

Tom Lipton had told him that he was going in number eleven and not five as in the first innings. There was no longer need to deceive the Australians. They certainly knew Horton's role now.

He felt relaxed and at ease.

He got a message to Sarah and met her in the Museum for ten minutes.

He was really enjoying himself.

If only the England batsman could make a respectable score. Three hundred and fifty. Or even three hundred at a pinch might do.

Thirty one for two wasn't good enough.

Still, with Hughes and Farr there and Lipton, Young and Ames still to come things were not desperate.

*

Sharp at ten past two O'Rory opened the after lunch session.

It was obvious that both Hughes and Farr were going to continue the festina lente policy.

Loose balls were hit carefully for runs.

Anything like a good ball was treated with immense respect.

The score grew.

Runs came.

The fifty was up in the twelfth over after lunch. Hughes carefully steered a very short ball from Fleetfoot-Jones down fine of Bardman for two. It was typical of the policy. On his normal form it would have been four.

Farr just stood and took everything that came.

O'Rory bowled him two vicious bouncers in one over.

The first zipped past his head practically parting his hair.

The second rose fiercely off a length and cracked Farr full on the left ribs. He didn't even rub himself. He showed nothing at all. It must have been agony but he merely flicked the ball back to Prout and tapped in gently in his block again.

He was incredibly tough.

The runs came from Hughes.

Brian Farr was the anchor man again.

Sixty came up.

Sixty for two.

Four overs later seventy was on the scoreboard and Rose came on for O'Rory.

Hughes was on forty-eight and facing his second fifty of the match.

Farr was stuck on eighteen.

England were digging out of a nasty hole.

Harry was in the flat glued to the bedroom window.

He had brought the stool and a cup of coffee from the kitchen and settled down to a fascinating afternoon.

He saw Hughes get his fifty.

He saw him clean bowled by Rose two runs later.

He saw the scoreboard reading seventy-eight for three. Number four twenty. Number five nought. Last man fifty-two.

He watched thrilled, while Farr and Lipton built up a stand.

The hundred came up just as Daphne came in from shopping.

'Harry!'

'Yes.'

'Where are you?'

'Cricket.'

'Oh of course.' She came into the room. 'I spoke to the porter about the sheets.'

'That was damned silly.'

'He said, "what did I expect?" What did he mean?'

'Search me.'

'I think I ought to. *I* never took them so it can only be you.'

'Sure I took them. I had a cold.'

'What on earth do you mean?'

'Oh never mind.'

She looked puzzled.

'I think I might tell Inspector Crouch upstairs.'

'The policeman!'

'Yes.'

'For God's sake don't.'

'Why not?'

'Just don't. That's all.'

'I'll think about it.'

'Oh put it out of your mind – oh good shot Lipton. Gosh he's batting well. These two will knock off the deficit and pile on some runs.'

He kept on viewing through the binoculars.

When his eyes got tired he'd put them down on the windowsill and take in the whole view.

He saw Farr hit the two that brought up the longed for one hundred and thirty-five runs. One ahead and seven wickets in hand.

If only Daphne wasn't such a bloody bore.

Lipton and Farr went on.

A hundred and forty-four came up.

They looked set for a big partnership.

When Farr was out.

It was the first careless shot he'd played in two and a half hours.

He cut halfheartedly and late off O'Rory who had come on for Fleetfoot-Jones.

He got a touch and Prout took an easy catch at shoulder height.

A hundred and forty-four for four. Farr out for fifty-two invaluable runs.

Harry made another cup of coffee.

He added a measure of rum. Returned to his perch. He wondered what Margot was doing.

Lipton and Young fought on.

Tea came up with the score on a hundred and fifty-two for four and Harry slipped out for some cigarettes.

At that moment Margot was letting a tall, elderly, distinguished man out of her flat.

Teddy Blackman had got interested in the cricket.

For long moments he forgot he had killed the postmaster. He wasn't on the run, probably identified and nowhere to go. He hadn't got the measly two hundred nicker in his hip pocket.

He was gay, carefree Teddy Blackman again, taking a smashing blonde called Lucy to Lords.

The feeling didn't last long at a time.

He was enjoying England's Captain, Lipton, knocking the score along with Young. He saw them put on thirty-six smashing runs.

Then he saw O'Rory bowl a faster one to Young.

He saw Young play and miss.

He saw the wickets fall apart like the postmaster had when he dug the knife in under his ribs.

He saw the stumps crumple backwards, splayed out and useless as the postmaster had been.

The whole bloody, miserable, unintended scene came back to him.

The postmaster and Young's stumps were one and the same thing.

Whatever happened he'd never forget that violent death was a wicket falling.

On the verandah outside the England dressing room sat a bunch of worried men.

On the left Michael sat next to Ivor Hughes.

The sun beat down.

They were all in their shirt sleeves.

Young had disappeared into the pavilion below them and Peter Ames was walking confidently to the middle.

England a hundred and eighty-two for five.

Forty-eight runs ahead and the last accredited pair of batsmen in.

Only the tail was to come.

They were facing almost certain defeat.

No one spoke too much.

They knew they needed another hundred and seventy runs to even stand a chance – and they weren't going to get them.

It would all be over on Monday and Australia would hold the Ashes.

Even when Ames started with a four square to leg off O'Rory they could only get mildly interested.

'Peter wearing your new pads?' Hughes asked Michael.

'Yep. He asked to try them. I'm very pleased.'

'Wha' d' you call them?'

'Super Protecta.'

'Clever chaps you manufacturers. What put you onto them?'

'Well everything's going lightweight these days. The stuffing's made of foam used by the Yanks in the aero space industry. They made the pads and gloves possible.'

'Maybe we all ought to have them.

'I wish you would.'

'I'll bet you do.'

They went silent again.

Tom Lipton got his fifty.

The crowd were ecstatic. The England players relieved.

Mallor came on for Rose.

At once Lipton looked in trouble.

The spinner dropped straight on a length and turned the ball appreciably.

'Tom should close up,' said Farr.

'He won't,' said Hughes.

And he didn't.

On the third ball he took two paces down the wicket and drove the ball high over Mid on's head to land in the crowd near the sight screen.

The spectators rose in enthusiasm.

'That's the way to deal with Mallor,' said Bolte.

'It's not,' said Hughes, 'it's fatal.'

Three balls later Lipton repeated the shot.

Two quick paces forward. Right up to the pitch of the ball.

He swung – and missed.

Prout had the bails off like lightning.

Eleven Australians howled an appeal.

Umpire Derby had no doubt.

His finger flashed up.

Lipton was out. Stumped Prout off Mallor.

Superintendent Roger Martin gave his eyes a rest from searching the crowds for Blackman.

He looked up at the huge scoreboard.

Changes were being made.

The total stood at a hundred and ninety-seven for six.

Number six batsman was removed and the number eight came up in the slot.

Last man changed to fifty-seven.

Number seven stayed on four.

He wasn't following the cricket but he knew England were in deep trouble. So was Blackman if they could lay hands on him. Deeper trouble than losing a Test.

He wondered how the zoo team were doing. He'd know when he got back to the car park and the radio van.

He'd begun to think Lords was the wrong place. Blackman may be miles away. Not in London at all. Yet a crowded place to hide was the M.O. of Blackman – and where more handy to Motlam Street than the Test Match?

Martin looked across the field and saw Overton making his way slowly to the wicket.

He knew he'd got to think of some better way for four men to scan thirty thousand faces.

' 'Core Card. 'Core Card. Want a 'Core Card?'

'Hey Ginger.'

The little man selling Score Cards turned round.

'What is it?'

'They want you back in the printing room.'

'Wha' for?'

' 'ow do I know? They just said.'

'Bloody 'ell. This is 'ow I make an honest penny. Not in the bleeding printing room.'

'The boss said you was to come back.'

'O'right. Give us a minute.'

'Miss Playdell asked me to lunch tomorrow,' said Stephen.

'Yes, I know. She told me. She's awfully sweet. I'm having a marvellous time staying with her.'

'Got a crush or something?'

'Don't be silly. I'm past that.'

'Really!'

'Yes. Really.'

They watched Overton playing Mallor quite confidently. Ames was at the other end.

'What do you think goes on between Dad and la Playdell?'

'I'm not sure.'

'What does that mean?'

'I'm not sure.'

'But you think something.'

'Could be. She's super attractive.'

'She certainly is.' Stephen agreed.

'You got a crush?'

'Now that could be. Yes.'

'Your father's girl friend?' Mary laughed.

'Do you think she is?'

'It's not impossible.'

Stephen said, 'Is Playdell the reason why Mum's gone off? I mean is she the other woman?'

'Gosh no. Daddy didn't even know Sarah when Mummy made all the fuss. I don't believe there was anyone else – in fact I'm sure not – but I think Sarah and Daddy are more than just good friends.'

'The randy old bugger.'

'Stephen!'

'What?'

'You're dreadful. You really are.'

'Well how else would you describe it?'

'I think Daddy's fond of Sarah and I think she may be in love with him.'

'How touching.'

'Oh shut up. I'm watching the cricket.'

Ames took one off Fleetfoot-Jones.

Overton got three.

Whatever happened the situation looked hopeless. Sixty-seven runs on and only the tail to come.

It was no surprise to anyone – not even Overton – when Mallor clean bowled him for three.

Two hundred and one for seven.

A pathetic stand of eight followed between Ames and Frost.

It lasted twenty-five minutes until Fleetfoot-Jones had Frost L.B.W. for six.

Now the end really was near.

Only Bolte and Horton to come.

As the clock neared six thirty the crowd started to move.

England seemed destined to lose in three straight Tests. The Ashes were gone.

Australia would surely be able to knock off a miserable seventy or eighty runs on Monday.

'Score Card. Score Card. Thank you. Thank you. Thank you very much. Score Card.' Sargeant Dibly of the C.I.D. had taken over from Ginger.

He was a pretty rotten example of a Score Card seller but that didn't matter now.

The cover got him right in among the people sitting on the grass and that's what he wanted.

'Score Card. Last Score Card of the day.' He eased in among the crowd.

'Can I 'av a Score Card, our dad?'

'Wha' for?'

'Cos. To remember.'

'Yer soft.'

'I aint.'

'Y' are.'

'Can I?'

'Yer can't read yer silly bugger.'

'If I 'av a Score Card I'll learn.'

'That'll be the day. O'right. 'ere y' are.' He passed over ten pence.

'Hey Mister. Mister Score Cards,' called out the boy.

Sargeant Dibly leant forward. He took the coin and passed the kid a card. As he did so he looked at the man on the boy's right. Even before the head turned he knew it was Blackman.

Dibly hardly thought.

He took a pace forward to grab the knife man. But Teddy Blackman had recognised Dibly in the flash of turning his head. He leapt to his feet and jumped over the boundary board onto the fine grass. He ran ten steps and stopped. He was lost.

The girl Lucy screamed, 'Teddy!'

Dibly ran forward onto the field.

Uniformed police appeared from nowhere.

There was a lot of noise from the now frightened crowd round the area.

Blackman drew a commando dagger from his trouser belt. He stood. Defiant. Thirty feet onto the cricket ground. He backed off as the police approached.

Umpire Derby saw what was going on. He stopped play.

The fielders and the batsmen were still.

Sergeant Dibly ran for Blackman.

The knife flashed and Dibly clasped a rent in his jacket from which blood poured.

Two uniformed men rushed forward.

Blackman ran backwards. He was getting nearer and nearer to Bardman at Square Leg.

The whole crowd were now watching, aghast.

Two uniformed police came on. They were ten paces from Blackman.

Bardman took four flying leaps towards the man's back and lunged with a low rugby tackle round Blackman's ankles.

He went down like a sack of potatoes falling off a lorry.

The police pounced.

They got the knife.

They got Blackman. Put a half nelson on him. Nodded to Bardman and frog-marched the wanted man off the field.

Umpires Fox and Derby removed the bails. It was exactly 6.31 p.m.

Superintendent Martin ran onto the field. He took Bardman by the arm and they walked off together.

England two hundred and eleven for eight. Ames seven. Bolte two.

A lead of seventy-seven miserable runs.

Blackman was charged with murder.

THIRD TEST MATCH 4th DAY

Monday dawned overcast.

The lovely weather had lasted over Sunday and ended in thunder storms.

The players had relaxed.

Some had played golf at Woking.

Mallor and Prout sailed at Burnham.

Farr did nothing.

Michael walked with Sarah in St. James' park. He had lunch at Sarah's flat with the children.

They all did their own thing.

Now Michael sat on the verandah padded up and in a long sleeve sweater.

He was next in.

Ames and Bolte were struggling to build up a partnership. The prospects were pretty poor.

The ground was little over half full. Coats and mackintoshes had taken the place of shirt sleeves and summer dresses.

Only the very hardy sat on the grass.

Within ten minutes Bolte was back in the pavilion, bowled by O'Rory and with two to his name.

Horton had walked slowly to the wicket.

The crowd had met his arrival with a great ovation. His staggering bowling on the Friday had made a great impression.

Now he was in a position of responsibility again when he thought he would be able to bat with complete abandon.

The position was really hopeless – two hundred and eleven for nine – but he'd got to try and stay while Ames made the runs. He feared O'Rory and his pace. He feared the whole situation. He was as frightened as he took guard as he had been in the first innings.

The field was all clustered round. Slips and Gullies and Silly Ons and Offs. He seemed surrounded.

O'Rory came from miles away. Steaming in.

He flashed past Umpire Fox – and bowled.

On the leg stump. Horton played bat and pad towards Mid Wicket. He got an edge. The ball flew – he knew not where. Ames called 'one'. He ran. He felt like a heavily loaded Jumbo Jet trying to get off the deck with too little power. Ames passed him going fast and athletically. Horton pounded on. He made the crease and slowed up.

He was blowing hard.

'Where did that go?' he asked Umpire Fox.

'Third Man.'

'Good God.'

He suddenly realized he'd scored.

There was a one opposite number eleven on the scoreboard.

Ames and Horton struggled on.

Michael playing bat and pad the whole time.

Peter trying hard to get one at the end of each over. Succeeding often.

The score slowly crept up.

Two hundred and fifteen. Two hundred and twenty. Two hundred and thirty. Ames on nineteen. Horton five.

Michael's runs all came from the edge.

He didn't mind.

At two hundred and thirty-one for nine Mallor came on for O'Rory.

He bowled Horton a full toss outside the leg stump. He pulled – with all his might. Smack on the drive. What a feeling. The ball hurtled to the square leg boundary. Horton nine. God, that felt more like it.

He hit the next one through the covers for two. He was beginning to feel confident.

Ames walked down the wicket to him.

'Look Mike, don't overdo it. I'd sooner you just stayed and left the runs to me.'

'No way. If I get a bad ball I'm going to hit the bloody thing.'

'Well for God's sake hit it down. Not up.'

'I'll try.'

Michael promptly took a one off Mallor down to Long Leg and fairly shot down the other end.

His tail was up.

Rose came on for Fleetfoot-Jones and Ames took four off his first over. Ames twenty-three. Horton twelve. England two hundred and thirty-nine for nine. The fourth biggest partnership of the innings.

Michael earned two leg byes by trying to sweep Mallor for six and promptly repeated the shot next ball to get four down to the Grandstand fine of square.

Two runs later the end came.

Michael tried to cut Rose.

The ball was too good and too close to the bat.

He got a top edge and Ian Church took the easiest of catches – if slip catches are ever easy – at Second Slip.

An appalling total.

Two hundred and forty seven all out.

A lead of a hundred and twelve.

' 'Core Card. 'Core Card.' Ginger was back on his beat again. 'Latest 'Core Card. Thank yew.' He moved round the ground.

Mary bought another.

She'd got six now.

She was horribly afraid the seventh would be the last.

Australia would win so easily.

England.	First Innings.	217
	(Hughes 67. Lipton 45)	
	Second Innings	
I. A. R. Hughes	b Rose	52
J. R. Porthead	b O'Rory	3
L. A. Sheddons	ct Bardman b Fleetfoot-Jones	1
B. Farr	ct Prout b O'Rory	52
T. A. M. Lipton	St. Prout b Mallor	57
G. Young	b O'Rory	18
P. E. G. Ames	Not out	24
B. Overton	b Mallor	3
P. A. R. Frost	L.B.W. Fleetfoot-Jones	6
A. L. Bolte	b O'Rory	2
M. V. Horton	ct Church I., b Rose	17
Extras		12
	TOTAL	247

1 for 8, 2 for 10, 3 for 78, 4 for 144, 5 for 182, 6 for 197, 7 for 201, 8 for 209, 9 for 211, 10 for 247.

Australia.	First Innings.	351
	(Graypath 107. Bardman 90. Oliver 61)	

Australia require 113 to win.

Ben Hendricks sipped a glass of champagne.

It was just twelve thirty and the players had gone off with England in a desperate situation.

Nothing to celebrate, he thought.

It was comfortable up here in Bob Salter's luxurious box above the Grandstand.

There were eleven – no twelve of them.

A bar. Chairs. Even a television if you wanted to see the play-backs.

Ben sighed.

He's have preferred to be sitting on the grass in the light rain that had begun to fall, if England only had a lead of two hundred and fifty.

So much depended on Mike.

The trouble was he couldn't use a new ball – yet Hendricks knew very well that he'd got to. Lipton would have to get Horton on damned quick.

'All be over by three, don't you agree, Darling?' Ben heard Mabel Anderson asking Wells.

'Not if this rain gets going. Could save us yet. It may bloody easily rain for two days. Hope it does.'

'Isn't that . . . well, rather cheating, Darling. I mean to say.'

Ben Hendricks moved away.

He walked past Bob Salter who was talking quietly to Basil Kemp.

'Maurice Kerr will have to go. No doubt about it now.'

'Bebington's still O.K.,' Kemp stated.

'Good God yes. One of the best. To tell you the truth Basil I think George Manners is the chap for Kerr's job.'

'My dear chap. There's only one person to take Maurice's job.'

'Who's that?'

'Why you me dear feller.'

'Think so?'

'Of course. Stands out a mile.'

'What can you do about it?'

Kemp said, 'Leave it to me. I've got a fair bit of power. Tell you what I'll do . . .'

Ben moved on.

He was horribly bored.

He saw Elizabeth Penning sitting alone.

At least she was pretty.

'Hello Elizabeth.'

'Hello Ben.'

'It's bad, isn't it?' he asked.

'Yes,' she said. 'It is. But isn't your friend Mike Horton going to save us?'

'If we had even two hundred in hand I think he could. The ball won't be old enough for him to use properly for a couple of hours.'

'Well then that,' she shrugged her shoulder, 'is that. Will the rain save us?'

'I hope not.'

'So do I.' She crossed extremely attractive legs. 'Ben don't you hate this private box way of watching cricket?'

'Loathe it like poison.'

'Why do you come?'

'Mr. Bob Salter is one of my prize customers and a fellow must eat. If he wants me. There I am. Oh thank the Lord the umpires are coming out so they *are* going to begin.'

'Perhaps that drizzle's stopped.'

'Suppose so.'

'Field for Frost,' said Lipton. 'Field for Frost.'

The Australian openers were on their way out.

Everyone was swathed in two sweaters.

Michael was in his hidy hole at First Slip protected by Ames and Hughes.

The ball looked very shiny as Umpire Fox took it out. A few overs and it would be slimy too.

The rain had stopped – there was only a little of it anyway. Now it was just overcast with one black cloud hanging right over Lords.

Once again Michael noticed the incredible difference in speed between Frost and O'Rory. By comparison the Sussex bowler was only just fast of medium. O'Rory had real bite. So for that matter did Fleetfoot-Jones and Rose. Where were all the English fast bowlers now. The Truman's and Tyson's didn't seem to exist.

Graypath took a four off Frost's third ball and the target went down to a hundred and nine.

Tom Lipton made the field slighly more defensive.

He opened at the Nursery end with Young.

Here was a really medium pacer, thought Michael, but God he could move the ball. In the air and off the seam. But he should be England's first change – not an opener.

The weather stayed foul and the runs came.

After eight overs, thirty was on the board.

It began to drizzle. Not hard. Just very fine like being in a cloud.

Graypath had gone off like a rocket. Scoring twenty-six of the first thirty runs. He had most of the bowling.

At thirty-four Young bowled a beauty.

It pitched middle and off and cut away sharply off the seam.

It was good enough to get anyone.

It got Graypath.

He tried to withdraw at the last moment. Got an edge and Hughes picked it out of the air in front of Michael's face.

'Sorry,' Hughes said.

'Thanks,' Michael replied. 'I hadn't had it in mind to catch it.'

'I thought you wouldn't object.'

'I don't.'

Graypath out for twenty eight. Australia thirty four for one.

Better than nothing – but not good enough.

Bardman came in.

'Stop picking your bloody ...'

'I worn't.'

'Course you were. When weren't yer?'

'Not then.'

'Liar.'

'I ain't. Truth.'

'Y'are. Bloody little nose pickin' liar.'

'Oh come off our Dad. Be fair.'

'Be fucking fair! Every time I take me eyes off the cricket your bleeding finger is 'alf way dahn yer throat.'

'It ain't true.'

'It is.'

'It ain't.'

'It is.'

'It ain't.'

'It is.'

Bardman scored two.

The drizzle turned to rain.

For a moment the players hesitated. Then ran as one for the pavilion steps.

Umpires Fox and Derby followed with the bails, more sedately.

Terry's father pulled his coat up over his head.

Terry copied him.

They looked like a big monk sitting next to a little monk.

'What yer doin' under that bloody coat?'

'Nuffink.'

'Y'are.'

'I ain't.'

'Y'are. Your pickin' your fucking nose again ain't yer?'

'Yus. Our Dad.'

The run ups were covered but the wicket remained open to the rain unless Umpires Fox and Derby called off play for the day.

The forty minute lunchtime came and went.

The rain had set in.

The forecast round London was 'thundery showers or persistent rain all day.'

At four thirty, the Umpires announced no more play for the day and the covers came out onto the wicket area.

Most of the crowd had gone.

A few optimists remained and the bars were full.

Harry got back from the office to see an empty, miserable Lords with the heavy covers all over the playing area and pipes taking the water into the outfield.

The Union Jack and Australian's flag hung wet and limp on their poles.

'I think I'll take the day off and go to Lords tomorrow.'

'But Patrick I thought the whole thing was virtually over. Surely Australia have won – or at least they're going to.'

'I don't know. You'll think this pretty stupid Darling, but I dreamt last night they didn't win.'

'Good God. You of all people.'

'I know. It's not my line is it? Still, it was all very vivid and if the weather's better I'd like to be there. Pretty silly I agree. But if you'd had this dream. Well – there it is. I think I'll take the day off.'

'All right, Patrick Love. You do that.'

THE THIRD TEST LAST DAY

Tuesday morning early was beautiful.

The sun rose through a shimmer of mist and slowly lit up London.

The milkmen and the bakers' roundsmen knew first that it was going to be a wonderful summer's day.

Michael knew when he woke up at eight thirty. It was already warm.

As he shaved he talked to himself in the mirror.

'This, my lad, has got to be your day. Those chaps Frost and Young and Bolte can only help. This is what you've been aiming for and . . .' He hesitated. 'Please God give me a hand. You know how badly I'm going to need one. These Aussies only want another seventy seven and they've got nine wickets to go. It's a big problem for you God, but if you can help I'd be extremely grateful. I'll try and do my bit but if you could just assist we might do it. Sorry to trouble you.'

He cut his chin.

'Damn.'

Two and a half hours later he walked onto the grass at Lords.

It was damp.

Oh Lord you might have dried the grass. The ball will slip like hell.

Young bowled the first over of the day to Oliver. It was a maiden.

The night before, at the team meeting, it had been agreed that Frost would have two overs and Horton would replace him whatever the state of the ball.

That's what happened.

With the score at fifty two for one Michael was tossed a very shiny, slithery, wet ball.

He tried to spin it from hand to hand. It was almost impossible. The damned thing was like soap. Wet, soggy soaked-in-the-bath soap.

'I don't think it's going to work.' He murmured to Tom Lipton.

'It's got to.'

'I bloody know it's got to. I just don't think it will.'

'There's no will or won't about it. It must.'

'Of course it must you young idiot. I just don't think it's going to.'

'Well get on with it.'

'Look Tom. I might throw the whole thing away. Why not keep on with the boys?'

'See here, Horton. I'm not asking you. I'm telling you. Get these buggers out.'

'Oh very well.'

It was a chaotic over from the start.

Whatever happened Michael was *not* going to bowl any wides. He couldn't afford them. With only sixty-one runs needed wides were a luxury he couldn't be allowed.

They took thirteen off the over.

If it hadn't been for some remarkable fielding it would have been twenty-six.

Farr at Silly Mid Off stopped a flat out drive from Oliver that had 'Four' written all over it.

Bolte used his shin to save at least three and nearly broke his leg.

'Take me off,' Michael said.

'I won't,' replied Tom. 'You'll bloody well stay on.'

'They only need forty eight.'

'Well it's about time you got moving on them, isn't it?'

'Oh God.'

At the end of Young's over Australia were sixty-seven for one wicket towards the one hundred and thirteen required to win.

Michael bowled again.

They only got five off him but he looked anything but dangerous.

The ball spun. Yes. But not the terrific tweeks that got Horton his wickets.

Seventy-two for one. Forty-one needed. Nine wickets to get them with. Oliver. Bardman. Ian Church. His cousin Graham. Mallor. Prout. Even Rose – still to come.

It was impossible.

Young bowled a maiden.

There's no point in mucking about, Michael told himself. Spin the bloody thing like hell and if it's wide, it's wide – that's all.

He signalled a massive leg break to Peter Ames.

He came in.

One, two, three, four-five.

He bowled.

It pitched well.

Dug in and bit.

Shot towards the stumps.

Oliver fenced at the last moment.

Got a touch.

The ball deflected off the bat.

Bolte dived forward at Leg Slip.

The ball bounced off his wrist. Hit his shoulder.

He twisted.

Caught it.
Australia seventy-two for two.
Oliver caught Bolte bowled Horton twenty-nine.
The situation was still hopeless.
Bardman settling in well and on eleven.
Ian Church at the wicket obviously determined to avoid the 'pair' he was on.
Forty one runs needed. Eight wickets in hand.
Young finished his over.
Michael bowled. With complete abandon.
The fourth ball whipped through at grass height and spread-eagled Church's wicket.
The crowd rose – only a half filled ground, but the noise was deafening.
Church looked disbelieving.
Bloody well out for another Duck.
Sod it.
He walked.
'What do you think?' asked Freddy Barrington.
'Afraid it's hopeless,' said Kerr. 'If the batsmen hadn't let us down. If we even had two hundred to play with there would have been a hope. But this ... Well, it's all over, isn't it?'
'I don't know. Your Horton man's got two damned useful wickets.'
'We need another seven.'
'I think it's rather interesting.'
'I think it bloody awful.'

Young and Horton persevered.
Graham Church got off the mark and looked like the fine batsman he was.
Two runs after Ian Church went Horton trapped Bardman with a tremendous leg break that bowled him round his legs. He never even played a stroke.

Seventy-five for four.

Three wickets had gone down for three runs.

Young was bowling immaculately.

Horton was getting wickets.

The England team suddenly got lighthearted.

The best Australians were out.

If only Mallor and Prout could be disposed of cheaply.

Patrick turned to his neighbour.

'I had a dream about this innings the other night.'

'Oh yes. And who won?'

'England.'

'Do you have dreams that ... well ... come true?'

'No.'

'I don't think that dream was right either. The Aussies only need thirty-eight runs and a couple of them are bound to come off. I mean it's only a matter of averages. They can't help winning.'

'I expect you're right.'

'I'll have a tenner on it.'

Patrick thought a moment.

'O.K. Done.'

They both produced ten pound notes.

'Dad's looking tired.'

'I'm not surprised.'

'Me too. If only he can keep going.'

'He's fantastic. Isn't he?'

'Yes,' said Stephen. 'I wish Mum was here.'

'How funny. I was just thinking that.'

'I wonder where she is.'

'Lord knows. And he's not telling.'

'Dad's rather marvellous. Heavens it's exciting. And to think a couple of days ago we were ashamed of him.'

'You were.'

'So were you.'

'Not really.'

'Oh yes you were.'

'Well, a bit perhaps.'

'You really are ... He's bowled Church! Oh how bleeding wonderful. How absolutely super. These Australians have no idea what to do. It's fabulous.'

His voice was drowned by the cheering spectators.

Two boys ran on the field.

They tore over to Michael.

Clasped his hand. Patted his back.

Dodged two policemen and shot back into the crowd.

Australia eighty for five.

It was becoming touch and go.

'Stop ...'

'I worn't.'

'Yer were.'

'Oh bother it.'

'I think you're going to lose your tenner.'

'Not yet I'm not. They only want thirty-three with five wickets in hand.'

'You'll still lose.'

'I won't you know.'

'We'll see.'

*

The ball caught the bat's shoulder.
Hughes flung himself square at Gully.
He took it right handed at full stretch.
Prout out. Nought.
The England players jumped like footballers scoring a goal.
The crowd followed suit.
Michael sagged and sat down.
He leant on an elbow.
He felt terrible and marvellous at the same time.
If only he could last out.
His hands were quivering with pure exhaustion.
He lay flat and tried to breathe steadily.
Rose arrived at the crease.
Michael struggled up.
Please help me God. There's a good chap.

He took Rose first ball with a perfectly simple back spinner.
Rose played forward defensively.
He had to play. It was on the stumps.
The stroke was from the book.
Angled.
But the spin was far too much.
It came up in a silly little arc straight into Horton's hands.
Michael held it firm for a moment and then, with a burst of energy flung it far over towards the crowd under the Grandstand.
Eighty-three for six.
Thirty still needed to win.
Great God they were going to do it.
Horton felt huge.
And irreversible.
He sat on the grass with his forehead bent low between his knees.
The rest of the team kept clear.
They seemed to sense his concentration.

The first time for England at the age of fifty-three. And standing on a hat trick!

Five wickets in this innings under his belt on top of eight in the first.

Never, since he first set eyes on Vittorio, did he imagine this.

He knew victory in the Third Test lay in his hands.

Keeping the Ashes afloat was up to him.

He dug his head even lower, feeling the huge bulk of his waist-line.

Christ. He'd got to get these wickets. How many runs did they need? Thirty. And four wickets still to fall.

It was possible.

Get Cornwall and his hat trick.

Then take O'Rory and Fleetfoot-Jones.

Leave Mallor be. He didn't matter.

Let him half read the spin. The others couldn't

As he analysed the players Michael realised it could be done.

They could all be out for ninety.

A victory by twenty-three runs.

He caught the flash of Cornwall walking past to the wicket.

Michael stood and glared after him.

He called to Tom.

'Can we close the field?'

'Of course.'

They ringed Cornwall like a defiant bull.

He kept calm.

All he had to do was prevent this hat trick and then calmly go forward with Mallor towards the thirty needed.

He was sweating all the same.

Umpire Fox gave him guard.

Two leg.

Cornwall looked at the circle of close fielders. Only Lipton was any way off – at Cover.

Michael sent Ames a code signal.

He looked up at Father Time on the Grandstand roof. He smiled at him. Thought of his scythe.

The field settled.

Horton came in.
One, two, thre ... He missed his step.
He ran through and never bowled.
Cornwall came up from his stance.
The field eased.
Horton walked back.
Damn and bloody hell. What caused that?
He stood for a moment. Looking down at his marker.
He counted up to ten.
Came in again.
The ball was bad.
Too short.
Too far off.
Cornwall wouldn't have to play.
He did.
He struck hard to massacre the close field.
Made contact. With an inside edge.
The ball deflected passed his legs.
And rattled the stumps behind his shoulder.
He was out.
Carelessly, stupidly out.
Off a bad ball.
And this sod Horton had got his third wicket.

As the crowd poured onto the field Cornwall walked, hitting his pad with the bat in anger.

Bowled off the edge.
Played on.
Out like a fool.
Bugger this game.
Eighty-three for eight.
Thirty needed.
Only two wickets to go.

O'Rory came in and carefully steered Horton towards Lipton. No score.

He looked confident. At ease.

Young and Horton bowled two maiden overs each. The danger was that Horton seemed to have melted.

He spun the ball viciously to leg, to off and top and back spin but his pitching control was loose.

His head hung low. His shoulders stooped. His zip was gone. He was no longer dominantly on top.

Then Mallor took a single.

Three overs later he got another.

The scoring rate was like treacle but the wickets held.

Another single by Mallor took the score to eighty-six.

Twenty-seven looked for.

When Young bowled Mallor.

The ball shattered the wicket.

Ames, standing up was cascaded with bails, ball and stumps.

The cheering roared.

England were going to win.

At that moment they all knew it.

Australia, the spectators, the new crowds flooding in the gates free of charge, Maurice Kerr, Bob Salter and Ben Hendricks, the England team, the listeners to B.B.C. 3.

All would have put their shirt on an England win.

Michael Horton knew it.

He knew it as he saw his partner, Young, pile in to bowl to Fleetfoot-Jones.

The ball was alive.

Michael could hardly wait to get his hands on it. He hoped and prayed that Greg Young would leave this one to him.

Young's over seemed to last an age. Fleetfoot-Jones played carefully.

For him the match was not over – just yet.

He got his head down over Young and put his foot and pad out to the ball.

And then the over finished.

Ames threw Michael the ball.

He rubbed it on the ground.

Now.
Look out O'Rory.
This is it.

•

Michael Horton had bowled hundreds of overs in practice. He'd cut his run up down to the minimum to conserve his energies. He'd known that if he ever played for England he might be called upon to go beyond his physical capacity. He'd put the thought from his mind. If Lipton took him beyond the physical barrier then he'd just ask to be taken off.

Now the worse situation possible had arisen.

He *was* physically beyond his limit – and he couldn't come off. Even Michael knew that.

Very well, Mr. O'Rory. Then it must be short and sweet.

He came in.

More slowly than before.

He lumbered past Umpire Fox.

He bowled.

A bigger wide than even Horton had bowled before. It was nearly to Cover.

He trudged back.

Bowled a bad one.

O'Rory took two to square leg. Overton chased it and saved the third.

Another bad one that O'Rory swung at and missed.

Followed by a prodigious wide on the leg side.

And a rotten short ball that beat O'Rory it was so bad – and nearly beat Peter Ames.

The over dragged out.

In the end Michael was just trying to pitch them and to hell with the spin.

He sloped off to his position at first slip. Hughes joined him.

'Pretty shagged Mike?'

'Too true.'

'Tom can't rest you.'

'I know.'

'What're you going to do?'

'Take an easy over and try and get back in the next one. Got a Dextrose, Peter?'

'Hip pocket. Help yourself.'

They settled down.

Michael chewing glucose.

Greg Young bowled a tight over.

Fleetfoot-Jones took a single off the fifth ball. He looked neat and better than a number eleven.

Michael slung a straightforward six balls. He didn't try to spin it. Just to pitch the damned thing a good length on the off stump. It worked. He bowled a maiden. Fleetfoot-Jones wasn't looking for trouble.

Four maidens followed.

Michael still rested from bowling his massive breaks.

The Australians were willing to wait.

They'd got all the time in the world.

In the last over before lunch Horton put everything into it.

All that happened were two huge wides and a lot of loose stuff that didn't need playing at all.

He came off the field exhausted and low in spirits.

England seemed to be losing the throttling grip it had had on the match.

'Hello. Hello. Oh damn. I want Sarah Playdell.'

'. . . .'

'Oh it's you. Bloody awful line. It's Mac.'

'. . . .'

'Mac, you idiot. Your editor.'

'. . . .'

'Yes. Mac. Can you hear?'

'. . . .'

'Good. Well I've found that dame you wanted. The Horton woman ...'

'....'

'Yes it was clever. I'm rather proud.'

'....'

'No. I didn't do it myself. Harvey did. But I'm taking the credit.'

'....'

'In the south of France.'

'....'

'Yes France. Antibes.'

'....'

'Staying with old Cheshire-Bourne.'

'....'

'Yes. The writer.'

'....'

'All alone as far as I know.'

'....'

'Yes. Harvey says no trouble at all. They're due in at Heathrow tonight at nine.'

'....'

'No. She had no idea about it. Hadn't heard a word. Seemed astonished.'

'....'

'Well you know Harvey. He'd sell a eunuch french letters, wouldn't he?'

'....'

'I'm not being crude. Merely illustrative.'

'....'

'Illustrative. Oh it doesn't matter. Anyway she's coming back. That's what you wanted isn't it?'

'....'

'You extraordinary thing.'

'....'

'No. I'll take no notice of you. We're putting her in the Intercontinental. O.K.?'

'....'

'If England win,' said Bob Salter, 'I presume Kerr will stay on.'

'Almost certainly. Yes.'

'Damn.'

'Don't worry. I don't think they stand a snowball's chance in hell.'

'I hope not.'

'So do I.'

Michael walked over to Tom Lipton.

'I'm all in.'

'I know you are, Mike. But can you keep going?'

'If I've got to. I'm feeling very shaky though.'

'Migraine?'

'Good God no. I'm just flaked. Exhausted.'

'Like a Dextrose?'

'Um. Yes.'

'Peter's got some. I'll have a word.'

'Thanks. That might help.'

Mallor cut Horton for three.

Eighty-three for five.

Thirty to win.

Michael bent down and put his head between his knees. He stood up. He still felt shaky but better than he had.

He came in to bowl to Prout.

Past Umpire Fox.

– two, three, four-five.

Five feet outside the off stump.

It careered in towards the wickets.

Prout moved across to block it.

He jabbed.

'You do that. And I'll expect your thanks later.'

'. . . .'

'I know you are. Just get me the bloody story. 'Bye.'

'. . . .'

Michael spent the forty minutes of the lunch break lying on the massage table. He had a sandwich and a glass of milk. The doctor checked him over.

Young took his boots off and lay flat on the bed. Then got up and did exercises.

Tom Lipton had lunch with Kerr.

At eight minutes past two the umpires were out. England followed with Hughes and Horton trailing.

Fleetfoot-Jones and O'Rory were there by ten past and Young bowled the first ball of the new session.

It was a beauty and O'Rory just kept it out.

Horton began with yet another wide.

He felt desperate.

What the bloody hell to do?

He'd try to bowl a semi spinner pitching in the leg stump and cutting away sharply towards Third Slip.

He did.

It was a gem.

Exactly what he'd intended.

Fleetfoot-Jones leapt out two huge paces.

He clobbered the ball on the half volley.

It flew back over Horton's head and landed full pitch in the pavilion.

A massive crowd chilling six of the kind that wins matches.

Horton stood and stared.

Australia one hundred for nine.

Only thirteen wanted to win.

*

Fleetwood-Jones went back into his shell.

He blocked and stopped everything Horton threw at him. He seemed, like Mallor, to be able to read the spin.

O'Rory took two off Young. And then a single.

Ten wanted.

Horton bowled a poor maiden to O'Rory.

He was already tiring again.

Fleetfoot-Jones edged one to leg off Young.

A hundred and four for nine. Chasing a hundred and thirteen.

Michael knew it was now or never.

He signalled a huge off break to Ames.

It nearly worked.

The trouble was it spun too far.

Horton saw Umpire Fox signal a wide.

Oh shit!

He could *not* afford these wides.

He bowled two up and downers.

The third good ball of the over was a straight top spinner pitched on a length.

Even as he bowled he saw Fleetfoot-Jones move forward.

It was too late. There was nothing he could do.

The Australian was three paces down the wicket. He hit the ball full toss. It arced back over Horton's head again, buzzing as it went.

It landed deep in among the Members in the pavilion.

Another marvellous six. High and handsome.

Michael was shaking with tiredness and fury. Damn. Damn. And damn again.

A hundred and eleven for nine. Only two wanted.

Tom Lipton came across.

'What're you going to do, Mike?'

'Same again. Nearly.'

'Want a man out?'

'No certainly not. I want him to try again.'

'It's all yours.'

'I bloody well know.'

It looked like the previous ball – but had twice as much back spin.

Fleetfoot-Jones came out two and a half crisp paces. He drove – hard. Right on the meat of the bat.

The ball came back over Horton going like a rocket – but lower than the last one.

Horton jumped.

Somehow he got his huge weight two feet off the ground.

His right hand stretched up towards the blue sky.

The ball hit his raised arm. There was a noise like stumps being hit.

The ball fell.

It passed his face. His chest.

He grabbed rather hopelessly with his spare left hand. It was somewhere round his waist.

He felt a wall of pain. And cried out.

The ball fell into his left hand.

Fleetfoot-Jones caught and bowled Horton.

Australia a hundred and eleven all out.

England win by two runs.

The crowd explodes.

They dash wildly onto the green that is Lords.

And Horton is lying doubled up in the centre of the wicket.

'Did you have the glasses on that, Trevor?' asked George Allot.

'Yes I did. I'm afraid Mike Horton's hurt rather badly. He caught that fantastic catch after stopping the ball high up on his right arm. Must have done quite a bit of damage. He's lying down clutching his arm and I'm afraid there's rather a lot of blood about. All over the front of his shirt.

'They're trying to keep the crowd off. Hughes and Farr are lifting him. They're not waiting for a stretcher. He's being rushed off and the crowd are parting to let him through.

'He's on his legs all right – but he looks very pale.

'Now this is exceptional.

'The Australians have come down from their dressing room and they're lining the way to the pavilion gate. They're all clapping Horton and he's raised a smile for them. This is really remarkable. I've never seen such a thing before.

'And Horton goes up the steps into the pavilion.

'What an amazing reception.

'The Members are cheering too. Standing.

'Surely this must be known as Horton's Test.'

'Get an ambulance.'

'It's coming,' said Kerr. 'How bad is he?'

Bad enough. If I hang on I can stop the bleeding.'

'What is it?'

'Wrist's gone. Compound.'

'Is he in pain?'

'Not now. I gave him a pretty big shot. Where's the bloody ambulance – and tell those buggers to be a bit quieter. It's not helping him.'

'It's on the way.'

'I think it ought to hurry.'

'Right. I'll put a bomb behind it.'

Kerr left the first aid room. He ran down the stairs to Bebington's office.

Behind him the doctor sat on the hard chair next to Michael on the bed. He held his right arm bent across his chest and pressed hard on the artery.

Michael never moved.

His eyes were half open but he took little in.

All the England players were on the balcony drinking champagne. All except Ivor Hughes who leant silently on the massage table.

'Ambulance here.'

The doctor moved. He handed over to the two men in blue uniform. He passed a few instructions.

'St. Martin's?'

'St. Martin's.'

'O.K. Well go fast as you can. I'll talk to Mr. Maxwell. This chap'll need some blood.'

They eased Michael Horton into a carry chair and holding him as the doctor had done took him down and out the pavilion main doors.

There were crowds of spectators.

Silent.

A woman waved and said, 'Good luck'.

Others took it up.

Into the ambulance.

And away.

'How bad is Daddy?'

'My dear, I don't know,' said Sarah. 'He'll be well looked after.'

Stephen said, 'I didn't like all that blood. What the hell did he do?'

'A bad compound fracture which broke through the skin I think.'

'But where?'

'I don't know, Stephen. We'll find out at the hospital.'

'Poor Dad.'

Meg Horton was on the way to London from Heathrow.

Mac was in the car with Harvey Baker and a driver.

'I understand the accident,' said Meg. 'What I don't follow is what on earth he was doing playing cricket at Lords.'

'Oh Mrs. Horton – that's a long story,' said Mac. 'I'd sooner leave that to our cricket correspondent, Sarah Playdell, to tell you. She may be at the hotel. With your children.'

'Do they know all about this?'

'Yes.'

‘It seems I’m the only person who doesn’t.’

‘We’ve been trying to find you for days.’

‘Oh I know it’s my own fault. I just feel . . . well, rather out of it.’

‘I’m sorry.’

‘So am I.’

Michael lay in a small white room.

His right arm was propped up on a plastazote structure down his side and his hand lay on a moulded board.

He felt nothing.

No pain.

No fear.

No elation.

He opened his eyes and looked around without turning his head.

A nurse moved.

‘Mr. Horton.’

‘Yes.’

‘How do you feel?’

‘I don’t know. I’d like some water.’

‘Just a small sip then.’

She helped him.

‘No more.’

‘Oh hell that was damn all.’

‘You can have some more in a minute.’

Michael closed his eyes and lay still.

For five minutes he rested.

‘When is it?’ he asked.

‘I’m sorry?’

‘What time is it? What day?’

‘Wednesday morning. It’s eleven thirty.’

‘We won.’

‘Yes, Mr. Horton. You won.’

‘Good.’

He slept again.

An hour later he woke. Maxwell was there.

'How are you?'

'Who're you?'

'My name's Maxwell. I'm your . . . doctor.'

'Well why the hell are you asking me how I am? You bloody well tell me.'

Maxwell laughed.

'Well there's not much wrong with your spirit. That's for sure.'

'What about this arm?'

Maxwell hesitated. 'That's not quite so clever.'

'What've I done?'

'Made a mess of it.'

'How bad?'

'I'm bringing a Mr. McLure to see you this afternoon. I think we'll wait 'til he comes.'

'Why.'

'Because he's a very clever chap.'

'And you're not?'

'Not as clever as McLure.'

'I'd like to see Sarah Playdell.'

'Who?'

'Sarah Playdell. She's on the Daily News.'

'Oh yes. She came in this morning with your children.'

'God. The Kids. How are they?'

'They all seem fine.'

'Can I see Sarah?'

'Tomorrow.'

'O Christ, Maxwell. That's a hell of a time away.'

'You must be patient.'

'I'm not. I'm bloody impatient. In fact I'll be the worst bleeding patient you've got.'

'I can see that. I'll have to give you something to calm you down.'

'Over my dead body.'

'We'll see.'

*

McLure walked away from the x-ray photographs.

He sat down slowly and carefully in the chair in Maxwell's office.

He re-read the medical report clipped onto a plastic board. Flipped the pages over.

'Unpleasant.'

'Yes.'

'I was there.'

'Where?'

'At Lords. I saw it happen. It made quite a noise.'

'The wrist going?'

'Yes.'

'Nasty.'

'Very.'

McLure walked back to the x-rays.

He stood. Comparing the picture with the report. He turned to Maxwell.

'I imagine Horton's a pretty tough egg.'

'I should say so. Yes. He won't want leading up the garden path. As I read him he'd sooner have the facts – however bad.'

'He looked like that on the field.' He flipped the papers again. 'Who's the next of kin?'

'His wife.'

'No point in talking to her,' McLure said. 'We'd just better tell him.'

'You think it's hopeless then?'

'Oh utterly. The chap's got no alternative. Neither have we. Plain as a pikestaff.' He hesitated and tapped his teeth with a pen. 'Like me to tell Horton?'

'I think we both should,' said Maxwell.

'The sooner the better then. Let's see him now. Are you free tomorrow?'

'Yes.'

'Well you fix the details. Just tell me when.'

*

'Mrs. Horton?' Sarah spoke into the telephone.

'Yes.'

'You don't know me. My name is Sarah Playdell. I'm . . .'

'I know of you. Your editor explained.'

'Explained, Mrs. Horton? Explained what?'

'That for some unknown reason you are to tell me what my husband has been doing.'

'Well. You've read the papers today?'

'Yes. It seems he's front page news on nearly all of them. But what does it mean? I . . . I mean . . . how did it all happen?'

'I think I'd better come and see you, Mrs. Horton. If I came round to the hotel now could we have coffee or something? In your room? I'd really like to talk with you.'

'Very well. But you're not after some story are you? Because if you are I'll . . .'

'No I am not.'

'All right then. If you promise me . . .'

'I do.'

'Very well come round. I'm in room 630.'

Three days later Horton had his first visitor. Ivor Hughes.

The Welshman only stayed five minutes.

They laughed and talked about the match.

They never mentioned Michael's injury.

Hughes left Michael a cricket bat signed by all the Australians and at the bottom –

'We were Hortoned'.

The nurse showed Ivor out.

'When can I see Miss Playdell?'

'Tomorrow.'

'Every day you say tomorrow, you old cow.'

'Flattery will get you nothing, Mr. Horton. I've said you'll see her tomorrow and tomorrow it will be. After Mr. McLure and Mr. Maxwell have been.'

'I'd like some paper and a pen.'

'Whatever for?'

'I want to sign my name you idiot woman.'

'Hello, Sarah.'

'Hello, Mike.'

She stood near the door.

'Well come here. I'm not going to break.'

She walked slowly to the bed. Took his left hand. Stood there. Tears in her eyes.

'Yes,' said Mike, 'you'll have to hold that one. They've chopped the other off.'

'I know.'

'Seems I made a frightful mess of my wrist. The whole thing was shattered. Bones, nerves, ligaments, blood system. The whole bloody lot. Muscles. You name it I bust it. I'm sorry, Sarah.'

'Oh, Mike.'

'Well a one handed fat man of fifty three is hardly a catch. Is he?'

'Don't be stupid.'

'I feel stupid if you want to know. If I'd just broken up the few bones I had left they could have stiffened up the bloody thing. But oh no. I had to go the whole fucking way and lose it.'

'Mike. Don't. Please.'

'Oh come on, Darling. You can't expect me to be hilarious about it. Not for a while anyway.'

'Mike. There's someone else to see you.'

'I don't want to see anyone else, Sarah. I want to see you. Sit down. I want to look at you.'

'It's Meg.'

'Meg!'

'Yes.'

'What's she doing?'

'She was in France. Antibes. The Daily News found her. She

knew nothing of you playing for England. Nothing at all. When she heard she realised what an ass she'd been and came straight home. Then you were hurt.' Sarah stopped. She took a full breath. 'And now she's come to see you.'

'I don't want to.'

'Don't want to what?'

'See her.'

'Don't be bloody ridiculous. You've got to. She's your wife.'

'So are you.'

'I'm not. And anyway that's nothing to do with it.'

'It damned well is.'

'Of course it's not.'

'Don't argue with me Sarah Playdell. If I say it is. It is. If I have to, I'll hold you with my stump or whatever you call it and beat you with my left hand.'

'Oh, Mike.'

'Oh shit.'

She stroked his hand gently.

'You must see her, Mike. I want you to.'

'Why?'

'Well you must. God you must know you must.'

'What a bloody awful sentence.'

'Oh Mike. You fool.'

'O.K. So I see her. What then?'

'I'm going to Australia.'

He lay there silent.

A full two minutes went by.

'Did you hear?' she asked.

He said nothing.

'Mike. I said I'm going to Australia.'

'Why?'

'A major Sidney daily have been after me for two years to edit their whole leisure section. It's a wonderful chance. I'm going to say "yes".'

'Why now?'

'Because I love you.'

'That's why not. That's not why yes.'

'It is why yes, Mike. Truly it is.'

'When do you think you're going.'

'Next week. Tuesday. Look Mike. I'm going out for three months. Then I'm flying back to tidy up things here.'

'How long will you be home?'

'About two weeks.'

'And you'll tidy up everything. I mean everything?'

'Yes.'

He touched her cheek with his good hand. He pulled her head down to him and kissed her – terribly softly.

'You really mean you'll tidy up everything?'

'Yes, Mike. Absolutely everything.'

He stared at her. Sighing deeply and shaking his head.

'All right.' He shrugged. And then smiling at her,' You'd better ask Meg to come in.'